Praise for

NOVEMBER MOURNS

"No one else *writes* like Tom Piccirilli. He has the
lyrical soul of a poet and the narrative talents of a man
channeling Poe, William Faulkner, and Shirley Jackson.
His people are as real as pain and his ghosts are as
terrifyingly surreal as an evening alone on the razor-thin
boundary between reality and nightmare. After you begin
reading *November Mourns*, you will not be able to put it
down: and when you have finished it, and have returned it
to your bookcase, you will not be able to forget it. Ever."
—T. M. Wright, author of *Cold House* and
A Manhattan Ghost Story

"Piccirilli is one of the most compelling writers working
in the field today. He creates a burgeoning sense
of unease, and his lyrical writing and insightful
characterizations make *November Mourns*
as intoxicating as moonshine."
—Tim Lebbon, author of *Face* and *Fears Unnamed*

"A mesmerizing, one-of-a-kind backwoods meditation on
death, madness, and moonshine. Tom Piccirilli's voice
is unique, and his fever dream storytelling
is spellbinding and surprising."
—Mick Garris, director of *Desperation* and *The Stand*

"A novel of supreme and mesmerizing power that reads like a head-on collision between Flannery O'Connor and M. R. James. The overwhelming sense of dread, grief, anger, and place that permeates this book are only a few of its many triumphs. This novel is—in the correct, dictionary sense of the word—a masterpiece."
—Gary A. Braunbeck, author of *In Silent Graves*

"Tom's best novel to date. What impressed me most was the intensely provocative story, character development, deft handling of the material, and the high quality of the writing and imagery throughout."
—Bill Pronzini, author of *Spook* and *The Alias Man*

"*November Mourns* teems with a strange, beautiful, disturbing life. The writing's tough as jerked beef yet seasoned with pinches of poetry. The further you read, the more the spare realism at the novel's core is pierced by unexpected assaults of the unnervingly spooky."
—Jack Ketchum, author of *The Lost* and *She Wakes*

"A powerful, passionate, poetic examination of tormented souls and their Graham Greene-like struggle for redemption."—Ed Gorman, author of *Blood Moon*

"Piccirilli is fast becoming the Pied Piper of supernatural suspense, leading a legion of readers to the genre. The author's sensitivity toward his characters is reminiscent of William Faulkner with a Dean Koontz twist and a Peter Straub chaser with a dash of Charles Grant."
—Robert W. Walker, author of *Absolute Instinct* and *Final Edge*

"If you go down to the woods with Tom Piccirilli, make sure you have eyes in the back of your head. Scary, engaging, this story gives a totally new meaning to the phrase 'cliff-hanger.'"
—Graham Masterton, author of *Unspeakable*

"*November Mourns* rolls in over the reader like a thick, encompassing mist. It's vivid and ripe with dread and tragedy, with characters who live and breathe. Tom Piccirilli is a writer whose talent glows on the page."
—Ray Garton, author of *Seductions* and *Scissors*

"A sparkling rich gem of a novel . . . Tom Piccirilli is a master of literate darkness, and he's at his best with this ghostly tale of passion, mystery and murder."
—Tamara Thorne, author of *Haunted*

A CHOIR OF ILL CHILDREN

"A wonderfully wacked, disorienting, fully creepy book from which I never once reeled in revulsion . . . I didn't reel because the poetic nature of the prose and seriousness of intent carried the day in every scene." —Dean Koontz

"Riotous, surprising, and marvelously gruesome."
—Stewart O'Nan

"Beautifully written, ingeniously plotted, richly atmospheric . . . Piccirilli is one of the few living authors who can mingle with the masters of the genre."
—Thomas Ligotti

"In this compelling Southern Gothic, Piccirilli...
presents a searing portrait of twisted souls trapped in a
wasteland.... Will appeal both to genre fans and to
readers of Flannery O'Connor and even of William
Faulkner. James Lee Burke and Harry Crews devotees
should also take note." —*Publishers Weekly*

"Lyrical, ghastly, first-class horror." —*Kirkus Reviews*

"Piccirilli has a gift for pitch-black humor that makes
much of this novel outrageously funny, until laughter
finally drowns amid murderous phantasms." —*Locus*

"*A Choir of Ill Children* demonstrates the author's
versatility and penchant for the bizarre.... Piccirilli has
created a world that is disturbing and compelling."
—*Rocky Mountain News*

"*A Choir of Ill Children* is a full-on Southern Gothic... a
surreal melange of witchcraft, deformity, and ghosts.
Piccirilli explore[s] his ongoing theme of memory and
knowledge as damning elements... adding a further level
of surreal absurdity to the proceedings, until you're not
quite sure which way is up." —*Fangoria*

"A marvelous fable about family, responsibility, and
owning up to your nightmares." —*SF Site*

"In *A Choir of Ill Children* Piccirilli explores monsters of flesh and mind, intermingling abominations with unlikely saviors in a narrative puzzle as intellectually challenging as it is slap-your-knee entertaining." —*Cemetery Dance*

"Tom Piccirilli writes with a razor for his pen. *A Choir of Ill Children* is both deeply disturbing and completely compelling."
—Christopher Golden, author of *Wildwood Road*

"This is a Gothic tale of sustained invention, told in colorful prose. I loved the characters, the prose (which alternates, deliberately, between jazzy and/or bluesy tones and a clipped sort of Faulknerian picture-making), the imagery, the incidents, and the smart balance between the humorous and the horrific."
—Michael Bishop, author of *Philip K. Dick Is Dead, Alas* and *Brighten to Incandescence*

.

"A resonant title for a resonant, powerful, lyrical, and disturbing piece of work. I enjoyed *A Choir of Ill Children* enormously."
—Simon Clark, author of *Stranger* and *Darker*

"Whether writing horror, mysteries, or thrillers, Tom Piccirilli delivers the goods. His characters have heart, smarts, and guts. They come to life in fine stories you'll not soon forget. I'm a big fan."
—Richard Laymon, author of *Night in the Lonesome October* and *The Cellar*

"Tom Piccirilli's work is full of wit and inventiveness—
sharp as a sword, tart as apple vinegar. I look
forward to all his work."
—Joe R. Lansdale, author of *The Bottoms*

"Tom Piccirilli is one of the best stylists working today—
not simply in the horror genre but in fiction in general.
His characters are quirky and fascinating, and his
imagination is a scary, amazing thing."
—T. M. Wright

"*A Choir of Ill Children* is spellbinding. Piccirilli
writes like lightning, illuminating a dark landscape
of wonders."
—Douglas Clegg, author of *The Hour
Before Dark* and *The Infinite*

"This book is brilliant. Surprises abound on every page,
and every one of its characters is unforgettable
and sublimely imagined."
—*Flesh & Blood Magazine*

"Brilliantly grotesque, beautifully written, and yet
shockingly morbid, pulsing with blood that seems a
little too real for fiction. This is not just another
genre novel, it's a macabre work of art."
—Edward Lee, author of *City Infernal* and *Monstrosity*

"Tom Piccirilli never backs away from a disturbing or disgusting scene in the dubious interest of self-censorship, but neither does he seem to relish it as some perverted writers do (guilty, guilty, guilty). He faces it and follows it through to the consequences, and that requires bravery."
—Poppy Z. Brite, author of *Lost Souls*

"*A Choir of Ill Children* is effing brilliant—Carson McCullers by way of William S. Burroughs . . . or Ellen Gilchrist on really, really bad acid. It's the kind of novel that makes me shake my head in envy and awe. . . . A powerful meditation on isolation, pointless anger, and familial obligation that ranks right up there with *Geek Love* and *Tattoo Girl*." —Gary A. Braunbeck

"Tom Piccirilli's *A Choir of Ill Children* is rich with poetry, his characters are vivid and sharp, and his writing peels away layers of everyday reality. Like all the best authors, he leads readers into the strange and dark places inside themselves."
—Gerard Houarner, author of *The Beast That Was Max* and *Road to Hell*

"Piccirilli courageously walks a dangerous line, telling his story in a fast-paced stream of consciousness narrative that drops the reader into fascinating circumstances with the very first sentence. *A Choir of Ill Children* does not disappoint. You won't be able to stop reading."
—David B. Silva, author of *Through Shattered Glass*

"The hypnotic power of Piccirilli's writing draws you into a world you might otherwise run from. It's easy to believe that this man won a Bram Stoker Award for his poetry because his narrative is infused with a lyrical voice. I can't imagine who else's mind *A Choir of Ill Children* might have sprung from."
—Robert Randisi, author of *Blood on the Arch*

"Better start revising your favorite author list—Piccirilli deserves to be at the top." —*Book Lovers*

"[Piccirilli] invests his work with potent atmosphere and realistic characterization while maintaining an economy of words and seamless plot cohesion. His horror fiction is mysterious, and his mysteries border on the horrific, and no matter what genre he employs the plots hold true, developing organically from the actions and reactions of the players." —*Gothic.net*

"Piccirilli is a master of the snapshot, of the slice of life— he plunges you headlong into various worlds, makes his points, then ushers you out, leaving you to reflect on what you've experienced." —*Hellnotes*

OTHER BOOKS BY TOM PICCIRILLI

NOVELS:
A Choir of Ill Children
Coffin Blues
Grave Men
A Lower Deep
The Night Class
The Deceased
Hexes
Sorrow's Crown
The Dead Past
Shards
Dark Father

COLLECTIONS:
Mean Sheep
Waiting My Turn to Go Under the Knife (Poetry)
This Cape Is Red Because I've Been Bleeding (Poetry)
A Student of Hell (Poetry)
Deep Into That Darkness Peering
The Dog Syndrome & Other Sick Puppies
Pentacle

NONFICTION:
Welcome to Hell

Tom Piccirilli

November Mourns

BANTAM BOOKS

051270

DOVER FREE PUBLIC LIBRARY
32 EAST CLINTON ST.
DOVER, NJ 07801

NOVEMBER MOURNS
A Bantam Spectra Book / June 2005

Published by Bantam Dell
A Division of Random House, Inc.
New York, New York

All rights reserved
Copyright © 2005 by Tom Piccirilli
Cover photo copyright © Kevin Radford
Cover design by Franco Accornero

Book design and title page photograph by Karin Batten

If you purchased this book without a cover, you should be aware that this
book is stolen property. It was reported as "unsold and destroyed" to
the publisher, and neither the author nor the publisher has received any
payment for this "stripped book."

Bantam Books, the rooster colophon, Spectra, and the portrayal of a
boxed "s" are trademarks of Random House, Inc.

ISBN 0-553-58720-X

Printed in the United States of America
Published simultaneously in Canada

www.bantamdell.com

OPM 10 9 8 7 6 5 4 3 2 1

For Jack Cady
another of my fathers
who will be dearly missed

and to my wife Michelle

Acknowledgments

A debt is owed to the following for their friendship, support, encouragement and inspiration over the writing of this novel: Gerard Houarner, T. M. Wright, Patrick Lussier, Stewart O'Nan, Dallas Mayr, Lee Seymour, Bill Pronzini, Tom Monteleone, Ray Garton, Caniglia, Graham Masterton, Michael Bishop, Al Sarrantonio, Gary A. Braunbeck, Brian Keene, Rich SanFilippo, Tim Lebbon, Thomas Ligotti, Mick Garris, Dean Koontz, and Thomas Tessier.

More thanks go to Ed Gorman, for sending all the boxes of great old books. Gold Medal rules!

Extraspecial thanks to my editor, Caitlin Alexander.

November
Mourns

YOUR BLOOD WAS ALWAYS WHISPERING, EVEN if you didn't want to listen.

Shad awoke on his feet, standing on his bunk, staring at the cement wall. He turned, peering into the darkness of the C-Block tier. In a pale flash, his sister's hands pressed toward him through the bars of his cell.

"Mags," he said. He opened his mouth to say more but was afraid he might whimper. Sometimes the depth of night hid you from your fears, and sometimes it brought them right to your bed.

He gritted his teeth, grunted her name again from the center of his chest. It was too easy to give in to the sorrow of your life. All it took was one instant of letting the pain in, and the flood would never end.

His father had phoned him this afternoon to tell him Mags was dead, and now here she was, visiting him. But why out there on the walk and not beside him? He waited for her to move closer, so she could talk to him, tell him who had done this to her.

If your kin had something to tell you, they'd come after you, no matter how far they had to travel. Even if your sister had no mouth anymore.

He stepped off his bunk and her hands receded into shadow as if she might be frightened. Like he might've shoved her away. "Mags?" he called, then much louder, "Megan!"

On the tier, their eyes glittered. He must've been at it for a while, yelling and walking around in his sleep. Other cons stood at their cell doors, staring out at him, silent except for a few of the Mexicans saying prayers.

The heat that always crouched at the back of his skull now burned more intensely, his rage alive and eager within him. Protective and loving. He reached up and touched his lips. He was smiling like an idiot, but there were tears on his face.

PART 1

Blood
Dreams

Chapter One

YOU COULD ALWAYS GO HOME AGAIN, THE trouble was getting back out.

Flames lit the surrounding banks of the Chatalaha River, which wound through the mountains in a whitecapped rush. Streams of orange and gold washed over rocks where centuries ago the Indians stoned their elderly in the shallows.

After nearly two years in the can, Shad Jenkins had returned to Moon Run Hollow and hit the first bonfire in the fields he heard about. He figured he'd see everybody there who might be interested, tell his story once and get it over with.

In the twenty-one months he'd been away nothing had changed except that Mags was dead.

He could've been gone for eighteen years, the way his pa had been, and still walked into the roadhouse and seen those gray faces hunched over the pitted bar, their breath making slow ripples in the scratched glasses of whiskey. The men telling the same mediocre stories that circled the place like crows that never set down, going around forever from one hoarse voice to another.

Fathers passed the tired tales to their sons and grandsons the way they bestowed their potbellies, sour-mash stills, and empty wallets. The tin-shack trailers, three acres of rock-cluttered pasture, and their taste for warm, flat beer and moonshine. In a few generations they had gone from being tradition to genetic.

What you really wanted, you could never have. You needed a tragic father to give your life meaning.

Shad broke from the darkness and walked across the clearing until he found the ring of Jeeps, pickups, and 4x4s that had tracked across the field, headlights glowing against the cane. Maybe fifty people in all, about half of them passed out on their feet or jacked on meth and crushed Ritalin.

Jake Hapgood reached into his open cooler and handed Shad a bottle of beer as if they'd seen each other only twenty minutes ago. Jake was one of the very few slick people in Moon Run Hollow. Five-eight in his cowboy boots, wearing a corduroy jacket and tight black jeans, with his dark hair combed into a casually disheveled style, maybe a half inch shy of pompadour. When he smoked he liked to snap the Zippo off his ass, light up, and let the cigarette dangle from his bottom lip, give a half-turn glance over the shoulder to see which girls might be watching. At the moment he was making do with a stalk of grass. It was one of the props that gave him a boyish charm he cultivated to the limit.

Shad checked around. The only woman nearby was Becka Dudlow, the preacher's wife. She was midfifties with angry teeth and perpetually hard nipples that passed harsh judgment on anybody who looked. She was also the main supplier of coke and meth in town, though Shad had never been able to figure out where she imported her stuff from. She'd had a thing for Jake ever since he was in her Bible class.

"If you want something with a little more bite," Jake told him, "Luppy Joe's got a couple jugs of moon making the rounds."

Shad's mouth dried just thinking about the harsh taste of it, a quiver working through his belly. Sometimes you needed it so bad that you had to stay away. "The only liquor I've had for two years was a raisin pruno the cons distilled in their toilets."

"Any good?"

"Other guys used to say it was the hardest stuff they'd ever had, flopping around on their bunks and giggling like crazy. Luppy's moon would've taken out most of C-Block in one sitting."

"Jesus Christ," Jake said, giving Shad the long once-over. "You look good. I thought you'd be pale and jittery, but you're more tan than me and I'm outside all afternoon every day. You must've put on at least fifteen pounds too, and it's solid. Works for you." He champed the stalk with his back teeth and it bobbed, twirling this way and that, while Becka Dudlow's eyes followed. "How the hell do you gain weight on institution food? I didn't think prison actually agreed with people."

"It doesn't."

"But I mean, isn't that the whole point? This is where my tax dollars go? Making you better-looking than me?"

"I didn't mind doing time much," Shad said. "They let me have plenty of books."

051270

"Uh-huh. So all you did was read for two years. Developing your mind."

"More or less." It was the kind of thing that didn't sound true but actually was. Everyone in the hollow would be expecting him to talk about shanking guys in the kidneys, which bubbas tried to pull a train on him. You told them what you could, let them understand as much as they were able, and the rest you kept to yourself for when the right time came.

The world tilted red, then black. He turned toward the back hills, trying to concentrate. A soft dangerous heat began to twine across the back of his neck. Up there in the woods, a vague figure without enough form watched him, luminous broken threads wheeling from its faint pain-filled aura. Somebody up there thinking about him, focusing too deeply.

A soft chortle floated from Jake, the kind of murmur he gave when his lips were pressed to a girl's throat. "I'm surprised the Chamber of Commerce didn't throw you a parade."

"Why's that?"

"You're near a hero in these parts, you know."

Sure, except that nobody ever visited him, and only Elfie wrote. Three letters, in the beginning, until it got too rough on the both of them.

"If you're gonna kick the snot out of somebody," Jake said, "make certain it's a piece of shit like Zeke Hester. You were right about that. Reverend Dudlow did a nice bit of preaching on your behalf too, gave the rallying cry down by the river, took up the cause. He likes when folks smack hell out of miscreants." Voice dropping to a whisper, but still loud enough for Becka to hear. "Gives him hope that he might beat up his wife one day and they'd praise him in the pulpit for it."

Nothing ever changed, except Mags was dead. Shad had to keep reminding himself, and the rage would surge through him for a moment, get his heart rate up, as he readied himself for what had to come.

"Anyway, don't be shocked if people start clapping you on the back."

It would never happen but Jake made the scene sound almost possible. His brand of sleekness would've gotten him through ten years of prison without a scratch, then killed him half an hour before they let him out.

"My old man told everybody the story, that's why," Shad said, suddenly wanting to speak with his father. "I think he was sort of proud to have a con in the family. Made him feel righteous for a while. He needed that more than anything."

"Have you seen him yet?"

"No."

Jake nodded, scanning the crowd, searching for anybody who might get a kick out of seeing Shad again after all this time. A delicate tension hovered between them. Jake wanted to give his condolences but was unsure how to actually get around to it, or how Shad would react.

It was going to be like this with everybody in town, Shad realized.

Jake's gaze landed on Elfie, over there on the other side of the burning stacks of timber, barely visible through the fire, but he said nothing. Shad waited, anticipating a bit more, but maybe he was expecting too much as usual.

"You staying with your pa while you're back?"

"No," Shad said. "Over at Mrs. Rhyerson's boarding-house."

"Christ, she's still alive?" Jake let out that laugh again, hissy and honeyed. It could get on your nerves after a while if you let it. "I thought she'd be long gone by now. You must be her only boarder. Where's your car?"

"In town."

"Still got the 'Stang?"

"Yes," Shad told him, knowing what was coming next. "Sat in the garage behind Tub Gattling's used auto parts the whole time I was away, but Tub kept it charged and shined."

"You bought it from him, didn't you? After them other guys died in it, hands on the wheel?"

"Yes."

"Must've made Tub feel like one of his babies had come back to him for warmth and a little tenderness. He loves getting his hands back on the cars he's tuned so fine and let out into the world."

"I suspect you're right."

Jake's stance shifted, his legs set wider apart, shoulders dropping, leaning forward to tell secrets. You learned to look for the subtle body language. "There's still good money to be made in hauling whiskey, if you want to build up a stake to help get you back on your feet. Luppy's always on the lookout for someone who knows the back roads and trails and isn't afraid to jump a crumbling tres-tle bridge."

Shad took a sip of the thin, watery beer and couldn't figure out why he'd wanted one so badly for the last two years. "I've been out of prison for two days, you looking to send me right back?"

"I know you've mostly kept clear of running moon, but just in case you needed some quick cash. Something to consider. I don't see the 'Stang. Who brought you up here?"

"I walked."

"That's near two miles back to Main Street."

"Needed the exercise."

It was true, in a way. He wanted to become part of the hollow again, even if he hated it.

The lines of Jake's confident face softened again for a second. He searched Shad's eyes and didn't like what he found there. His teeth lost some of their shine and the hip hair sagged. He backed off a couple of feet and tried to let his cool slip over him once more, until he was grinning.

Even so, Shad's stomach tightened, the breeze on his neck wafting by like a girlish hand. You could put some things away and they'd only show up when you were ready to take them out again. Others you had a touch more trouble grabbing hold of and locking down. He'd done okay in the can, but already the hollow was beginning to shake him loose inside.

It didn't take anything much. Just the mounting realization, as he watched them and they watched him, that the embrace of the familiar he'd been hoping for was not coming. He could feel the turning of the world around him, the way a boy does when his voice changes and life draws him across the boundary of manhood. That you're moving from one place to another, and no matter how much you want to go back, you can never return.

Part of Jake's poise was taking things slow, backing off when the mood changed. "Enjoy yourself," he said. "You deserve it. Go catch up."

"Nobody's come over yet."

"They're scared."

"Why? I thought I was near a hero in these parts."

Hearing his words flung back at him got Jake grinning again, though he stared at his feet. "Only time anybody's done federal time is 'cause of running moon. You're the first to go away for almost murdering one of their own. Miscreant though Zeke Hester may be. They're afraid of stepping up on you wrong. They're drunk. And excited. They think you're going to kill somebody."

"Do they want me to?"

"I reckon so. It'll break up their day pretty good. But they won't be inviting you over for boysenberry pie for a while." Jake started to drift off. "Still, these people are your friends, don't forget that. Go have yourself some fun, I'll catch up with you later."

A few of them were his friends, and none of them close, but Shad nodded, took another swig, and watched Jake edge in among the others.

He waited for their approach but nobody did. Some of the guys he'd spent most of his life with did little more than cast uncomfortable glances in his direction and tramp off the opposite way. He could understand the discomfort he caused now that he'd become peculiar in a fashion, a curiosity.

Jail was nothing new to them, but a stint upstate was. Maybe they also decided he'd been talking to the feds and spilling the names of moon makers. That he'd been gone for two years and nobody back home had been busted didn't make much of an impression. It gave their lives a little more definition, thinking that the government was coming after them for tax money on homemade liquor. A lot of them still picked up only three channels with the rabbit ears on their television sets.

He could see it in their eager eyes, imagining how he'd been taking it in the ass from his cellmate for the last couple years, or spending all of his time sharpening scrap metal in the tool shop and cutting throats in the shower stalls.

That was all right. You could make peace with anything so long as you had one spot, no matter how small, that nobody could touch.

Shad turned and spotted Elfie Danforth coming at him around the flames, shadows of the others weaving against her. They were spitting moon into the fire because nobody had any more wood or cane to burn. There was nothing better to do so they spewed Luppy's liquor and sort of danced and chased each other around. It wouldn't stop until somebody fell in.

Elfie wasn't quite giving him her usual devastating smile, but at least she wasn't scowling. That familiar, rough tickle started working through his chest. His breathing became ragged and he rubbed his fingertips together, trying to shake off the electrical tingle. These had once been the signs of his affection, and he felt a barely contained sorrow making a grab for his heart.

Sparks scattered, framing her contours as she glided toward him with a calculated thrift of motion. Hips swinging just enough to make him groan. She wore a stylish heavy sweater that didn't conceal any of her natural curves, with her shoulder-length blond hair rising and fanning wildly in the wind.

Her face remained thin and sharp, but in a way that worked. It made you want to run your palms along the angle of her nose, the jut of her chin. Elfie had eyes that weren't entirely fierce but made you think they could easily fill with anger, and you'd do whatever it took to keep that from happening. She squinted when she smiled and really threw everything into it when she laughed, her whole body shuddering, hand on her belly trying to hold it in. She guffawed, low and resonant, none of the silly little-girl snigger that made you wonder if it was all an act, what she might really be after.

They'd made love the night before he'd been arrested. Lying in bed in her trailer out behind her parents' house, listening to the willows swipe at the roof, the metal ringing with a strained note that never let up for a second. Her mama doing the dishes with a fixed regularity, the plates slapping down hard in the sink. Silverware clattering on the porcelain as she took one fork, one spoon, one knife after the other, and rinsed them, dried them, stuck them back in the drawer.

The heavy aroma of low country gullah chicken and hobo bread slid into the trailer's open window, just over his head, and made his stomach rumble. Elfie moved her hand slowly over his stomach, gently scratching through his moist pubis, dipping into the sweat and smoothing the wetness along his thigh. Five minutes later he'd been busted.

Now he could barely control the urge to haul her forward into his arms, hide his face against her neck.

She reached out to brush her fingers through his hair but stopped short, as if his new flecks of gray might be catching.

"Hey, Elfie."

And there it was, the smile that opened him wide. His breath caught and he could only stare—at the perfect teeth, the way she cocked her chin, and how she hit that pose in the moonlight. With an awful clarity he knew she would always symbolize this emotion, the one too intense to have a name.

"I wasn't sure if I'd ever see you again," she said.

"Were you hoping for or against?"

Her lips remained fixed in that modest smirk, but he saw her stiffen. There were some things he shouldn't ask because he didn't really want to know the answer. Waiting to see where they stood only broadened the breach within him.

"I'm not sure."

"I don't blame you."

"I have missed you though."

It was nice of her to say it anyhow. He wanted to believe, as the lust began to do a slow crawl through his guts, and was again surprised at how weak prison had made him in some ways.

She took his hand and drew him farther from the others until they reached an outcropping of rock perched above the river. He kept seeing a pale hand gesturing to him from the corner of his eye, and he had to force himself not to turn. Maybe he'd totally flipped over the edge on C-Block, or maybe coming home again had done it. You didn't need much of a push.

Elfie rubbed her thumb over his knuckles—the nail a dusty blue of glitter—back and forth like settling a baby, the same as she'd always done in school after he'd been brawling. He wondered who she'd dated while he was gone, what new loves, regrets, and heartaches she'd found. He looked back and scanned the gathering to see if any guy was watching intently, somebody pouting, ready to yank a squirrel killer .22 from his pocket and come charging. But there was no one.

"Have you been all right?" he asked, and hoped it didn't sound too dull.

But the way her face closed up, it must've. She held back her questions, her lasting dismay. Her thumb kept brushing over his knuckles, like she was trying to get into his skin and down into his blood. He didn't know what the proper response was supposed to be.

"Yes, I've been fine," she said.

"I'm glad."

The wind continued to heave and abate. Elfie nodded, her hair tangling under her chin, until she slipped it back behind her ears. It kept coiling, flowing toward his throat. You could find your paranoia anywhere.

"I'm working at my father's bait and tackle shop. I do his accounts and the books for a couple of other stores nearby. Chuckie Eagleclaw's art gallery, Bardley Serret's Rock Museum, and the Craftsman and Leather."

Shad almost said, *You were always good with numbers,* but managed to stop himself in time. It was something her father had told her from the start, because he never had anything important to say. Shad had watched Elf go to her pa and admit she was pregnant, asking for his help, and had heard the man say right then and there, *You should go to that banking school in Washatabe County, you always were good with numbers.*

Elfie started talking about Chuckie's books and how you could beat the IRS, but Shad could barely hear her. Mags's pale hand kept distracting him.

"I kept your letters," she said. "They were lovely. You write beautifully."

"I kept yours for a few months too."

It stopped her. "Only a few months?"

"Well, somebody filched them."

She gave a sidelong glance. It was a natural enough reaction, this kind of fear, thinking there was somebody out there who'd read your mail, knew your home address. "Really?"

"It's what guys in the joint do. They're bored. I read a lot of novels and used the envelopes as bookmarks. I'd reread your letters every couple of days, but eventually someone got around to stealing the books."

"Did you know who did it?" she asked.

"Sure. A guy they called Tushie Kline. He was always nosing around my bunk. Tush liked to cause little difficulties where he could. Inconveniences really, general annoyances. Nothing big, just the kind of crap that would ruin your afternoon."

She grew more interested, leaning in now, maybe a touch excited as her eyes grew more serious, hoping to hear about a shiv in the jugular. "Did you do anything about it?"

"Like what?"

"Did you hurt him?"

This was the part where he could really push the story if he wanted, throw in all kinds of nasty action. Hanging somebody in the shower stalls with the elastic from their own underwear, setting them on fire and locking the cell door. Making a gun with a twelve-penny nail, a steel tube, and a rubber band.

But he decided his time as a conversation piece was over. "I taught him how to read."

She drew her chin back like he'd slapped her. "What?"

"Tush always stole books and tore them up, flushed

them down the john. He hated them because he was illiterate, like everybody in his family, and he lashed out."

"That sounds familiar," she said.

Half the county did the same thing. Kept their kids home from school because they thought it was a waste of time. Put them to work on the farm or hauling moon by the time they were eleven or twelve. The best runners were about fourteen years old—young, stupid, and juiced with immortality. Almost everybody had a relation who had died before hitting sixteen. Rolling over down an embankment, broadsiding a semi, head-on into a tree and rupturing the gas tank.

Burning moonshine, if it was the good stuff, couldn't be put out. The flames just kept going for hour after hour. Scorch marks and rusted, burned-out GTO husks littered the hogback paths of the hollow.

"So I taught Tushie to read. Prison libraries have an extensive catalogue of children's literature. The Dick and Jane, A is for Apple type of stuff; and the middle-grade books. He picked it up quick, quit trashing my stuff and we started hanging out together a little, talking about the stories. Got to be okay pals."

Night swarmed around them, alive and malleable. Water lapped across the flat stones and grumbled in the weeds. There were still people who brought their cats down to these rocks in croker sacks and drowned them in the shallows. Elfie shuddered against him and it reminded him of where he was. A cloud of her breath burst against his chest.

She looked into his eyes and he stared back, thinking of how he'd first beaten the hell out of Tush Kline. The guards had urged it on for a few minutes before stopping him. He remembered the troubled looks he'd gotten from other cons in the library later on, making Tush practice his alphabet, the guy's tongue prodding the corner of his mouth as he struggled to spell out Dog. Money. Gun.

Elf had her lips slightly parted, perhaps welcoming a kiss or just feeling him out, see what he'd do next. Shad wasn't certain they'd ever actually been in love, though they'd come pretty close. Maybe they'd been on their way to some kind of happiness, as much as anyone could hope for in the hollow, before she'd become pregnant. It had shocked them both but also infused them with a tenuous sense of joy. Something to look forward to, a new significance that might count for more than they'd believed.

Shad had walked around for about a week wearing a stunned smile, and by the time he'd finally come to fully accept the situation, that he was actually going to be a daddy, she'd miscarried.

Elfie had cried for three days straight until her electrolyte balance was shot. He had to force-feed her salty soup and clean up the constant vomit. Her mama stared out the kitchen window at the trailer but only came over to read the Bible, pray, and order things off the late-night shopping channel without her husband knowing. Painless Nostril Hair Waxer. Anti-snoring Throat Lubricant with Uninterrupted Airflow Pillow. A four-gallon tub of Dissolve'a'Grit.

Elf spent another week mostly unresponsive and staring through the ceiling. He'd heard about this sort of thing before but watching her lying there inert and totally silent, only her lips moving a little, scared the shit out of him. Even more so because when she wasn't holding herself responsible for the baby, he knew she was blaming him and hating him to death.

One morning she came back a little and started dressing herself again. She cleaned the trailer constantly, dusting the high corners. Prying up the floorboards with a spackle blade, really smearing on her mother's Dissolve'a'Grit. You didn't have to be Freud to figure it out.

Eventually she became herself again, never mentioned the baby, and acted as if none of it had happened. Shad played along. They continued seeing each other until he took his fall, but they both must've felt some relief that it was done with.

Now he wondered if enough time would ever pass for him to bring up the kid. If he could tell her what he needed to say. It grieved him to have this secret burden. He always felt it did an injustice to the child as well, without so much as a whisper about it.

"Are you planning to get a job?" she asked.

"No."

"I suppose you'll just run moon like the rest of them."

"You know me better than that."

"It's what everyone does. A few years ago, they still had the option of farming, fishing, working the fields or the cane. But it's different now."

"Is it?"

"It's all make liquor or run liquor. All your old friends are working moon, except for Dave Fox. Jake, Luppy Joe, even Tub sometimes moves whiskey when he's not doing the road shows or the stock car derby."

She mentioned more names. The ones he hadn't thought about since he'd left, coming back to him one after the other. It went to show how elated he'd been to get out of the hollow, even if it was only into the slam. Maybe he'd have time enough to do what needed to be done.

"It's not their fault," he said. "It's just the way things are."

"Don't you want to do more?"

"I haven't thought about it much lately."

"I assumed you would've thought of nothing else."

"You shouldn't have," he told her, and there was more indignation in his voice than he'd meant.

"I see that now."

Naive, a touch too judgmental, but resolute in her convictions. It saddened him some, how much he'd learned behind bars, how forgiving it made him.

"Why'd you come back?" she asked. "You were one of the few people who actually got out of this town."

"I wasn't exactly out," Shad said. "I was in prison."

"For being a man of admirable qualities. You stood up to that Zeke Hester when nobody else would."

"My intentions weren't exactly noble. I just wanted to kill the son of a bitch."

"That's noble enough around here."

Maybe anywhere. She could always crack through the bone of any conversation, reach right in and get to your deepest place. Even if she was wrong, she never let you pull any shit with her. He probably still needed that in his life, even though he'd been waiting two years to find someone he could be soft with once more.

"Shad? You didn't answer me."

He looked at her with the blue awareness that whatever had once held them together had already departed. He could hunt for his passion for the rest of his life and never find it again.

"Why'd you come back?"

"To find out what happened to Megan," he said.

The sound of his sister's name had an unearthly quality to it, ephemeral as an echo. He suddenly felt thirsty and glanced around hoping to see one of Luppy Joe Anson's jugs nearby. The need for moon was suddenly on him.

"I was awfully sorry to hear about her."

Shad wanted to ask a dozen questions, but he couldn't go about it that way. The proper place to start was with his father. All the rest would be rumor, hearsay, and gossip.

"You're a very stupid man, Shad Jenkins."

He shrugged and gave her the grin that used to make her tilt forward to nuzzle his chest. Now she just stared at him, wary and nettled. "You're not the first to tell me that, Elf."

"It's no surprise. You're going to get yourself into very bad trouble in the hollow. You ought to leave. You have to go."

"I will," he said, feeling the rage fragment until slivers prodded his neck, his wrists, "as soon as I find out what happened to Mags."

The ebbing bonfire suddenly burst apart with rekindled life. Swirling flames heaved and bucked. Somebody shouted and the others laughed, still spurting streams of moon.

Shad saw arms whirling and waving, covered in red, and thought somebody was bleeding before he realized it was a guy on fire, trying to put his blazing jacket cuffs out. It was Jake Hapgood, his swept hair singed. Becka Dudlow, the reverend's wife, eased beside him and led him away into the dark, smoke rising from his collar.

"Shad, you're gonna die here," Elfie said.

"Sure," he told her.

Whatever it took. As if any of them had a choice.

Madness in the air, wanting him.

Chapter Two

NOVEMBER WINDS SWEPT THROUGH THE SCRUB oak ringing the property. Stands of slash pine swayed and lurched to the song. The dry creek bed, lush with moonlight, cut a swathe toward the stunted orchards to the west. Shad could feel the abhorrent vacuum of his father's house from a quarter mile away. He stopped his car on the road, unsure that he had enough strength to go on tonight.

The Mustang held meaning. Life and death had been packed tightly in here. It was a sky-blue '69 Boss 429, with 375 horsepower and 450 lb-ft. Bigger and heavier than the preceding year's model, with much-improved handling. Four headlights to slice through the mountain mist, and the interior was more rounded off, with separate cockpits for the driver and passenger.

The seat now perfectly adjusted so that he didn't even really have to press down hard on the pedal, it all came naturally. The thrum of the engine worked into his body, became a part of his pulse.

There was a history to the machine. The two previous owners had died in it, pretty much behind the wheel. You couldn't feel sorry for them.

One was showing off for his girl. He had his hand up her skirt and was tearing donuts through her uncle's cornfield, knocking down the scarecrows. It proved how crazy you could get with boredom when you weren't blocking state troopers for the haulers. Standing on the pedal and cutting off the cruisers so the hunkered-down trucks of moon could slip away.

You lived stupid and died ridiculous. A prized sow had slipped her pen and escaped through the rows, came across the tire tracks and started to eat the crushed corn.

When the driver stopped short the point of his chin snapped down against the steering wheel. It showed where his heart was—you never hit another man's animal. In an instant, his jawbone had shattered and he'd had a heart seizure, dead before the car came to a rest. His fingers still twitching inside the girl while she flipped.

The other guy was Luppy's cousin from the next county over, and Shad had met him once. About twenty-five with a prim manner, vain to the point of carrying a pocket mirror all the time. He dreamed of making a break for Hollywood and becoming a soap opera star. Didn't give a damn about movies, just wanted to do soap operas so his mama and aunts and lady cousins could see him every day on television.

He'd become so obsessed with his prematurely receding hairline that he couldn't quit looking at it. In the car he always checked himself in the rearview, fluffing his curls up in the front, doing whatever he could to cover his broadening forehead.

While tugging at his thinning forelock he missed a stop

sign in the middle of town. The blaring horns caught his attention and brought him back to the road, but not in time. He panicked and stomped the brake, skidding up a curb. The 'Stang did a slow, complete 360 in the intersection out in front of Chuckie Eagleclaw's place, bumped the Civil War cannon on a little plot of turf there. His door sprang open and the guy flopped out into traffic. He managed to make it to his feet before getting smeared by Chuckie's mom, who was turning the corner in her pickup, coming to bring Chuckie his lunch. Hush puppies and sweet-potato pancakes.

Not even a scratch on the car from where it hit the cannon. Chuckie came running outside to check on his mother, shouting, "Ma, you all right?"

She shouted back, "The hell you worrying about me for? I ain't the one snarled in the fan belt."

It gave you strength, being directly connected to death via the machine. Just driving it around in circles, going out to the highway but never getting on, passing the exit and heading back again. It made you feel invincible in an ass-backwards way. Like the black angel was sitting behind you, watching over you so long as you didn't piss him off. That was the trick.

Shad put the 'Stang back in gear and rolled slowly toward his father's house.

Something about the place suggested sorrow. Maybe the lay of the land, or because it had been built—mortar, brick, and log—by Pa while Shad's mother lay dying of pneumonia, in a trailer at the edge of the grounds.

The lengthening shadow of her headstone on the foothill struck the road when the moon rose halfway across the sky. Shad never walked through it.

Mags would be buried up there now as well. It would

take Pa a full five months, perhaps six, to cut the stone from the quarry and chisel and smooth the marker. He would put more love into the rock than he'd ever shown anybody in life. It was the man's way, and Shad felt no resentment about it. You couldn't pass judgment on your own father, no matter what he'd done. There were boundaries of blood that couldn't be crossed.

Almost midnight, and Pa sat on the porch in his rocker, a hound pup flopped at his feet, shivering. The dog's name was Lament. Every dog Pa ever owned was named Lament. There was a reason for that, but Shad didn't know it.

Somehow the cold never bothered his father, regardless of how far the temperature dropped. Even after the ice crystals formed in his beard stubble, he'd still sit there rocking, waiting.

Pa was playing chess against himself, as usual, moonlight flickering in the polished, hand-carved quartz pieces. The old man made only three or four moves a night. He took the game more seriously than others might think—it gave his life an even greater simplicity than anyone would suppose. He just didn't know what to do with himself since his third wife had left him.

The shotgun, always loaded, remained propped across his father's knee.

Collar up, with the heat of his grief keeping him warm as he edged the 'Stang forward. The car helped to keep him in the past, where he needed to be.

A shiver worked between his shoulders as he thought of Mags's empty room inside the house. He gripped the steering wheel tight and drove through the shadow of Mama's headstone, teeth clenched. Symbols like these had the power to torment. You always had to be on your toes.

He felt it again, that somebody in the hills was thinking about him, worried, bitter.

Shad parked and walked up the porch. His father looked over and a rare smile crossed his lips. "Hello, son."

"Hi, Pa."

"You should've let me meet you."

Shad shook his head. "I preferred it this way. Gave me a chance to reacquaint myself. See some of the folks gathering out in the fields, down by the river."

"Any of them right enough in their minds to say hello?"

"A few."

"Can't expect more than that."

You could, but there wasn't much point to it. His father furrowed his brow but said nothing else. He stared at Shad's hands as if inspecting them for prison tats, wondering exactly what tales the new scars might betray. Brawling, knifing, the puckered flesh around his wrists from the tight handcuffs.

His father handled grief and remorse even worse than Shad. You didn't want to think of him as a hypersensitive beat-down disappointment, too often lost in self-pity, but there it was. The old man had discarded everything that ever belonged to each of his wives, damn near every dish, sheet, or couch cushion they'd ever touched. He walked around his own home like it was tearing off his skin.

His memories were already too powerful and he didn't need anything more to remind him of the experiences. Pa couldn't bear to own anything with a history that he hadn't made with his own hands.

Karl Jenkins had turned sixty-three years old last month, and he'd finally aged into his flat broad face as hard-featured as bedrock. Firm-muscled and compact, he contained a coiled energy that made him always seem a second away from leaping forward into your chest. Pa moved with a bearish and terrible grace, a relentless sense of force.

He usually kept his thick silver hair short, but since Mags had died no one had cut it for him. Shad liked how it had grown out, giving him an easygoing appearance that offset his impenetrable dark eyes. Shad had started to go gray when he was seventeen, and now at twenty-two he had white at his temples and a patch in front that at first glance made him appear older than his own father.

Pa had passed a determined sort of melancholia down to his children, but not much of his despair. The man's first wife had run off with a farm equipment salesman trying to sell them a used corn thresher. It didn't take much to seduce and persuade folks to leave Moon Run Hollow.

His second wife—Shad's mother—had died less than a year into their marriage, three weeks after Shad's birth and long before the final log had been shaved and laid into the roof of the house.

You could wind up with a wretched history without having to do a damn thing on your own. Just sit around long enough and it would just happen around you.

His third wife, Tandy Mae Lusk—Megan's mother—had given birth to Mags, stuck around for about three years, then skipped town with her own first cousin whom she'd always been in love with. She hadn't gotten far. They lived less than twenty miles away in Waynescross now, burdened with a brood of crippled ill children. Two with flippers instead of arms, one hydrocephalic with a wet brain and enormous head, another with no bone in his jaw and hardly any spine.

Mags never saw her mother again. But on occasion Shad would drive out to the neglected Lusk farm near a diseased cherry orchard, watch the kids rolling and crawling around the yard, and try to figure out exactly what it all meant.

Pa wouldn't ask any questions, and he'd never bring Mags up on his own. He propped the shotgun in the corner, pulled a beer off the porch rail, and passed it to Shad, gesturing for him to sit. Shad slid into the love seat swing and pretended to sip from the can.

His father had never asked him to play chess. Pa did on his own, at his own pace, in order to keep his own footing in the world. He sat in the night for his own reasons, some of which Shad could guess at, most he never wanted to learn. You had to let some things slide.

They'd have to get around to Megan's death slowly. The weight of Mags's presence was a solid pressure on Shad's shoulders. He could feel it there caressing his back the way she used to do when he'd wrenched himself chopping wood. The women in his life were always rubbing him, patting him like, *Baby, baby, all will be fine, go sleep now.* He knew it was his own fault.

It was going to take a while to think of her in the past tense. He still occasionally spoke of his mother as if he'd just seen her a couple of days before, instead of never having met the woman at all. When you needed your family, you built one from whatever you had on hand.

He peered through the window, but the inside of the house was too dim for him to see anything. The dog sat up, furiously scratched his ear, then lay down again with a lengthy sigh.

"Zeke Hester come around looking for you three or four days ago," Pa said. "He was keeping tabs on when you got out."

"Did he hassle you?"

"No, but he's got a short memory, that boy. Doesn't quite recall what happened to him last time."

"He remembers."

"Not well enough, I reckon."

Maybe that was true, maybe not. Shad supposed he'd find out soon enough. The pride in his father's voice was more jarring than he'd expected. If only Pa had ever sounded that way about something that hadn't sent Shad to jail. "Did he say anything about Mags?"

"You don't want to know what he said about her. I went for the shotgun but he was already gone by the time I got back to the door."

Pa was like a cop standing watch over a crime scene. The body removed, but the blood still on the floor.

"He's a fool, Pa. He isn't even worth getting mad about."

"That your advice to me after spending two years downstate for trouncing hell out of him?"

"But I didn't get mad," Shad said.

"You split your own hairs, son, I'll split mine. That's the way of it."

"Sure enough."

The rage started working through Shad again, but he kept it down where it could be handled. It wasn't anger though, not the usual kind. He swallowed a groan, felt the living confusion inside him swell for an instant, then settle. The hound let out a whine, keeping an eye on Shad. Zeke Hester had wanted Megan, there was no other way to

say it, but she'd always managed to elude him as she flour-
ished into womanhood. Shad did what he could, which
amounted to giving Zeke a few even-handed threats that
the guy was too ignorant to heed. He simply may not have
understood what Shad was getting at.

It went on like that for a couple of years, until the night
Zeke caught her behind Crisco Miller's still on Sweetwater
Creek. While Shad was just starting to put the butter
knives back out for Elfie, Zeke was throwing his all at
Mags. He battered her pretty good, fractured her wrist
and dislocated her left knee, but he never got what he was
after. Mags had hellfire in her when she got going. She had
Pa's hands, small but hard with meat to them.

She succeeded in slugging Zeke in the mouth hard
enough to crack a rotted front tooth he had hanging
among the rest of the brown train wreck. The pain cata-
pulted him sideways, and she kicked free and crawled into
the tree line to hide.

She refused to go to the doctor and only lay in bed for a
weekend before she got back to doing her chores. Mags had
a resolve that Shad had never acquired. They talked a lot during those couple of days, but he couldn't remember a word of
it. He was having a difficult time even hearing her voice
nowadays. It was the kind of thing that made you knot your
fists and drive them into your temples, trying to loosen
memories. The only voice she had was the impact left on him.

When Shad caught up with Zeke Hester outside of
Griff's Suds'n'Pump, he broke the bastard's jaw, cheek,
nose, and left arm in three places.

True enough, he hadn't gotten mad. A cool lucidity had
somehow draped over him, a calm he hadn't experienced
before. By the time Zeke was weeping on his belly and

baying in pain, Shad felt only an ample amount of pity and sadness.

When Sheriff Increase Wintel asked him why it had happened, Shad refused to explain. Some circumstances you kept quiet about if you could. When you managed it, you found your assurance in the silence.

Perhaps it was a talent he'd picked up from his father. He willingly took the deuce in prison and managed to finish three semesters' worth of college courses. All in all, he'd read about a book a day for the two years he was inside, and he'd only had to watch one man die.

His father studied the chessboard for a minute before he moved the white bishop.

Shad looked off at the brush-shrouded terrain and tried to discern movement. Already the old caged-in feeling was beginning to overtake him. You could prepare for it but you couldn't get away from your smallest apprehensions. The dark land led back into the surrounding weed-choked pastures, and the air seemed thick with a sickeningly sweet honeysuckle even at the end of autumn.

"What happened, Pa?"

His father's perfect control wavered, and the angles of his face fell in on themselves. The old man opened his mouth and shut it again. Cleared his throat and moved the white bishop back where it'd been.

"She never came home."

Shad waited but his father said nothing more. "The hell does that mean?"

"She went to school like always and just never come back."

Okay, so he was going to have to pry it loose. Shad

flipped the beer can across the porch and stood, moved in on his father. "Tell me about it. That afternoon."

"You can't change nothin', son."

"I realize that." His fingers flexed, like he was ushering the words out. "But I need to know. Do it for me. As much as it pains you."

Pa pulled himself together, sluggishly. He shut his eyes and his chin began to lower to his chest. It stayed there for a while. Shad rapped the chessboard with his knuckles, careful not to jostle the pieces. His father opened his eyes.

"I tried not to get nervous that afternoon," Pa said. "I thought maybe she went off with that Luvell girl. Malt shop, the junior rodeo over there in Springfield. However they keep busy. You know your sister was a good girl, she doesn't do what them others all do. When it came evening I made some phone calls but nobody's seen her. Come ten o'clock I called the sheriff's office. She'd never been out past that without telling me before. That damn Increase Wintel didn't pay me no heed, but Dave Fox went off looking right then. He found her the next morning."

Leaning closer, Shad remained poised, but his father had hit the wall again.

"And what happened to her?"

"Nobody's sure. She just . . . went to sleep there on Gospel Trail Road."

"That's not what you told me."

"Yes it is, boy."

"You said—"

"I know what I said. I told you the truth is what I did."

His father's voice had cracked painfully when he'd phoned the prison over a month ago. It was the only call Shad ever received on the inside. He knew it was going to be awful the instant he touched the receiver. Pa had said exactly thirteen words and hung up before Shad could respond.

Your sister's been killed. Come home 'fore you get on with your life.

Pa couldn't see the disparity of what he'd said on the phone and what he was saying now. Shad had to let it go.

He chewed his tongue, kept staring into darkness. "There's nothing up that way at all. Gospel Trail leads to the trestle, doesn't it? Why was she near the gorge?"

"I ain't got no answers."

"But what did she die from?"

"I don't know that either. They never found out. Doc Bollar ain't a big-city medical examiner. All he told me was her heart stopped. How's that for putting a father's mind at rest? That bastard!"

Mags had just turned seventeen. He searched Pa's face to see if the old man was hiding anything, but there was only the usual frustration in his features, the endless disappointment.

"It's a bad road, son."

The words, spoken as if they held a terrible meaning. "What's that?"

"I told you kids to keep off it, didn't I?"

"The road? When did you ever tell me to stay clear of it?"

"Since you were both children!" The veins on his father's wiry forearms stood out, the thick muscles in his neck corded and going red. "Not to go up there on Gospel Trail! It's a bad road! Didn't I say that?"

"Did you?"

"Stay away from Jonah Ridge! There's nothing there

but murder in wait. Don't neither of you ever listen to me?"

Now that Shad thought about it some, he realized that he'd never been up there to the top of the gorge in his life. His father had told him, many times, but Shad didn't stay away because of that. He simply never had a reason to go into those hills. And neither had Megan, so far as he knew.

"Tell me what you mean by that."

"Don't you know yet, boy?"

"No. Why would there be murder waiting?"

"I can't explain it no better."

His father stood, with that coiled explosive force inside him about to propel him forward. Shad reached out and took his father by the shoulders, held the old man where he was. They both began to tremble, fighting one another like that, will against will. Shad understood that his father was no longer going to be of any help. Whatever had to be done, he had to do himself.

"I'll take care of it," he said.

"Don't talk such damn nonsense!"

"It'll be okay."

The pressure inside Pa suddenly eased. He deflated and slumped back into his chair, weakly started to rock again. The dog began to crawl around in circles. Shad patted his father's back, rubbing him, like, *Baby, baby, all will be fine, go sleep now.*

"Have you told Tandy Mae?" he asked. Shad didn't feel comfortable bringing it up, but had to do so.

"I got no truck with her anymore, son."

"She's Megan's mother."

"That isn't much of a truth to tell. Tandy gave birth to her, that's all. 'Sides, she got enough worries with them

other lame and afflicted children. Every one of us got
enough burden already, don't you think?"

When you got down to it, when somebody put it like
that, you couldn't do anything but agree. Shad nodded.
"Yes."

"You gonna stay the night?"

"No."

"Didn't think you would, but you're welcome to stay,
a'course. Your old bedroom's still fixed up. Megan always
cleaned it, put clean sheets on while you were away."

His father's steady motion began to waver. As if he
consciously forced himself to keep going but kept forget-
ting, from second to second, what he was supposed to be
doing.

Shad started to turn. His father was instantly on him,
an inch away and hovering. "Son—"

"I want to see her room."

"There isn't anything left that might help you."

"Show me."

"It's gonna do nothing but kill you, if'n you stay."

Everyone thinking he didn't have a chance, that he was
already dead.

"What is?"

"The hollow."

Shad spoke gently now, softly, the way you had to talk
to Tandy Mae's hydrocephalic pumpkin-headed son. "Pa,
you wanted me to come home. Now I'm here. I want to
check her room."

The hound rose slowly and stood at Shad's knee as he
pulled open the screen door and pressed inside.

Immediately he could feel the oppression of common
failure and everyday defeat. You could smell it like the

stink of terror. Anybody who had it on him in prison was finished by the end of the first week.

You didn't have to be murdered to haunt a house. And the place didn't have to do anything more than exist to harass you. He wondered why he'd never felt it in his cell, with a century of caged men's energy imprisoned along with him. No, only here, surrounded by family.

He entered Mags's room and stopped short. All her belongings were still in their appropriate spots—the schoolbooks and teen magazines stacked neatly on her desk, closet door open and her clothes draped on hangers and hooks. Shad gritted his teeth and almost glanced away.

"You didn't touch anything."

"I couldn't."

"That's not like you. She's been dead six weeks." About twenty minutes after Tandy Mae had taken up with her cousin, Pa had cleared every remnant of the woman from the house. Whatever she didn't take, he burned in a bin out back.

His father shrugged, appeared almost sheepish. Was it because he'd lost yet another woman in his life? Or had he finally learned that removing the effects didn't push out any of the memories?

"Five and a half," Pa said.

"Did the police show up here?"

"Sheriff Wintel never came around at all, not even to offer his commiseration and condolences. Dave Fox searched through her things. Wore a pair of latex gloves the whole time. He inspected different parts a'the house, looked around the yard some. I'm not sure what he might've been hunting for. Drugs, I suppose. But she never touched none of that. There was nothing suspicious. So he told me, anyways. But if there was nothing peculiar, why was he lookin'?"

"Good point."

So Dave didn't consider her death to be from natural causes. Shad checked for something he could use to help him hold his course. "Letters? A diary?" He unmade the bed and, despite himself, tore away the blankets, and pulled up the mattress, the box spring Pa had made himself. He stared blankly at the clean slats of the floor beneath.

"Nothing like that. You knew your sister."

Of course he had—but no, of course he hadn't. Not anymore. He'd strayed off for two of the most important years in her life. When he'd gone into the can she'd just begun the transition from girl to young woman. It made him ache to think of what he'd missed.

"Don't go up there," his father said again, the man talking the way he did when Shad was a kid. "Stay away from them woods."

"Pa, did you ever think that maybe someone just left her there? A boyfriend?"

"She didn't have none."

"Maybe you just didn't know."

"I knew everything about my baby girl."

Except why she was dead. "They probably went up there to make out. Had a fight. She—"

"There wasn't no boy, son."

He'd been priming himself for weeks to avenge a killing. There had been cruelty in his father's voice, whether the old man admitted to it now or not. He'd been calling down the rage, hoping to set it in motion.

Shad walked out but couldn't help staring over at the

chessboard. Both sides had mate in three moves. Pa always played a losing game.

Most of them did. Shad knew he had to fight, all the time, without hope of finishing, to keep from doing the same. The blood dreams had violent, beautiful needs that were entirely human.

Chapter Three

WHEN HE GOT BACK TO MRS. RHYERSON'S boardinghouse he called Dave Fox from the phone in the hallway, and said, "It's Shad Jenkins. I want you to show me where Megan's body was found."

Even a call at midnight didn't surprise Dave. When you stood six-foot-four, went 250 of brawn and assurance, and could shoot the asshole out of a junkyard rat with an S&W.32 at two hundred yards, there wasn't much that could shake you. He'd never been rattled in his life, over anything, but there was a trace of concern in his firm voice. "Maybe that's not such a smart decision. The hell are you doing? You shouldn't even be here."

"It's about time people stopped informing me of their opinions on where I should be."

"You nearly gained yourself a college degree in the can. That puts you on the highway out of this county. You got a start on something new."

It surprised Shad. He hadn't known Dave Fox or the sheriff's office would be so plugged in on him. He leaned against the wall, trying to ignore the pink wallpaper and a framed paint-by-numbers portrait of Conway Twitty shaking hands with Jesus.

"Is that how you'd play it?" Shad asked.

He was almost grinning and wasn't sure why, until he reached up and felt his lips and realized it wasn't a grin at all, he was baring his teeth. You could lose control for an instant and not even know it.

Never show what's inside. If you didn't hide it, they'd use it against you. He touched his mouth again and his expression was tranquil.

Dave still hadn't responded and wouldn't put it into words, but they both understood that hollow folks always paid their debts, and went after whatever was owed. "Will you take me up there?"

"Yes. I'll pick you up at seven."

"Thanks."

It made sense. Dave had been keeping tabs on him and already knew Shad was staying at the boardinghouse.

He could hear it in the deputy's voice, and sense his fortitude even over the phone. Dave Fox remained imperturbable, solid as mahogany, a tower of finely carved muscle, unwavering but purposeful. They'd never been particularly close but Shad guessed that was about to change now.

He hung up and thought of Mags's beautiful face, dead at seventeen, laid out in the middle of a road no one ever traveled.

When he got back to the room his mother and the white bishop were waiting for him, standing there together smiling, breathing heavily as if they'd just been dancing. Shad looked down and saw himself sleeping on the bed with his eyes open.

It hadn't happened like this for a while.

With her hand against the white bishop's chin, drawing him to her, the robes flowed around them both as they whispered to one another and giggled. Shad noticed the inside of the window was steamed, and a word was written on the glass.

Pharisee

Someone had spelled it out using an index finger.

Shad stepped toward his mother but she wasn't aware of him yet. It would take time, he knew, and he tried not to let the dread build within him. The bishop moved away from her and leaned over Shad's body on the bed, put a hand on his shoulder as if trying to wake him. Failing that, the bishop slid away and came to rest beside Shad where he stood in the center of the room, and spoke to him from the corner of his mouth. As if they were conspirators in a grand royal treachery.

The white bishop's voice was the voice of his father. "So there you are."

"Yes," Shad said.

The three roles of the bishop were illustrated in his vestments. His role as ruler was denoted by the crown. As a guardian, by the shepherd's staff. As a guide, by the bells on the *saccos,* the short tunic with box sleeves. The sides were buttoned up with bells, beginning at the wrists and flowing to the bottom of the hem. The bells called worshipers to follow.

The *Omophorion*—the long band of cloth marked with crosses that passed around the neck—wafted as if a steady breeze was loose in the room. The vestments were styled after the official's robes at the court of the Byzantine Emperor.

Shad had no idea how he knew such things. His cellmate, Jeffie O'Rourke, was probably the only Catholic he had ever met.

The staff stood midchest high and had a small crossbar as a handle. The white bishop tapped it on the floor to get Shad's attention. "She forgets more every year."

"I know," Shad said. "It's better that way."

"She wants to give you advice, though."

He tried to imagine what it might be, the form it would take, and if there was any chance that it might prove useful. Usually his mother's guidance—if this was his mother—came in tangled meanings and bewildering prophecies that never came to pass. He kept waiting, hoping she'd help him out along the way, but so far she wasn't proving to be much of an oracle.

Mama's ghost slowly became cognizant of him standing there and glanced over, searching, but without seeing him yet. She stared off into the distance, and said, "Son?"

"I'm here, Mama."

"Son?"

"I'm right next to you."

"Shad?"

"Yes."

"Oh, there. Hello."

"Hello, Mama."

She smiled and held her hand out to him. If he took it, she would vanish and he'd awaken on the bed and immediately begin spitting up blood.

Now, he had an awful anxiety working through him that Megan had somehow willed this visit and was watching from nearby. He wanted to ask the white bishop about Mags but decided against it. You could only handle one ghost at a time. It unsettled him to think his sister might begin appearing to him like this, lost and perpetually confused, the way his mother had been coming to him since he was eleven or twelve years old.

When he was a child, his mother's spirit had been full of anger and bitterness, and spent most of her stays doing little more than railing against his father. Since then, she'd lost more and more of her interest in this world, but he couldn't figure out if he was somehow calling her to him, and if so, what he could do to stop it.

"Shad? You listen, son. You listen to me."

"He is," the white bishop said, by way of helping.

"Shh. Leave her be." Shad moved to his mother until her gaze fell on him once more. "I'm listening, Mama."

"Stay off that road."

He had to be sure he knew what she meant. "Which road?"

"The Gospel road. They get taken away up there."

"How did Megan die?"

"She's not my girl. That isn't my daughter."

"No, but she's my sister."

The blunt angles of her face sharpened with anger. "The harlot. He lay with the harlot. I still had skin, the earth wasn't cold, and he sanded his stone and cleaved to another."

Shad was surprised. It was the most emotion she'd shown him in years. "What happens on that road, Mama?"

"There's bad will."

That was true everywhere you went. "Who did it to her? Did somebody hurt her? What was she doing there?"

"They don't prove love with their teeth," she said, and the bishop nodded. He appeared weaker, grieving, and she glanced over and gave him a look of anguish. "They leave their marks and they can even kill, yes, but it's all in vain. Listen to me, they don't demonstrate, you see. They don't *represent*. They don't represent the savior. Instead, it's the land. One with the river. It's him. He represents."

A word that had a whole different meaning in the can—the gangbangers and car boosters used it all the time. She kept at it, swaying now. "But he can demonstrate his belief on his belly. Our Lord, our Lord. My God. But they all manifest nothing more than poison. Do you understand that?"

"No," he told her.

Manifest wasn't a word his mother would know, even in the afterlife. It was a word he wouldn't have known himself before all the books in prison. "You stay away from there. They will take you."

The white bishop, acting the guardian, raised his shepherd's staff over Shad's body on the bed. The band of cloth around his neck continued to flap and waver as if buffeted by winds. As guide, he shook his arms and allowed the bells to ring quietly.

Shad's hands tightened into fists, the sheets twisted and bunched around him. Mags had been a part of the spot inside him that no one could touch. She had kept him alive in prison and now he'd never be able to thank her. He began to sob in his sleep but the despondent sound choked off quickly.

Groaning once, he dreamed of revenging himself on whoever had taken his sister from him, and soon began to whimper. His mother clawed the air, advanced like an animal, and sprang at him. The moment they touched he opened his eyes, flailed aside, and coughed blood onto the floor.

Chapter Four

THE TEMPERATURE HAD DROPPED DURING
the night. Over the wide curve of the ridge the
countryside sloped into an area lined with virgin stands of more slash pine. The scent of matted cedar rose and wafted along the rutted road. Around
them grew thin white oak and the heavy grasses only occasionally trimmed back by the chain gang road crews. Off
to the east were thickets of briar and heavy thistle that
could flay a hiker who'd taken a wrong turn.

Shad stood staring at the hard-packed earth where
Megan's body had been discovered, trying to confess to her
how sorry he felt, through the endless veil.

"My pa tells me this is a bad road," Shad said.

Dave glanced over. "Mine says the same."

"He ever explain why?"

"You know the history of the area. The plague victims.
It gets him edgy. Something left over from their fathers
and grandfathers, I suppose."

Shad thought of his old man twisted out of shape, his

mother's elusive warnings that would probably never be
unraveled. "There's more than that."

"There always is."

Deputy Dave Fox, dressed in his sharply creased gray
uniform, crossed his massive arms over his chest. He
shifted his stance until the leather of his gun belt creaked.
With his jacket partway open, you could see that the neat-
ness ... the *straightness* of his pinned tie was so perfect it
appeared to be nailed to him.

You couldn't get away from the feeling that Dave was
about a hundred years displaced. Someone who should've
been out there driving cattle across the plains, fighting
Indians hand to hand, or walking down the middle of a
boomtown street heading for a shoot-out. Shad had always
held a tremendous admiration for Dave, even in school
when they were kids. Back then, it had bordered on something like reverence. Now Shad didn't know what it was.
Maybe the same thing.

After joining the local police force at eighteen, Dave
had broken up the Boxcars ring in Okra County, all on his
own. Over on Route 12, with the whores' rusty trailers out
back, the hole in the wall barroom had become a hot spot
of loaded gambling and contaminated moon in the space
of six months. The white slavery ring had brought in un-
derage girls from as far off as Poverhoe City. The Southern
mob guys would come around for some fun and go off
their nuts, and they still held lynching raids when they
got drunk enough.

Dave had kicked it all down in about two hours. Killed
three men and the madam, who'd just finished beating a
teenage girl unconscious with a car antenna for not being
perky enough with a businessman from Memphis. He

arrested seven other thugs before Sheriff Increase Wintel even showed up. Dave had been shot twice in the thigh by a .22 and it hadn't slowed him up a step. He received a commendation and had his photo taken with the governor.

"I've never been out this way," Shad admitted.

"Not even when you were blocking moonrunners for Luppy Joe Anson?"

"I only did it for one summer, and he had no buyers anywhere near here."

"None of them do, but sometimes when they're trying to slip the highway patrol, they come out because of the turnoffs, hide in the brush or around the creeks. Powder the cops' faces tearing along the dirt roads and kicking up dust."

"It doesn't work. I stuck closer to town."

"That's why you never got caught."

Some of the runners, they were only in it for the game. If the police weren't involved, coming at them from all sides and putting up roadblocks, it just wasn't any fun.

"What's over that way?" Shad asked, looking up the trail. It annoyed him that he didn't know the lay of the land here, as if it had been hidden from him. "Is it just the trestle leading to the other side of the gorge?"

"Pretty much. The road heads into the mountains, threads north to the trestle bridge. There's a trail on the other side of Jonah Ridge that peters out in some bramble forests. Used to be sort of a lovers' lane, a hundred forty or so years ago, before the war and the outbreak of yellow fever. They'd go courting and bring their whole families. There's nice grasslands around in summer, wildflowers all over. Horse and buggies would head up toward the gorge and couples would picnic after church, quote scripture and sing gospels."

His mother telling him, *They die up there.*

Shad got that feeling again, that someone was focusing on him, calling up their forces and aiming their intent. He wavered on his feet and began to sweat. He saw nothing, but still sensed movement around him—flitting, dancing even. The back of his neck warmed and his ears were suddenly burning. He concentrated but couldn't center himself. It took a minute for the November breeze to cool him.

Dave asked, "You okay?"

"Yes."

Leaning back against his patrol car, Dave said, "Probably started getting its reputation right around the time of the Battle of Chickamauga. Some captured Union troops were corralled up there by the Rebs and tossed into the gorge."

Shad hadn't thought of that in a long time, but now that he heard it, he abruptly remembered the story. "I almost forgot about that."

"It's not the kind of Civil War moment people put plaques up about to commemorate. After that, the hollow had its share of epidemics. Yellow fever in 1885. Cholera in 1915. When the disease reached its worst they'd bring whole wagons of the sick into the hills and leave them there."

"Jesus."

Dave spoke with great clarity, completely without emotion. "Suicides would come up this way too."

"That's right."

"The lonely, the elderly. They'd throw themselves off the precipice."

Shad caught vague, fleeting impressions of Mags around him, and spotted her pale hand again. Reaching, trying to touch. It was time to get down to hearing whatever facts there were.

"What killed her?" he asked.

"The autopsy didn't reveal any cause of death," Dave told him.

That stopped Shad, made him turn and cock his head. "The hell's that mean?"

"Exactly what I said."

"My father suspects she was murdered."

"I know. He spreads his suspicions high and low around town. But officially her death is listed as 'by misadventure.'"

Shad waited, counting the snap of his pulse to ten while Dave patiently influenced himself upon the world. "What?"

"Death by misadventure."

It could get like this at the oddest times. He wished he had a cigarette—this was the kind of circumstance where a guy would take a drag, allow the seconds to roll by while he kept his lungs busy, then let the smoke out in a thin stream, everything cool and hip and effective.

He fought to make his voice casual. Never any show of consternation, especially with someone that much bigger than you. "Dave, are you going to keep making me say 'what the goddamn' all day long? Or will you just lay it out?"

"We don't have any answers."

"I got that much."

"Misadventure means it's an accident we can't explain."

"And that's an *official* report?"

"Yes."

"You guys really cover your asses." No matter how hard you tried, you'd never figure out the carefully constructed mystification of the justice system. "If you can't explain it, then you don't know she was actually killed."

"That's right."

"Her heart simply stopped."

"That's right."

"For no reason."

"That we can ascertain."

"So why's my father say she was murdered?"

Dave's expression didn't change but he settled back on his feet, and the slight adjustment in his body language let Shad know he felt a touch embarrassed. Not for himself, but for Pa. You had to have been around Dave Fox for most of your life in order to pick up on little things like that, and even then you wouldn't know what it really meant.

"She had a scratch on her cheek," Dave said. "He takes it to mean she was attacked."

Shad searched the deputy's face and came up empty. "And you do too?"

"I didn't say that."

"No, you didn't." Dave made you fight for everything, but his silence still gave him away occasionally. It was one way he could stay true to himself and still let people know what was on his mind. "Doc never cared much for moon, he's more of a Jack Daniel's drinker. I'd come across him on the lower banks while I was hauling whiskey, out cold with his feet in the water."

"He's got bunions."

"I'd stop and pick him up, drive him home before he floated off. His wife always tried to pay me forty dollars when I'd bring him inside. I'm not sure how she arrived at that price."

Telling Dave pretty much what he thought of old Doc without having to come right out with it.

But Dave Fox would never talk out against someone in authority, not even against the sheriff, who everyone knew was on the take. He drew his line in the sand and kicked the shit out of everybody to one side and let everyone on the other side slide.

"Who found her?" Shad asked.

"I did. She was lying there, like I said, as if she were sleeping."

"What made you think to look all the way out here?"

"I looked everywhere. I started when your father called at about ten o'clock or so, and discovered her at four-fifteen in the morning."

"Don't you ever sleep?"

"No."

Shad thought about his sister so far from town, in the night, alone, surrounded by darkness. How different would it have played out if he'd been home? Maybe the same, except he would've been the one to find her.

He could imagine himself there beside her. Hear himself groaning, cradling her, kneeling in the dirt with her body in his arms. His breath hitched until he was almost snorting. His hands clasped into fists as if he were trying to grab hold of her, there on the ground, and pull her back toward him.

He started to walk up the road and Dave fell in line beside him. They worked their way toward high ground that was dense with oak and heavy underbrush. Farther off, near the ridge, the willows loomed and swayed in the crosswinds.

He'd missed too much in the two years he was gone, and it was hobbling him. There would've been more boys around, a part-time job, other activities. He didn't know Megan well enough anymore, and nobody was filling him in.

"She was seventeen," he said. "She wouldn't have come up this way alone."

"I talked to her friends, classmates, and the closest neighbors. They all said she wasn't seeing anyone. Had no beau. Did she ever write you and say different?"

"No. She never wrote me. I told her not to."

"Why?"

"It would've only made it harder."

The closest neighbors were more than a mile off through the fields in any direction from Pa's house. They wouldn't know anything. Who were the girls she used to be friendly with? He couldn't remember.

"Maybe a new boy," Shad said.

"If so, nobody ever saw them together."

"A party?"

"I checked with all the parents. No one was gone for the night. No parties. One of the kids would've mentioned it."

"A bonfire that night? In the fields?"

"No signs of one at all. No fresh tire tracks, no ashes, no trash. Somebody would've said something."

"Even if they were trying to hide her death?"

With a slow, heavy breath Dave tried to reach out with

his own will and composure and calm Shad down. "What group of teenagers can keep their mouths shut about anything?"

None. Shad realized it but was already grasping for whatever he could. In the can, locked down with assholes and killers everywhere, he never lost his confidence or ease. Now, standing here, he knew he was shaking apart inside. It was almost enough to scare him, but not quite.

"Was she raped?"

"No. There was no indication of a struggle."

"Did you . . . ?"

"You need to stop acting like a private eye, Shad Jenkins. You're not very good at it. Stop asking so many questions."

"You're right," Shad admitted, "but it's not going to happen. Did you talk to Zeke Hester?"

"He was in Dober's Roadhouse, same as every night. Drunk and causing his usual misfortunes and woe. Had one altercation with the bartender, threw a pool cue across the room."

"He likes throwing things. The day I broke his arm he took off his boot and hurled it at my face."

"He's a sniveler, but twenty witnesses put him there until closing at two A.M. His mother says he got home quarter after. He tripped over her loom and busted her paint-by-numbers picture of Elvis and Jesus smiling on a cloud."

"Not Conway Twitty?"

"I know Elvis when I see him. So Old Lady Hester hit Zeke with an iron skillet and he passed out on the living room rug. And she's not covering for him. His mama hates him even more than you do."

"Maybe."

Mags's hand, waving to him from the corner of his eye, snagged his attention. If he turned his head, he'd lose her, so he froze, kept her in frame. Dave kept going for another yard, then stopped and looked at him. Shad tried to inspect her nails, see if they were broken or caked with grime, maybe somebody's skin.

It took a few seconds to slip into the shrouded, quiet place inside himself where he could handle whatever life threw at him. He couldn't get all the way there, but the effort helped, even as Megan's fingers flitted at the edges of his vision. Her hand looked clean. She drew it away.

Much calmer now, he asked, "Anything else out there? In those woods?"

"Not nearby. A few overgrown logging paths that lead to the old McMueller Mill. It's only ruins now, even the stream has dried up. Some stunted orchards, I think. I'm not really sure."

"Who lives over that way?"

"A few of the bottom hill families on the other side of the gorge. They stick to themselves, hardly ever come down into town. The Taskers. The Johansens. And the Gabriels too, as I recall. They have their own community, sort of an extended village up there near the briar woods. They're snake handlers, way I hear tell."

"I don't know any of them."

"I've met a couple and run into them now and again, but they keep their church goings-on to themselves. No phone among the bunch of them. Never cause any trouble. Red Sublett and his brood dwell nearby there, but he's not a part of their camp. He's got nine kids now. No wonder he looks half-dead when he comes in for supplies."

Shad thought of Red's wife, Lottie, hangdog and toothless, and he had to control a shudder from going through him. "Goddamn, he only had five when I went in."

"He got himself a set of premature quadruplets last year. All of them with club feet and stunted legs, and none with the correct amount of fingers. That Lottie, she's pushing them out too damn fast."

Shad didn't say aloud what they both already knew, that Red and Lottie were siblings though they usually denied it, but not always. Doing whatever they wanted to do, not out of love or even a fundamental need, but simply because of proximity. What a foolish reason to visit sins upon your babies.

He thought of Tandy Mae's children, who were Megan's deformed half brothers and half sisters, and so, somehow related to him by the narrow channels of blood.

"My grandfather used to tell me these hills were haunted," Dave told him.

The woods thickened with ash and birch and more slash pine, the land wild with sprawled logs and lightning-struck trunks clotted with weeds. Tangled briars, rosebay, Catawba, and rhododendron and dogwood knotted in mad, awkward patterns. Shad sighted areas of bark scarred with bullet holes and buckshot. There were flashes of light winking in the brush, reflections from beer cans and broken jugs of moon.

"Maybe they are," Shad said. It was true, at least for today. Megan, or something, wanted his pledge.

So now they were down to it. The milieu fluctuated a little, Dave taking full control again without having to do a damn thing.

"I don't want you to cause any trouble out this way, Shad Jenkins."

"I don't intend to."

"You're a god-awful liar."

"I have to find out what happened to her."

"That's my job." Voice firm, putting some bite into it. "Leave this to me."

It was Dave Fox's way of saying, no matter what the official report might read, that he would never give up on the case, he'd work it until the truth finally broke free.

"Let's go up there for a few minutes."

"Where?"

"Top of Jonah Ridge," Shad said.

"The hell for?"

"I want to take a look."

Dave pulled a face that only cops knew how to make—like he was dealing with a wiseass brat and ready to visit great injury upon that kid any second. But he obliged, willing to give Shad just a little more slack.

They walked back to the patrol car and drove up the Gospel Trail. The expanse broke into numerous dirt paths leading into the thickets and scrub tilting away from the rise. A split-rail fence had been put up to keep people from wandering off the edge.

The Chatalaha had, by its scouring violence, formed one of the most rugged chasms for hundreds of miles in any direction. The steep walls of the gorge enclosed the river for almost fifteen miles, clear up to Poverhoe. On the other side of the ravine, the terrain grew extremely steep and rugged, covered by a dense hardwood forest.

They got out. Dave Fox showed no sign of tension, but

Shad sensed he was getting antsy, wasting so much time talking, driving around, being idle, catering to a civilian. Shad did his best to ignore it.

The fence was weak and he could see black mold growing in the middle of the rotted slats. An ounce of pressure would send it over, and he could just imagine the rail giving away as he pressed his stomach to it, easing forward inch by inch, until he was plunging. Dave's powerful arm struck out and braced him.

"How far up are we?"

"Elevation averages about thirty-four hundred feet along the rim of the gorge," Dave said.

"Jesus—"

"Waters descend over two thousand feet before breaking into the open levels of the hollow. Jonah Ridge is on the other side of the chasm. My grandfather used to hunt grizzly and cougar up there."

"Even though he thought the hills were haunted?"

"He was a man of contradictions."

All of us are. You couldn't get away from it.

"Anybody live out that way?"

That tremendous torso filled with cold air, working like a bellows. Dave gave him that same look as before, sad and almost loving, but ready to backhand him hard across his nose if need be. "You going to hunt down everybody for a twenty-mile radius, Shad Jenkins?"

"If I have to."

"You're gonna cause yourself a lot of pain. That the way you gonna go at this?" He didn't wait for an answer. "It's mostly wilderness on Jonah. The grizzly and the big cats were wiped out. Now you've really only got deer, grouse, quail, and coon. Living off red chokeberry and wild indigo, they don't get as big as you might think. Plenty of timber rattlers too, in case you decide to go take a gander. Get yourself some real boots. They'll strike through the heels of what you're wearing and you'll probably be dead in two hours without treatment."

It was an exaggeration. Probably. "How much farther up is the trestle that covers the divide?"

"Maybe a mile. It's hidden from our line of view right now by the scrub and pine. The Pharisee Bridge. They were pure brimstone with naming things in these parts, weren't they?"

"They do appear to have been single-minded people back then."

"And some of their inheritors still can be."

"I suppose we can."

"The trestle was never the most stable structure, but the county used it for fifteen, twenty years or so beginning in the late thirties. They tried a couple of mining operations up there on Jonah but nothing ever came of it, and the tracks were abandoned and pulled up. Now the hill folk use the bridge to cut their trips to town in half, when they come down at all. Which happens less and less now. Nobody else would dare try it, not even the hunters. Easier and safer just to cross the Chatalaha at the bottom and drive up the old logging roads."

Shad stepped back over to the rickety rail fence and forced himself to stand there. To show whoever was pondering on him that he wasn't going to lie still or back off. He was coming.

He scanned the vista on the other side of the gorge, the dying orchards clustered with snarled catclaw brambles and briars.

A scratch on her cheek.

Pharisee.

If somebody hadn't taken Megan up to Gospel Trail Road, then maybe someone had brought her down from the back hills instead.

Chapter Five

THE LUVELL GIRL HIS FATHER HAD SPOKEN OF turned out to be Glide, who after dropping out of school in the fifth grade spent most of her days helping make sour-mash whiskey. She was a year younger than Megan—than Megan had been— but Glide already had 36C breasts and a natural cunning and understanding of men. Like her mother and sisters before her, she was built to bear children, designed by the hollow to pass on the burden of her general simplemindedness.

Shad remembered her as a crude kid always pouting and posturing, smelling of fresh cornstalk. She'd grown into a provocative teenager aware of her sexuality but too immature to do more than stick her chest in your face. She managed to hit all the right poses that accentuated her heavily freckled cleavage.

The Luvells had come out of the bottoms only to develop a taste for their own moon. Their patriarch, Pike Luvell, had blown himself up after drunkenly stuffing five sticks of dynamite in a chuckhole chasing down a gopher. His two sons were in various stages of chronic alcoholism. Instead of selling their moon they often never even finished distilling it, choosing to sit around their rock-strewn farm and eat the mash gruel.

It was an ugly sight. Neither of them had a tooth left in his skull. The oldest, Venn, was totally addled and rarely bothered to leave the barn. The younger, Hoober, yellow-tinged and bloated from failing kidneys, was a couple of years older than Shad and had reached the final stages of cirrhosis.

Their place crouched out on Bogan Road, nestled between a frog pond and a few acres of wire grass. Four shacks covered in crow shit faced one another.

Glide had a small potbelly but Shad couldn't tell if it was baby fat or if she was already pregnant. He made his guess as she kept on affecting mannerisms that would drive the guys at Dober's Roadhouse out of their heads. Shad hadn't had a woman for two years, yet he was somehow disheartened by the display.

It gave him pause. He was struck again by the alarming fact that he now understood C-Block murderers better than he did his own people.

Glide lived up to her name, swirling around Shad as she sleekly eddied about the yard, working the vats of bubbling mash. He could see the bottom of Venn's boots sticking out from beneath a thatch of hay in the corner of the barn. Broken pottery and mason jars littered the ground, half-hidden by tufts of crabgrass. Twisted lengths of converted radiator tubing connected the metal barrels and lay piled here and there among dried shucks of corn.

It sickened him thinking of how Mags must've walked

around here, viewing this scene of despondency. Did she ever gaze into Hoober's slack-jawed empty maw and listen to those befuddled slurrings? See Venn crawling around consuming his gruel? Could Shad have saved her from that at least?

He had to keep turning to watch Glide as she spun and circled the steaming drums. He wondered if he'd ever be able to drink whiskey again.

Glide stayed in motion, wriggling, the little belly quivering as she kept up a constant stream of chatter. Asking him ridiculous questions but showing a real curiosity. Wanting to know about the food they served in prison, the size of the cells, and if he'd gotten any jailhouse tattoos. If anybody had taught him how to break into a bank vault. She didn't expect any responses, didn't actually seem to need them. But it proved she kept her mind busy.

As she flowed closer to him, her shirt lifted, and he spotted a sloppy tattoo of a bumblebee on her left hip. Slightly below it, toward the base of her spine, a warm red devil face smiled affectionately. The needle hadn't been clean and the tats had scarred considerably.

He stood waiting for her to wind down, and when she didn't, he stepped over, got in front, and put a hand on her shoulder. It stopped her as if she'd run into a wall. She looked up, puzzled.

"Was Megan seeing anybody?" he asked.

"What do you mean?"

It got depressing, having to explain every word you said. "A boy. Did she have a boyfriend?"

"No, nobody like that."

"You certain?"

"A'course. After the trouble with that Zeke Hester

bastard, she never wanted much to do with the boys. Except some in the Youth Ministry. She thought they were all right 'cause they didn't do much 'sides go to prayer meetings."

"Know of anyone who would've wanted to do her harm?"

"No, a'course not."

"Think about it before you answer," he snapped.

She blinked at him, tongued the inside of her cheek, and let a few beats go by. "Everybody liked Megan. And Zeke stayed away."

He knew Glide was answering him marginally but honestly, and she wouldn't offer anything more than what was simplest and fastest to say.

He had to come at it a different way. "Did you ever go up there in the back hills with her?"

"Where? Which hills?"

"To Gospel Trail. The gorge."

With a surge of panicky strength, she snapped her arm away and broke free. "Hell no, I'd never go out that way."

The vehemence surprised him. "Why?"

"You know the talk."

"No, I don't."

"Yeah you do."

Shad was getting the feeling that he'd somehow missed an important facet to the county and was only now getting around to it. "Not really. Tell me what they say."

Glide appeared embarrassed by her outburst, humbled enough to actually dip her chin and blush. The rosy flush of her cheeks was authentic enough to tug at his guts.

She put on a moderately enticing girlish act, as if trying to throw him off the scent of her anxiety. There was a taunt in her eyes as well, the kind that made crazed lonely men run for shotguns to battle one another, and he knew better than to put his hand on her now.

"M'am gives tell that there's wraiths out that way. The suicides can't sleep. Hiding in the deadwood and brambles just waiting to catch folk. The land's got a taint to it, she warns everybody. I'm not saying I believe that, but if you ever heard my M'am going on about spirits, you'd give 'em considerable thought."

"You're right," he admitted.

M'am Luvell, Glide's great-grandmother, was a hex woman the superstitious kin of the hollow respected and feared. They brought their sick children to her, their cows that didn't give enough milk. The pumpkin heads and the kids with flippers. They came for love potions and charms to ward off the evil eye. They carried their chickens and their terror, and she would feed on it. All of it. Shad sort of liked the lady.

"Her mama was thrown into the chasm when M'am was a missy. Diptheria, I think. Or cholera. She watched it happen. She says the wraiths came out of the rocks and spent the afternoon with her, playing with her at first, then chasing and chewing on her legs."

After Shad's mother died, Pa went to M'am Luvell for a tonic to take his nightmares away—moon wasn't strong enough anymore. She'd taught him how to play chess.

"I'd like to see her," Shad said.

"Go right on," Glide told him, aiming her tits to show him the way. "It's not my place to stop anyone. Nor to urge 'em on, neither."

Venn squirmed beneath the hay for a moment, whimpered, and lay still again.

• • •

BULLFROGS ROARED IN THE POND AND THE WIRE grass appeared alive, agitated as it knifed into the breeze. Shad moved to the nearest shanty and stood at the ramshackle pineboard door. He reached out to knock and the walls groaned in protest, tilting horribly. The years of humidity, rain, and moss bleeding into the wood had rotted it to tissue paper. He tapped with his index finger and hoped the splintering door wouldn't fall off its hinges.

M'am's voice, low and almost dangerous, but filled with a quaint mischief, called out through the thick spaces between the slats. "Come on inside now, Shad Jenkins. Don't you worry none 'bout my home. It'll last long enough to serve me my remaining years, rest your mind on that."

He was still giving too much of himself away. He walked in and instantly felt as if he'd stepped into a pagan place of worship. A hallowed arena where the blood never finished soaking into the earth. Some areas had an innate sense of sanctuary about them. Another person's belief could wrap around your throat as tightly as your own.

M'am Luvell sat huddled on a small seat suited for a child, smoking a pipe. She nodded at him, eyes closed. Her dwarf's body was hidden beneath afghans and oversized sweaters, except for the stubby fingers with yellow cracked nails, wrapped around her pipe. Some of the folk in Moon Run Hollow carved their own from corncobs or hickory, but hers was store-bought and expensive. It gave the hex woman another element of contradiction.

Even so, he was a little surprised to realize she was

smoking marijuana. The sweet stink of it filled the shack and made him clear his throat.

He waited. Five minutes passed. It was a test of his patience, he knew. You learned more about people when they jumped than when they didn't.

The room was empty except for a small table in the corner, a plate and some utensils on it, and a kitchen area filled with wooden boxes and glass bowls filled with powders, roots, and herbs. Opposite that, a tiny bed with a cotton-stuffed mattress. At its foot rested the homemade wicker-backed wheelchair they would use to push her around downtown. Shad drifted over, inspected it, and recognized the work. His father had built everything in the house.

M'am Luvell had crossed to the point where age no longer mattered. There was a timeless quality to her, like a stone outcropping barely forming the shape of an old woman. The fierce decades had passed her in these mountains and done what damage they could, but she'd survived the forces thrown against her.

Shad tried to imagine how she might stretch her hand out and call him over to her. So that he'd crouch at her side while she patted his head with a diminutive hand, whispering words of understanding to him. You were always looking for somebody to trust.

"Commiseration," she said, opening her eyes. "Comfort and condolences."

"Thank you."

"First time you been by since you were a child."

He nodded, remembering back to when he was about five and Pa had brought him here. "You helped my father when he needed it."

"That wasn't so much." She noticed her pipe was out and laid it aside on the table. "I just gave him a game to take his mind off his troubles."

"It still does," Shad said. "Considering the burden of his worries, that counts for a great deal."

"For some neighbors, maybe," she told him. "But not all."

"Sure."

That was the end of it, these preliminaries. He felt it come to a close as if a cell door had slammed shut. M'am Luvell had pondered him long enough and was now ready. "So, what do you ask of me?"

"I'm not certain," he said.

"Well, you think on it some."

She cocked her head, watching him impassively. He glanced around and wondered what the hollow folk did with their chickens when they brought them to her. Did they just toss them on the floor so that you had squawking hens flapping all over? What other payments did they make? Since there was no place else to sit, did they kneel? He couldn't recall if his father had stood straight before M'am. Shad remembered lying on the floor, staring at spiders in the corner.

"They say my sister just fell asleep out there in the woods on Gospel Trail."

"But you don't believe it none?"

"I want to have an answer."

She broke into a quiet titter that sounded like bones clicking together. "I always did like the Jenkins men. You got an easy honesty about you. Sometimes leaves you stupid and exposed, but it's still a peculiar quality around these parts."

Shad was getting a little tired of people calling him stupid all the time, even if it might be true, but he said nothing.

"You afraid of me, boy?"

"No."

"Why's that? Hex women scare most hollow folk."

Telling her the candid fact that geriatric dwarves didn't hold much sway in the world most of the time just didn't much appeal to him, so Shad went at it a different way.

"I knew a guy in prison just like you. An older man who did a lot of smirking and chuckling. He knew people from the inside out and used it to his advantage. He talked up a streak and could slap you back into your place without half-trying. You looked at him and no matter who you were, you still saw somebody twelve feet high, with plenty of power in his face. It made a lot of cons cringe and hold their heads down."

"Who be that fella?" she asked.

"The warden."

M'am Luvell burst into a brittle laughter and shuddered in her seat. Drool slid down her billy-goat chin and clung to the curling white hairs. "You got wit. Your pa ain't got any of that wag."

Shad didn't exactly find it so witty, telling the truth. "He's got some."

"And what happened to this warden? I can see by the way you're leaning that there's more you got to say on him."

He looked down and saw she was right, he actually was leaning. No matter how hard you worked at it, you always had a tell. A way for them to see inside you.

"A bank robber named Jeffie O'Rourke used to work

for him in the office. As a secretary, an assistant sort of, but really they were lovers. Jeffie used to write him long, affectionate letters. They both liked to paint. The warden did seascapes, masted ships on the ocean. Jeffie did watercolors of children. Puppies. Flowers. The warden would tell him about the garden in his backyard, the hot tub, and the satellite dish. How he'd introduce Jeffie to the family when Jeffie got out."

"How you know all this?" M'am asked.

"I was his cellmate."

She let out a disapproving grunt. "Oh, you must've seen a lot."

"No, nothing like what you mean. But the warden fell for a new inmate, a straight guy called Mule. Mule was doing time for statutory rape, but he used to brag about how he would beat women, how much he hated them. The warden wasn't only gay but a misogynist too, and Mule appealed to him. He liked hearing the stories. He thought he could sway Mule's preference, bring him around. One night he came by the cell to break it easy to Jeffie and tell him it was all over. He probably did love the kid, in his own way. Didn't want to hurt him, said he'd help with his parole and hoped they could still be close friends."

"Uh-yuh."

Thinking back, Shad's voice dipped. "Jeffie O'Rourke had an easel with a self-portrait of himself looking serious. Fist under his chin, thoughtful, with his eyes very dark and deep. Maybe it was supposed to be sexy. He was painting it for the warden's birthday, which was coming up in a couple of days. He took the news about Mule poorly. Snapped his paintbrush and jammed it through the warden's eye and into his brain. Took half a second. Killed him on the spot."

Her disproportionately large head bowed to the right and the furry white chin bobbed, as if she'd heard the story many times before and was being tolerant by listening one more time. "What happened then?"

"They carried Jeffie away to solitary and he vanished."

Shad let it hang in the air like that, unsure of which way M'am Luvell might take it. Sounded like he was saying the guards killed Jeffie and buried him in secret. But the reality was, Jeffie truly had disappeared. He'd broken three prisons before and probably could've gotten out of this one anytime he wanted. He'd only stayed locked up because he was in love.

"And what lesson do you get from that?" M'am asked.

"I'm still working on it," Shad said.

A weighty silence passed between them, but neither looked away. It was a comfortable moment upset only when she beckoned him closer.

"And what if you find out it was Zeke Hester that done harm to that sweet child? Or some other mad dog fool on the loose?"

"I'll kill him."

"Without no regret?"

"Not too much."

He'd already decided that if events repeated themselves, he'd lie this time and do whatever he had to do to stay out of the joint. He considered any further dealings with Zeke to be an extension of what had already gone on before. He'd paid his price and wouldn't give up anything more.

"Without feeling?" she asked, prodding him a touch.

"There's always feeling."

"Not everybody can say that."

"Not everyone would want to."

She trembled at that, holding in the rancid laughter, but that sharp, clacking noise still rustled and rattled from her chest. Her hands came up in small balled fists and made him think of an excited child wanting candy. "But what if nobody killed your baby sister up on that bad road, Shad Jenkins? What if sweet Megan did go to sleep in the Lord's arms like they say? What if you never got nobody to blame?"

"When I'm satisfied I'll let it go."

"And if it's not to be?"

"Do you always ask this many questions of the people who come to ask you questions?"

She pursed her gray lips. "Yuh."

Okay, she was finally getting under his skin a little. "Do you accept it, M'am? That a seventeen-year-old girl's heart just stops out in the low hills? In a spot she's got no reason to be?"

The question took her back with a hint of sour amusement. "Asking my opinion, are you?"

"I suppose so."

"Heh. Been a while since anyone asked me my consideration on a subject. They want answers and blessings and ways to fend off spells. And fatter calves."

So maybe it threw her, having somebody in front of her who didn't bootlick. "Tell me about that place."

M'am fidgeted in her chair like she might want to hop off. Shad didn't know whether to help or not. He heard her ancient knees pop and winced at the sound, but she soon settled.

"I used to go up there with my ma and pa on Sunday afternoons after church. Dressed in pink with pretty bows in my blond hair. Hard to picture now, but so it was. Mama'd sing 'Gather at the River' while Daddy praised the Lord the whole ride up the mountain. In an ox wagon." She smiled, and he saw that, brown and crooked as some of her teeth were, she still had all of them. "But those hills were cross. Peevish. The land's got a taste for us."

"What's that mean?"

"Quiet now, you asked and I'm saying. So listen."

M'am Luvell pulled a wooden match from beneath her afghan and snapped her jagged thumbnail against it. She relit her pipe and allowed the seconds to roll by while she drew in a long, wheezing lungful of weed.

"We fed the gorge our ill and our hated, and now the ground's sick and full of scorn. It's hungry, but fickle. Storms come out of nowhere. Winds that'll take a man off his feet and hurl him into the chasm. There's outrage up that way, in those woods. It took my ma when I was but a girl a'four."

"Wraiths?" Shad asked. "That played with you first before they chased and bit your legs?" He said it without judgment or presumption.

"It's the reason why I never grew none. The young'un spoke out of turn. But she did no more than declare the truth. As do I."

Shad stared at her.

"You understand what I'm telling you?"

"Yes," he said. "I think so."

"But don't that threaten you none, boy? What you might find if you go digging in bitter soil?"

He shrugged. "There's evil everywhere."

The bullfrogs kept roaring, finding a nice contrapuntal harmony. Shad studied the old woman, trying to figure out if he was missing something here or if maybe she was. It didn't much matter one way or the other. She tilted her head again, this time in the opposite direction, waiting for him to ask something else, but he didn't see a point anymore. He walked out.

Chapter Six

YOU LEARNED TO PAY HEED TO THE DEAD breath on your neck.

Shad had gotten away without much trouble in the slam, but he'd still tapped into the sensibility of always having danger at hand. Knowing it was always out there, an inch to your left. You always had to be careful, never think you were one of the blessed, like you couldn't be touched. You could only be so stupid before you deserved to get taken out. Some cons thought their silvertongued charm might be a defense, as if the charisma that made women giggle and bat their eyelashes on the outside could actually make the gen pop *like* them behind bars.

Usually the violence wasn't aimed at Shad, but it sometimes got close enough that another man's blood wound up on the front of his shirt. His first week inside it happened twice on the cafeteria line when the guy standing directly in front of him had been attacked.

One got a sharpened toothbrush in his right ass cheek. Four days later the other took a seven-inch length of

shower pipe upside the head. Both of them had walked to
the infirmary under their own power, but it did a quick
job of fine-tuning Shad's slam instincts.

A few of the guys on C-Block started calling him a
jonah. That only helped to steer everyone clear. They
laughed it off but it was constantly in the back of their
minds, as they watched Shad standing there with another
con's blood on his clothes, knowing he had nothing to do
with it. Being in the wrong place at the worst time.

Like all institutions, the joint had plenty of its own ir-
rational and arbitrary beliefs. You had to study on how to
live within them.

If you did damage, or had harm done to you, that was
one thing. But if you were drawing the bad luck toward
you, and it missed and nabbed the guy on your left, then
you got a different kind of mark. Some of these men had
been in Vietnam, a few of the old-timers in Korea, and
they still had this war mentality that the new meat would
cause the most damage because he didn't know where to
step.

The Haitians and Mexicans were especially superstitious and gave a wide berth to Shad most of the time. Except for this one inmate called Little Pepe—Pepito—a
five-foot-nothing monstrosity as wide as he was tall, with
immense tattooed arms so huge they didn't look real.

Pepito got it into his head that Shad was giving him
the evil eye, putting some kind of curse on him and his
tribe. It had to do with Shad's books and always being in
the library. Pepito figured there was a great amount of
mystical knowledge and conjurings that could be found if
you knew how to use the Dewey Decimal System properly.
He thought Shad was a witch.

Little Pepe considered himself an honorable man. He was in for strangling his sister's husband with a Venetian blinds cord because the guy raised his voice at the dinner table, played poker, occasionally spanked his seven kids, and had taken too big a bite out of a coke deal they were in on together. Pepito's nephews and nieces were everything to him, and it still grated his soul a bit that he'd killed their father in front of them on Easter. Pepito was a stand-up guy if you caught him on the right day.

His indignation remained righteous. He had a family to protect inside the slam as well as out. Even though the leader of his tribe had turned down Little Pepe's request to shank the witch, he planned to do it anyway. On the cafeteria line, where the spells seemed to be landing on others.

Shad had a copy of *A Canticle for Leibowitz* in his back pocket, which, he realized too late, also miffed the Aryans, but not enough for them to take a poke at him. He had just received the second of Elfie Danforth's letters, and it held his place about halfway through the book.

He could already feel himself being forgotten by her, and was saddened by the fact that he didn't really mind. Her cursive script had a stop-and-go jitter to it, as if she had to walk away every few sentences and come back later after thinking up something else to tell him. She mainly wrote about people and events that didn't matter to him and never would. She asked him nothing. He thought about the determination it took to go through four pages to your lover and not ask a single question.

A new resolve had begun to fill him in the slam—as his detachment from the hollow continued to change him into some new version of himself.

Tushie Kline stood three or four guys behind him in

line, eyeing *A Canticle for Leibowitz* and planning to rob
Shad's cell in a couple of days. Shad knew there were plans
being formed that held him at their center, but he
couldn't pinpoint the who or why yet. He kept hoping the
jonah thing would help him out a bit more than it appeared to be doing.

That afternoon, he felt the angry heat on the back of his
neck and eyed Tush first, knowing there was going to be a
problem there soon. But not right at that second. He
scanned beyond the cons slopping mashed potatoes, beef
patties, and string beans onto the metal plates and saw the
insanely abnormal arms of Little Pepe swinging toward
him. If he had a shiv, Shad couldn't see it within those
enormous fists.

Not much time to do anything except bark a cuss,
reach over the counter, grab up the tray of burgers, and
hurl it into Pepito's face.

It was enough to get everyone yelling and laughing and
for the bulls to run over. Shad's luck held as he faded into
the crowd and the bulls had no one to grab except Pepito,
who was spouting off biblical passages in Spanish.

They didn't throw Little Pepe into solitary because he
hadn't really been fighting, but two days later the leader of
the tribe had him killed for disobeying orders.

So now Shad was coming out of Griff's Suds'n'Pump
holding a handful of change and a bottle of engine cleaner
when the dead breath whispered and got his hackles up.

He took two more steps across the parking lot as Zeke
Hester's belligerent presence descended upon him.

Shad paused, listening to the sudden rush of air swirling
behind him. He had compromised his hands, which was a
dumb but understandable mistake. You tried to be on

guard as much as possible, but you just couldn't do it all the time. Immediately he dropped what he was carrying and spun to his right as Zeke's fist plowed forward like a steam engine about to derail.

Zeke Hester stood six-four, weighed in at about 280, his body solidified from working on road crews since dropping out of school when he was fifteen. He was river bottom swamp scum who never bothered with pulling the legs off spiders or torturing small animals—he went straight to the weakest kids in grade school and started drawing blood. He moved up quickly to intimidating teachers, beating the drunks sleeping at the edge of the trailer park, and troubling girls at the roller rink in Waynescross.

Jake had been right when he'd said that prison had agreed with Shad. A crazy thing, but there it was. On the inside he'd lost his youthful clumsiness and earned a lissome agility. Working out in the gym every afternoon, honing himself, losing a beer gut and packing on an extra twenty pounds of crafted muscle. Two years with nothing to do but exercise your mind and body and try to keep from losing control. Sometimes it worked in your favor. It felt good to have real speed even when the highway patrol wasn't chasing you back and forth across the river.

Zeke did an ungainly dance, trying to keep himself from falling as he overshot and wheeled in a half circle. Shad planted his foot on Zeke's ass, kicked out, and sent him sprawling onto the pavement.

Here we go.

When Zeke looked up his face was filled with murderous frenzy. His cracked front tooth had worn away to a black nub. His gums were already rotted too, and he'd be down to eating nothing but succotash and applesauce by the time he was thirty. The busted cheekbone lay unnaturally flat and angled a little too far back toward his ear.

What Shad told M'am was true. He could kill this man with a very small amount of guilt. The realization disturbed him a bit, but not all that much, considering.

"I want to talk to you," Shad said.

Zeke hadn't shaved much or had a decent haircut since he was sixteen. His feral, savage appearance played well with the role he was going for. You had to cultivate your persona, your disguise.

If he was ever shorn down you'd see a pink face full of cutie-pie chubsie-ubsieness, all the weakness inside him scrawled into his soft, muddy face. When they were kids, the girls used to like him because he looked sort of like a lost puppy, until they got a look at his eyes.

Zeke scrambled on the ground for something to throw, but all he could find was the engine cleaner. He clambered to his feet and hurled the bottle at Shad like it was a brick. It flew over Shad's left shoulder and splattered against the gas pumps.

"Been waitin' two years to pay you back!"

"That so?"

"It is!"

Shad knew guys who liked to play the moment out, grinning before a brawl, warming up to it. All that mattered to them was ego and image. They went through the day acting like there was a camera covering their every move. Like there was a group of teenage girls sitting on a couch somewhere watching them, cheering them on, getting sweaty. It was much harder to fight when you were alone.

"You should've waited and put this off for as long as you could, Zeke."

"And why's that, convict?"

"Because I won't let you off so easy this time." Shad gave him the killing gaze so there'd be no doubt in Zeke Hester's mind at all.

"You think I'm scared of a jailbird like you?"

"You should be after last time. You're going to answer my questions or I'm going to hurt you again."

"You ain't got the brass," Zeke hissed, with a hint of fear in his dull voice. He was an idiot, but he had sense enough to know that everything Shad said was genuine. He tried to smile, putting some snarl into it.

They squared off and Zeke let out a nervous chortle, shrugging his shoulders, loosening up as if this might be a twelve-rounder. He slid out of his jacket and threw it wildly over Shad's head. He had on a sleeveless black T-shirt and hit a pose so his biceps bulged. He kept tightening and opening his fists, making his blood rush so the veins would stand out on his arms, hoping to look cut and strong. He scanned left and right to see if any girls might be around, but there was nobody except seventy-year-old Griff staring out the window, his lips covered in beer foam.

It was going to be tough getting through to Zeke Hester if he thought he was on a movie set, about to be the next action hero star. Already you could see he was hoping to come up with some snappy, sarcastic patter. Something they could use for the trailer and highlight on the poster.

Shad said, "Did you do anything to my sister?"

"What's that?" Zeke was still flexing, scared and unwilling to face the real context of the situation.

"Answer me."

"You—"

"I don't have all day. I won't ask you nicely again."

Zeke bolted up straight and his crude features, already cloyed with ignorance, grew even more moronic. "Megan? Your sister? You think . . . so you think I had something to do with what happened to her?"

"I'm asking you."

"I reckon you can just turn yourself around right now and go find yourself a knothole for you to stick your rod in 'cause I ain't—"

Shad flowed forward and covered the ground between them in one step. He brought his hand up from low and backhanded Zeke with a solid shot, but Zeke's unkempt head didn't even turn aside. He wasn't all flab. Beneath the matting of beard that chin was pointed stone.

"Goddamn you, Jenkins!"

"None of your usual posturing for the next five minutes, Zeke. What happened to her?"

"How the hell should I know!"

"You made a grab for her once."

"Now you listen to me 'bout that! You done sullied my good name—"

Again Zeke checked left and right, really hoping somebody would come along and listen to his script. He'd worked hard on it for the last two years. The word sullied wasn't an easy one to pull off, but Shad had to admit it sounded pretty natural. Zeke had been practicing.

"Did you try again?" Shad asked.

"What's that?"

"Don't make me repeat myself."

The longer they went without tussling, the more time

Zeke had to fan his anger and keep himself worked up. The fear was draining out of him too. "That ain't it at all, you son of a bitch!"

"Then why were you bothering my father?"

"Me? You blame me? That bastard's been putting the devil in folks' ears for weeks, telling 'em I had a hand in Megan's murder."

Shad tensed and stood straighter. "You think she was murdered?"

Zeke screwed his face into about as much of a pout as he could pull off. His fingers fluttered about like he was in front of a chalkboard trying to map out Sherman's March. "You're a damn fool. She was only seventeen. No young girl like that dies for no good reason, up in them foul woods."

"That's right."

"Don't you glare at me like that no more neither. You want to scrap, we'll have it out right now. But don't you give me that eye no more. I didn't have nothin' to do with what happened to yours. No matter what you and your miscreant daddy's got to say about it. And you better not be spoutin' gossip like that 'round town no more!"

Zeke Hester didn't have the temperament for any real slyness. Shad felt a small surge of shame even though he'd been attacked. He had known better. Zeke didn't have anything to do with Mags's death. He would've left marks.

"Get out of here," Shad told him.

"You don't tell me to move on, boy."

"It's time for you to be quiet now."

"You go on and stay the hell away from me, if you have any consideration for what's good for you. Or I'll beat you down and leave your ass out on the highway like week-old roadkill."

Shad sighed. Pa was right. Zeke didn't have a good memory. Already he was starting to flex again, weighing his odds, getting ready to push a little harder. You could see how he tongued his rotted tooth and the raw nerve gave him a painful kick that lifted him up onto his toes.

Whatever Zeke was going to say would be immensely unwise. It would be mean and it would be about Mags. Shad took a step backwards, as if urging the insult toward him.

Here it comes.

Zeke Hester smiled through that wild thatch of hair, and muttered, "The way she threw it around, driving guys crazy, I'm surprised it didn't happen no sooner. Now, you dwell on that some."

"Sure," Shad said, and he went for Zeke's bad arm, grabbing it at the elbow and wrist and giving it a vicious twist.

The snap was clean and loud as a gunshot. Zeke instantly went into shock and didn't even scream. He sat down heavily, twitched a few times, and started to cry.

Chapter Seven

HIS FATHER'S PICKUP WASN'T IN THE YARD when Shad finally decided to visit Megan's grave.

A trace of storm grew heavier in the air as the wind rose and gusted through the pastures. Crimson-tinted clouds swarmed across the sky, darkening it to the hue of trailer-trash bruises.

The rain let go for a while, stopped briefly, and began again, fitful and hesitant and cold. Stands of pine jerked and swayed, bowing as if determined to groan in your ear and confirm every apprehension. As he drove up the wet dirt road the Mustang hit every rut.

He parked at the base of the foothill and got out. The hound pup crawled free from beneath the house and trotted up the road to greet Shad. Lament's collar was old and oversized, but he'd grow into it. The tags were scratched and they jangled together as he began to lope.

"Come on," he said.

The dog followed as Shad worked his way up the knoll toward the graves of his mother and sister.

The sun had begun to hemorrhage in the west as the late afternoon cooled even faster. The nearest church, four miles away along the bottoms, crooned a despondent tune he'd heard before but could only remember while it played. The breeze in the boles of the oak trees hummed and occasionally drowned it out.

Standing in the weeds, he noticed again how stricken the land had become. The groves had thinned until they were little more than brushwood and briar patches.

His cool and calm seemed to come and go lately, and he knew he had to work on that before it got him killed. You played games as a kid that became the discipline of your adult life. He'd never realized it years ago—lying there in the darkness at the back of his closet, covered in sweat with his cheek pressed to the smooth hardwood floor, as the silence heaved around him, and he kept going further inside himself, hoping to talk to his mama, demanding it to be—that he was developing a skill that would come in handy in prison.

He tried to center himself before the tombstone of his mother, drifting for a second while he sought out the dark, quiet place behind his eyes. Your strength had a name that wasn't your own, and there were times you were going to need it. It would also need you.

With one foot set on his mother's grave, the other toed into his sister's, he kept his eyes open waiting for Mags's hand to flit into his vision once more and give him another sign. He shoveled the blackness aside like dirt covering her. The sound of his own heartbeat faded.

His depths parted. He went further, intent on her whisper. He didn't know what might happen if he ever hit bottom. It didn't matter. You went where you were called.

He kneeled, held out a fist to the ground, thinking how killers liked to stick close to their prey, even after it was dead. Would the malevolence in the hills climb down this far?

He aimed himself. The world shifted to red as Shad hooked on to somebody, or perhaps something, moving in and out of view, brooding about him again. He held his hand out farther and slowly wriggled his fingers, the way you do to get fish to rise to the surface. His chest grew warmer. Mags was helping. Maybe Mama too. He started panting, eventually hyperventilating, as the indistinct and somehow *imperfect* shape, the glowing broken threads of an anguished aura still wheeling from it, turned its unfinished face toward him. And beneath it, another face, slowly becoming recognizable.

There.

Easy.

He was almost there.

Another moment, Mags. This is for you.

He was almost . . . yes . . .

. . . when he felt a weak influence fuss beside him, like a kid tugging at his elbow. Intruding on his purpose. Tushie Kline used to do it all the time, jabbering on about books, his homeboys, and anything else that flitted into his head. Tush couldn't turn off his talk.

It was over. Shad's breathing returned to normal. The irritating force continued to pluck at his concentration until he looked over.

Preacher Dudlow stood beside him, staring down at the ground, with his hands clasped over his mammoth belly, sucking at the edges of his mustache.

Well now, Shad thought.

Most preachers Shad had run into were still brimstone types, thin as cottonwood and harsh as sun-scorched bone. They visited the hollow in their vans and set up tents out in the fields. They raved and slammed the meaty part of their palms into sinners' foreheads and commanded them to heal. They took crutches and canes and busted them over their knees. You watched the cripples struggling to stand upright on their diseased, gnarled legs. Folks threw silver. Gospel singers caterwauled like beasts. Deaf men leaned over mumbling, "*I cahn heh thuh voice'a Jehsus.*" Maybe they could. They were as punchy as if they'd knocked back a jug of moon.

But Dudlow had always been a happy, robust man, perfectly round but still sort of muscular, with his face tanned by his outdoor sermons in the pastures and his baptisms at the river.

This afternoon he was bundled tightly in a sheepskin coat and wearing a bright red hunter's cap with the flaps down over his ears. A mauve knitted scarf had been wrapped twice around his throat and still trailed over both shoulders, down to his ankles. Mrs. Swoozie, Dudlow's mother, lived next door to him, around the side of the church. The only thing she'd ever found to ease the pain of her arthritis, so she said, was to keep busy crocheting and cooking around the clock.

Shad didn't know if Dudlow was genuinely unaware of his wife Becka's lifestyle or not. The preacher might have simply repressed his knowledge beneath the weight of his religious beliefs. It was hard to admit to that kind of failure, especially to yourself. But Becka was usually crocked out on meth and a lot of the buyers came right to her back door. Perhaps Dudlow's whole act was only a performance and he was actually helping to cook the meth in the church basement.

No matter which was true, you didn't want the preacher knowing your secrets.

"Comfort and condolences, Shad Jenkins," Dudlow said.

"Thank you, Reverend."

"I've been meaning to stop by."

"And now you have."

He pointed down to the road, where he'd parked his microbus behind the 'Stang. "Yes, I saw your car, thought I'd come up. You look well."

"So do you."

Dudlow patted his stomach as if consoling a loved one. "Mama's got me on a strict diet of legumes. Problem is she bakes so much for the Youth Ministry, the Fellowship Hall, and the Ladies Coalition that she doesn't miss a few pies. And I can't help but indulge. I'm weak that way."

"So am I," Shad said, letting the lie ease out as if it might bring them closer together.

Dudlow let loose with a moist chortling, and Shad got the feeling that the man was somehow trying to patronize him. He wondered if the preacher showing up the way he did was a coincidence or had a greater design to it.

"Not so anyone would notice, Shad Jenkins. You're remarkably fit, I can see. More so than when you left us, I'd venture."

He stood there with an expectant air, as if he might want to get into it, ask some questions, find out if Shad had been anybody's bitch. Dudlow clapped his gloves together and began to jitter his way toward bad taste subjects, but then finally thought better of it.

"See, it's her boysenberry that keeps me awake at night."

"That so?"

"And I can't just have one piece either, I have to finish the whole thing off or she'd realize I was pilfering. I have to hide the paper plates at the bottom of the trash so she doesn't learn I'm off her vegetable platters."

Were they really talking about pies? "Mrs. Swoozie's baked goods are the best in the county."

"You're so right about that! And who can resist? I can't. If only I had more gumption!" His rotund torso wobbled and shook on those legs as if it might snap loose and roll free.

"We all have our temptations," Shad said.

"So true. So human of us. It's a divine test. We're fated to quarrel with our flaws."

Would the preacher mention Becka? Was this commentary on sins leading to drugs or Jake Hapgood?

Shad glanced at his feet and saw he was still standing on the graves. Could that be what caused the preacher's unease? He stepped away and Lament crept up from behind Mama's headstone, yawned, and sat at Shad's side.

"A fine looking hound pup!" Dudlow said, smiling so vacantly that Shad could almost see through his head.

"Yes."

"A terrific dog, that boy there!"

You cut slack where you could, and when you couldn't give any more you stood and waited. The warden used to play this kind of game, staring at you dead-eyed and talking in circles, imposing himself on the cons until they shrank away. Shad crossed his arms over his chest and kindly regarded Dudlow, unwilling to speak of legumes or cakes or puppies any more.

Dudlow sensed the change and went back to sucking the corners of his mustache for a minute. He toyed with his scarf, and said, "I thought I should visit Megan's resting place."

"That's kind of you."

"She was such a nice girl with a bright future. Very special. Such a loss."

"Yes."

"I spend several mornings a week down at the village cemetery, cleaning up the graves, saying prayers. But I like to make the effort to attend those who aren't buried on consecrated ground as well."

So that was it.

The things you could get hung up on.

Dudlow scanned the trees. "Lovely area. I hope your father finds some solace here."

"I don't think he does."

"That saddens me."

"Me too."

The preacher shrugged at that, and the ends of his lengthy scarf flapped against his boot laces. The chill breeze thickened around them. Shad let it at his hackles because he was still cooling down, while Dudlow clapped his hands trying to get some blood circulating. The solid whump of his gloves echoed across the embankment.

"I didn't merely come up here to pay my respects to your sister. I wanted to talk to you."

"Sure. About what?"

"To offer counsel, if you need it. I've dealt with ex-convicts in my parish before. The stigma they face, the prejudice and bias. Often there are great difficulties in readjusting to normal life again."

Only someone who'd never been inside would put it like that. Shad tried not to smile but wasn't sure if he managed to keep from showing teeth. Prison had its own methodical regularity, an even keel and conformity that made a lot more sense when you got right down to it. You didn't trust anyone. You kept out of the action as much as possible. It simplified life, made some things easier.

But the minute your time was up and you grabbed the next bus south, the sudden illusion of normality grew so oppressive that it could drive you crazy trying to wrap your mind around it.

"Thanks," Shad said.

"In the event you ever wish to talk to someone. If you ever need to unburden yourself over what you may have had to do to survive...and, ah, what might have been done to you, please let me know. I'm always willing to listen."

Here was another one who thought you did nothing behind bars except pull a train or get locked in the hot box for mouthing off. The preacher was eager for someone else's perversions. Like his own wife's wouldn't be enough.

"I appreciate it," Shad said.

That did the trick and Dudlow started to relax some, having offered his hand in friendship and spiritual consultation. He could get back to his boysenberry and jackoff thoughts now with a clear conscience. Good, whatever it took.

They stood like that for a while, listening to oak boles moaning, watching the skinks racing through a nearby clump of birch.

"She came to see me. Your sister. Just before—"

Shad tensed so abruptly that his elbows cracked. He really had to do something about this loss of cool. "Why?"

"I don't know. I was out and Becka said that Megan stopped by. I called around at your father's house but no one answered."

"When was this?"

"Three days before she . . . well . . ." Dudlow's voice cracked and a plaintive note chimed weakly. ". . . before God summoned her back to heaven."

Even he couldn't say that kind of shit with a completely straight face.

Toeing the dirt of Megan's grave as if making airholes for her, Shad asked, "Had she ever visited you at home before?"

"Only if it involved the Youth Ministry, and then she was usually with the rest of the group."

"She ever appear troubled to you?"

"How so?"

Sometimes you had to draw a picture. "That's what I'm asking."

Thinking about it for a second, Dudlow brought the big hard glove up to his face but couldn't work the fingers well enough to pinch his chin. "No, not after that difficulty between you and that Hester boy."

"Was there anyone she would have talked with? Somebody she was close to in the group?"

"She was friendly with Glide Luvell, but that girl had nothing to do with the ministry."

"How about besides her?"

"I believe Callie Anson."

"She kin to Luppy?"

"His wife."

See that, the things you miss when you're away from home.

Edging about on the heel of his boot, Dudlow looked over his shoulder in the direction of Luppy Joe Anson's place, maybe four miles east into the back roads where the moonrunners raced. A variety of expressions crossed his face. "She's seventeen, and they've been married for six months or so. Their love appears genuine enough, though I admit that if I had my druthers I'd request the juveniles of our community wait a bit longer before they made such important vows."

"I wasn't judging," Shad said.

"No, but perhaps I do in a fashion. It's so difficult for the children to stay young in a place like Moon Run Hollow."

"Or anywhere."

"So I hear tell. You've learned that firsthand, haven't you?"

Normal life on the outside.

Lament started scratching at the damp earth, sniffing as if he was tracking quail in the weeds. A whine escaped his throat and he flicked his heavy tail once. The hound dog stared at Shad with a solemn intensity, took a few loping steps around Mama's headstone, then sat in the dirt. Smoke wreathed Shad's face and it took him a second to realize the preacher was leaning in closer, his breath frozen on the air.

"Well, I'd best be off. Welcome home, Shad Jenkins."

"One more minute. What's a member of the Youth Ministry do?"

"Oh," Dudlow said, beaming, glad to talk about good and godly works. "Visits with our neighbors."

Shad knew that was usually a euphemism for knocking on doors and handing out pamphlets. "Anything else?"

"Helps with the elderly. Cooks food for those families who've fallen on hard times."

It sounded clichéd and a little forced, but Shad let it roll for now. "You let them go out in the hollow alone? Teenage girls? Into those hills?"

"The volunteers always go in groups of two or three."

"That's all?"

"Sometimes more," Dudlow said, on the defensive and gesturing vaguely with his hands. "We want to make our brethren feel embraced, but I'm not a naive man. I take my responsibilities in safeguarding my congregation very seriously."

With blackness creeping up to ply the back of his skull, Shad forced himself to see it.

Mags.

There she was. Seventeen years old, lovely and grinning, holding a Bible and some photocopied literature, maybe with donation envelopes or a mason jar for collections. Stepping up onto a shaky porch and knocking as the paint chips flaked around her shoulders, waiting patiently while some bitter, lonely wife-beating prick roused himself from a drunken stupor in front of the TV set. The game was over and he'd lost another twenty bucks on a bad defensive line. A bellyful of bile and three aching teeth. Got up with his belt unbuckled, only one sock on, kicked empty beer cans aside, and came to the door with the sunlight slashing his brain into juicy, throbbing slices. Just as Mags's shadow lengthened to cover his stubbled face, the beautiful smile something he'd rarely seen before—hadn't seen in years—while her gentle, buoyant voice asked for charity and offered an inviting hand. Talking about kindness, crafts shows, and church bake sales while his T-shirt, gummy with liquor and drool, slowly dried and stuck to his graying chest. His tattoos stretched and dull, the flesh pink as a sow's ass. Suddenly feeling fat and old and weak, unbearably needy, glaring at her legs in the golden afternoon. Watching the swell of her young breasts, the blond down and freckles at the base of her throat. Asking her inside with the promise of a few dollar bills on his dresser. Want some lemonade?

Shad looked into Dudlow's face and the preacher said, "Merciful Jesus." He took a step back, tottered in a chuckhole and nearly fell over. "Lord a'mighty."

"What?"

"Your eyes. So full of fury."

"You expect something else from a man who's just lost kin?"

"You're primed and set to go off, Shad Jenkins. I can see it." Wrapping the edges of his scarf in his fists, beginning to slip away. Scampering happily because murder was sort of pervy. "Who are you planning to kill? Who are you taking with you to hell?"

"I just want to find out what happened to my sister."

Dudlow paced backwards another few feet, as if he might turn and bolt on a dead run for his microbus. "She went to sleep. It happens. Not often, praise Jesus, but it does. That's the way of God."

"That's not good enough for me."

It made Dudlow look around for help, even glancing at Lament, hoping the dog would understand and agree. He let out a sorrowful breath but his eyes were gleaming. "The more's the pity."

"Maybe so. We all have our course."

"Come see me, if you need to talk. Before you . . . well, if you'd like to chat."

"Sure."

Preacher Dudlow trundled off so quickly that the orange flaps over his ears popped up as he made his way down the incline back to his vehicle. Pa's pickup still hadn't returned.

Lament shook himself, cocked his head. Shad went and plucked dying wildflowers from the thickets, putting half on Mama's grave, the rest on Megan's.

The hollow was getting on his nerves. He still had a few questions he wanted to ask. As soon as he had some answers, he'd drive up Gospel Trail, see if he could find whatever it was that had been thinking on him so decidedly.

Maybe Dudlow was right. Shad might have to kill some folks before this was all over, and take them along to oblivion.

Chapter Eight

THE BLOOD DREAMS RETURNED, SANGUINE and burning.

He used to have them a lot in the joint. He'd wake up and find himself standing naked at the bars, the entire cellblock awake but quiet, everybody staring into the dimness. Even the Aryans and the homeboys didn't say a word. Jeffie O'Rourke would have his face buried in his pillow, shrunken back into the corner of his bunk and pretending to be asleep.

Shad never found out what he said or did while sleepwalking. No one would ever tell him, and they'd give him a wide berth for a while. The Muslims kept trying to convert him even though he was white, saying that Mohammed and Allah had plans for him.

So, it was happening again.

He blinked and realized he was in Mrs. Rhyerson's backyard, looking up at the brightening sky. Maybe 5:00 A.M. from the purple hue of dawn, with the sound of the Freightliners barreling down the highway humming through the thickets.

He waited to see if he was out here for a reason. He was freezing, wearing only sweatpants and a T-shirt. The wind filled the trees overhead, and the ash and the oaks shrugged, leaves wafting against his knees. It kept him turning, facing one way, then another, the breeze shaking the brush. His hands were open at his sides, slightly raised, palms out. Knees bent, ready to run or jump. It was the most prepared you could be when you didn't know from which direction they'd be coming.

If someone wanted him, he was here. He was still being looked over, contemplated, deliberated on. He could feel a certain anxiety in the night but couldn't be sure if it was his own.

Shad had an urge to talk but checked himself. The more of your voice you gave away, the more power you consigned to your foe. Imagine the seventy-year-old woman clambering out of bed, stomping down the stairway, swinging through the kitchen and slamming open the screen door, holding an iron skillet.

Like he didn't have enough on his mind.

His feet were numb and his skin crawled with gooseflesh. He backed up, step by step, wondering if it would compel the hills to make a move.

Perhaps it had. Shad wanted to go back inside but suddenly grew immensely tired. A peculiar weakness trailed through his limbs. He stooped and sat under a spruce, and when he felt strong enough, he stood and started back to the house. He was almost at the door before he realized he'd left his body behind.

He headed back to the tree and his mother and the devil were waiting for him, both out of breath.

"Shad?"

Mama began calling to him again, like he wasn't there, or she wasn't. What would happen if he didn't answer? Did he have a choice? Would she finally leave?

Beside her stood Ashtoreth, evolved from the ancient Phoenician mother goddess of fertility Astarte, who in his male incarnation is a teacher of sciences and keeper of past and future secrets. A grand duke of hell that commands forty legions, one of the supreme demons.

Ashtoreth smiled affectionately through terrible scars covering his face. It took Shad a second to remember where he'd seen the devil before.

Tattooed at the base of Glide Luvell's back.

"Well now," Shad said.

Mama groped blindly for him. The red devil moved from her and crouched before Shad's body, which was still beneath the tree, breathing into his face and whispering something in his ear. Ashtoreth stared up almost contritely as Shad approached, quickly finished whatever he'd been saying, and stood.

The devil, dressed in the warden's finest suit, stepped forward and straightened the knot of his silk tie. Shad thought he should grab for his mother and get it over with now. Wake up, turn aside, and get the blood out of his belly.

Ashtoreth's voice was his father's voice. "She wants to give you a warning."

"She always does."

"You need to listen."

"No, I'm not so sure that I do."

But this was another of his faults. Holding out hope that the ghost of the mother he'd never met might actually be searching him, loving him in her own grotesque way. You never got free of your mama.

She drifted out there in the brush, tangling in the camphor laurel, the maple, and catclaw briars. Slowly she became aware of him standing there and looked over, held one hand out to the devil, the other toward Shad. He rubbed the creases in his forehead and sighed. She stared beyond him, and said, "Son?"

"I'm here, Mama."

"Son?"

"I'm right next to you. I'm always next to you."

"Shad?"

"Yes."

"Oh, hello."

"Hello, Mama."

Ashtoreth said, "Come closer. She wants you to come closer."

"Quiet, you."

Glide Luvell's devil revealed disappointment in his expression. "Believe me, you want to hear what I have to say."

"That right?"

The bizarre knowledge flooded him again, everything sharp and sensible as if he'd read it off a page many times before.

Instigator of demonic possession, most notably in the case of the Loudun nuns of France in the sixteenth century, who accused Father Urbain Grandier of unholy and perverse acts. After severe torture, Grandier scrawled a confession with his broken hands and was burned at the stake for consorting with Satan.

So, Shad thought, *this is the guidance I get.*

Ma smiled sadly, as if she too wanted this all to end as quickly as possible. Clutching for him so he'd wake up, get on with his life, and let her go back to the grave. She appeared even less interested in him this time than a few nights ago.

"Shad? You listen, son. You listen to me."

"Shh, Mama, I want to talk to your companion now."

"Son? I need to tell you . . . stay off the road." Confusion twisted and contorted her features as she moved off in the wrong direction trying to find him.

He figured what the hell, grabbed Ashtoreth by the warden's tie, and yanked him forward. "You got something that might actually help me or not?"

"Yes. I'm only here to deliver you a friend."

That stopped him. "What friend?"

"One you've been missing."

The devil faded from sight and soon Jeffie O'Rourke stepped up and stood there just a few feet away, dressed in Armani. His eyes had some new hipness to them that he hadn't possessed in the can, and his grin was knowing and a touch badass. Murdering your lover had a way of giving you a new confidence.

"Where'd you get to?" Shad asked.

"Been out and about," Jeffie said, taking a step closer. The three-thousand-dollar silk suit gave a gentle swish. Shad could see there was dried blood or paint on Jeffie's hands, the bitten-down fingernails caked with it. "Spending a lot of time sitting around on beaches, doing seascapes."

"Like the warden."

"Yes, just like him. He always said they were calming, but I don't find that to be the case."

"You should probably quit then."

"I'll give it a while longer though. Maybe it just takes time."

"Maybe so."

Jeffie gave a kind of frowning grin, like he was glad to be there and had arrived just in time. "Jenkins, I know this town is about as backass backwater backwards as can be, but are you telling me that you actually walk around this place like that? No shoes, no coat? You're young but you're not quite Huck Finn."

That slow crawling heat at the back of Shad's skull made itself aware to him again. It was always there, as much a part of him as the beating of his heart, but forgotten until the strain became too great. It grew more intense but wasn't yet too painful. He looked down and didn't see his body under the spruce anymore, and couldn't be certain if he was awake or asleep.

"Stay out of the woods," Jeffie said. "There are snakes in the dark."

"Jesus, you people and all these warnings about the fucking woods." He was starting to feel himself come undone a little. "Are you talking about the snake handlers up there? The community of the hill families? Did one of them kill Megan? Did her heart stop because of rattler venom?"

"How should I know? I've never been around here before."

"Why did you show up then?"

"You wanted me to."

Slouching a bit, Jeffie had a swagger now, something else he'd picked up off the warden. He let out a deliberate smirk and started chuckling, standing as if he were twelve feet tall, all this power in his face. Shad felt his shoulders go rigid as Jeffie reached out and touched him on the side of the neck. Flecks of red drifted against his skin. You could find some kind of goddamn symbolism wherever you looked.

"You ought to let it go. You're not doing this for the right reasons."

"Is that so?" Shad asked as the rage dug in deeper, putting the fire in his skin, kicking his heart rate up. "I'm going to find out what happened to her."

"No," Jeffie O'Rourke said, with that new merriment in his eyes. "I don't think you are. Not entirely."

When the calm wasn't there you tried to fake it as well as you could. Jeffie kept tugging at all the wrong nerves, the same way he sometimes did back in the joint. Dead maple leaves scuffled past their ankles, scrambling across the wide lawn as the morning winds staggered in and out of the brush.

"You having fun on the outside?" Shad asked.

"Not as much as you might think."

"Being an escaped felon might hinder your sense of cheer."

"It's not that so much, really. The FBI will never track me down. Those assholes spend most of their time tripping over one another, and they're into more crooked shit than all of C-Block combined. It's a machine working against itself. I've been number sixteen on the most wanted list for almost a year. They've never even come close."

"So what's the problem?" Shad asked, genuinely curious.

At last, a little of the old Jeffie came easing through.

The loving but distressed face shaping his heartbreak. "I miss him."

"The warden."

"Yes. It's not the same without him."

"Looks like you've got money."

"I had plenty stashed away. But, even with the cash, there's no ... reason in my life, if you can believe that shit."

"Okay."

Mrs. Rhyerson's yard began to take on more detail as the dawn broke against the mountains, a murky orange stewing behind the hills.

"Are you dead?" Shad asked.

"Hell no. I've assumed the name Prescott Plumber, and I've got a sweet deal in East Hollywood. I take care of Albert Herrin. He used to be a director. Pretty popular back in the fifties, did a lot of war movies and had a couple of hits. In the sixties he did biker flicks and cashed in on the drive-in exploitation market right when it was getting big. I invested in a production company, bought up the DVD rights, and we're making a fortune. Now he's seventy-eight years old and still has no problem keeping it up."

"The benefits of a pure life," Shad said, a little surprised at the sound of his own bitterness.

"Highly suspect, that." Jeffie checked the knot of his tie, the same as Ashtoreth had, the same way the warden always did. "Don't go up to the ridge. Your luck might not hold. There's things going on you won't believe."

"So tell me."

"I can't. I don't know what they are."

You never quite knew what was in your head and what was outside of it. "I've got to see this through to the end."

"Maybe she wouldn't want you to. Your sister. Ever think of that?"

"No."

It brought the greasy smirk back. "You know you're probably insane, right?"

"Sure," Shad said. "But it's the *probably* that keeps me going."

"Yeah, but still, everything I've told you is the truth. You can check on that."

"No need."

The moonrunners were starting early, their superchargers screaming down the dirt roads under the highway. The stink of whiskey wafted on the breeze.

That new flash of smugness in Jeffie's eyes turned ugly and came on a little bolder, and when he smiled his mouth was full of blood. "Do you want to know what you used to scream in the middle of the night?"

"No."

Bathed in sweat now, Shad turned to go back inside and heard drunken laughter in the undergrowth. He dug through the brush and saw Becka Dudlow and Hoober Luvell seated on a tree stump sharing a jug, hunched and leaning their heads together, lifting their chins to leer at him.

Hoober looked up with glassy red eyes gleaming, that toothless smile giving him a simpleminded expression. Some folks figured him for retarded because they never got any closer to him than the other side of the street. He was so bloated that his tawny skin seemed ready to peel away at any second.

Becka's angry teeth and antagonistic nipples aimed at Shad, and he felt the same way he used to feel when he was sitting in her Bible class and didn't know the correct chapter and verse. There was a smudge of cocaine on her upper lip.

It took a minute for Hoober to clear his head enough to actually speak. It was clearly an effort, and Shad wondered why he was even making it.

The nub of a tongue slid to one side, then to the other as the black gums parted. Hoober said, "Comfort and condolences."

"Thank you."

"Couldn't sleep?"

"I think I was."

"Nightwalking, eh? Got a pair of tricky feet."

"It happens."

"To me too, on occasion." Hoober couldn't quite open his eyes but his voice sounded sober and smart. "Some of us got a call we got to answer."

Becka Dudlow nodded as though the tendons in her neck had been clipped. Her lips quivered as if she might speak, but then her mouth closed again. Very slowly she slid off the stump in a well-practiced motion, curled up on the grass, and began to snore.

"Ain't you cold?" Hoober asked.

The moment Shad thought about it he began to tremble. "Yes. Did you hear me talking before?"

"No."

"You smell any paint?"

"Paint?" Hoober sniffed. His nostrils were caked with dirt and cocaine. "No."

"Or blood?"

"Damn, those must've been some bad dreams you've been having."

Or something else. Shad could still feel the sticky touch of Jeffie O'Rourke on his neck, but he couldn't see any of the red flecks on his flesh now. His shuddering became violent and he made his way to the back door of the boardinghouse.

He passed the phone in the hall. For a moment he thought he might call Information for the East Hollywood phone number of Albert Herrin, give it a ring, and ask for Prescott Plumber. But he didn't know what the hell he might do if Jeffie answered.

Chapter Nine

HE WAS ON HIS WAY TO SEE LUPPY JOE ANSON'S new wife, with Lament laid out and panting in the passenger seat, when Dave's cruiser filled the rearview mirror. Shad slowed and pulled over, got out, leaned against the 'Stang, and waited. He felt the same way he did when the bulls made their spot inspections.

When he used to block for the moonrunners, he'd hang a quarter mile in back of Tub Gattling or one of the other boys until the cops pounced from behind the bridges and billboards on the highway. On occasion, Sheriff Increase Wintel himself would circle around the twenty-foot-high stacks of planks at the lumberyard and hop the river on the outskirts of town. He had a girlfriend over that way and if the timing was right, he'd join the fray. The sheriff liked to lean out his window and take potshots.

The cops could always tell· who was carrying make-liquor because the weight would hunker the springs down under the trunk. When Shad suggested that the crews haul only half their loads and make two runs, or evenly distribute the jugs all over the car so the shocks didn't sag, the runners just looked at him like he was crazy.

You couldn't ruin the game, you simply had to play it. So Shad did his part, gunning in and cutting off the cruisers, taking the heat and blocking the cops until the runners got clear. Then he'd lead the police on a reckless chase across town before shaking them loose.

Everyone had their designated roles to perform. Too much money came into the county on untaxed whiskey. If the stills ever went out of business, a third of the population would suddenly be unemployed. The hollow would fold up in a weekend and reappear in a trailer park up in Poverhoe City.

The sheriff couldn't arrest more than a couple of haulers a month. The fun part was doing your best not to be one of the handful that got busted.

Dave walked over, and said, "Still in nice shape. Who kept it for you?"

"Tub Gattling."

"He do any extra work while you were gone?"

"No, just kept it cleaned and the battery charged."

"I'm surprised he could control himself, considering all the muscle cars he handles for the crews. Enhanced carriages and augmented suspension so they can bolt over rutted back roads, jump the creek beds without too much damage. He's got a real touch. He's doing new interior cage designs all the time."

Any other cop would've played it meaner, even if he was a friend. Coming up and hissing quietly in your ear. The bulls used to play it that way all the time on the tier, shove past with a grin and make threats under their breaths just to keep the cons off-balance. Hit you with a smile up front but their hands always wavered near their belts for the nightstick, just feeling you out. Bull goes home and finds out his sixteen-year-old daughter is pregnant, his son's selling weed and flunking geometry, his wife is maxing the credit cards out on new living room furniture, and he just doy-de-dums his way through it all until he gets to work. Then he cuts loose on some banger with a bad attitude.

Any other cop would've played it rougher, especially if he had the muscle behind him, but not Dave Fox. He took it calm and quietly. Shad realized he might be in trouble when Dave wasted time with small talk, but he couldn't do anything except wait it out. "The more money the state gives the police department for cruisers, the more seriously Tub has to take his part."

"I'm giving a nod of admiration where it's deserved. Even so, he should stick to his road shows or the stock car derby. He gets any more serious and someone will have to come down hard on him and even things out again."

Did Dave expect him to get right back into the game? Go back to running without a second thought?

Shad didn't want to show too much interest but knew it was expected of him, because this was about the only topic they had in common. "Goats still the ones they use most?"

"Yeah, Luppy and some of the boys still favor the GTOs 'cause their daddies drove them around after 'Nam. Makes them feel like they've got a bit of world history themselves."

"I always thought that 'Gran Turismo Omologato'

might've sounded too Asian for them to ever go for the make."

"Because none of them know that's what GTO stands for."

Your daddy's car had as much meaning and implication as your first lay. You were never quite a man until you'd passed through numerous fires and crossed a dozen lines scuffed across your front walk. Every time you advanced beyond one, another was waiting. The first time you carried your father home drunk. Your first night in jail.

Lament crawled into the driver's seat and was working at the knob trying to roll down the window. Pa had finally gotten a smart pup.

"Zeke Hester was in the emergency room last night," Dave said, and they were into it.

Shad made his face into a C-Block mask of blankness. "That so?"

"Seems he broke his arm again."

Sometimes you just had to be the asshole. On the rare occasion it was better than the alternatives. "Guess he should be more careful."

The November air swept by full of ash. Over the crests of rising fields, the farmers were burning branches of holly and poplar from the edges of their orchards. Dave crossed his massive arms over his chest and made a show of barely maintained restraint. It was a gesture that would've held more gravity before the days of Little Pepe. "I reckon the same could be said for others."

"Sure. Did he tell you what happened?"

"No."

Shad pinched at his chin with thumb and forefinger,

putting on his thinking cap, hitting the pose but trying not to go overboard with it. You didn't really want to fuck around with Dave too much.

"Maybe he tripped over his mother's loom again, coming in wrecked from the roadhouse. You got me wondering now. Did she ever do another paint-by-numbers to replace Elvis and Jesus up on the cloud?"

"No, she liked that one so much she just taped it back together."

You gave away nothing, but that didn't mean you couldn't have a little fun. He never would've tried it in the can, but he had to admit, being home made him feel smarter than he should've.

Dave glared, and his tie somehow became even straighter. "You gonna make me sorry you ever came back to town?"

"What a vicious thing to say."

"I know, I'm appalled at myself as well."

Lament had the window a quarter of the way down and was sticking his snout and jowls out, tongue lapping at the glass.

"I suppose you'll do what you have to do while you're home," Dave said, "whatever the price."

"You only know that because you'd do the same."

"I believe in stepping lightly until it's time to jump."

"So do I, but until you all decide what 'death by misadventure' means, I guess I have to go my own way on this."

"Look, I don't expect you to hand out buttered hot biscuits and gravy to your neighbors. But the sheriff isn't going to put up with too many problems."

"If that's true, then why isn't he here talking to me instead of you?"

It was a good question. Lament considered it too, head cocked and tail swiping back and forth, oversized puppy paws looking like they were too heavy for him to lift. Dave shifted his stance and Shad saw the hardness come into his eyes. "There was a stabbing at Dober's last night. Sheriff's busy with that."

"Anyone I know?"

"No. I followed up with you as a courtesy, and you ought to count it as such."

"I do." This sort of jab and feint was beginning to chip at his resolve. "If you're interested, Zeke came at me. From behind, charging like an ox. I wasn't looking for a fight."

"Learned to be nonviolent in prison, that so? Studied up plenty on the principles of Gandhi."

"I admit I didn't mind knocking him on his ass."

"You did a little more than that."

"Yes, and it could've been worse. Let's leave it go."

"All right, for the time being." Dave turned aside, stared into the deep reflection of his own face peering from the highly buffed hood of the Mustang. Dave Fox's daddy had once owned one just like it, when he'd gotten back from Da Nang. "Where you headed now?"

Already knowing where Shad was going, but making sure he realized the pressure was on, that the eye was on him.

"Luppy's place. I want to talk with his new wife."

"Callie. She's young, but has a real flair. I like her a lot. Joe's lucky, and she's gotten him to change some of his more dire ways."

"I look forward to meeting her."

"Wonder if she'll feel the same."

They let it go at that. When Dave pulled out and drove past, Shad had the angry urge to race after him, get in front, and smoke him all the way out to Waynescross.

Okay, so that hadn't gone as well as it might've. He got the distinct impression that he'd possibly lost the one friend around here who could actually help him find out what happened to his sister.

Lament picked up on the mood and flicked his tail cautiously, heavy hound dog face drawn into a grief-stricken look. The window was all the way down and Lament hung halfway out of the car, uncertain whether he should jump free. Shad knew how he felt. Hung up half-in and half-out, too scared to leap.

LUPPY JOE HAD BEEN THE KING MOONSHINE MAKER in the hollow for about ten years, running more than three thousand gallons a month. He had fifteen men working for his outfit, driving moon around to three counties, spreading it to the bars and shake shacks, the trailer parks and dice dens, where they'd use food coloring to turn the moon into bourbon, rum, tequila, and scotch.

Shad drove up the deeply grooved back road and swung toward the Anson farm, past clumps of birch and virgin white pine. He didn't know most of the men wandering around the property stacking boxes inside the barn and hiding the drums and sugar sacks around back.

He expected at least a little hassling but no one flagged him down or gave him any trouble. Luppy must've been paying the Feds and local law an even higher kickback, allowing them to pinch a couple of the sixteen-year-old haulers now and again. The kids would only get probation, and the department could spend their money and still look like they were doing their jobs. Nobody gave a shit about the hollow anyway.

Jake Hapgood squatted on the far side of the house near a vat of corn mash, working one of the old-timer stills. He was tapping at the coiled tubing with a wooden bedframe slat. He chawed on a stalk of grass, boots covered with pig shit. He'd trimmed most of the singed ends off and needed another shot of mousse, but his hair was hanging in pretty good, one curl uncoiled over his eye. More duck's ass today than pompadour.

Shad drove up slowly, watching out for the hogs, and parked. Jake turned and smirked. "Don't tell me you're thinking of getting back into the make-liquor business."

"I'll leave that to the professionals," Shad said.

"Run-liquor then?"

"No, I'm just here to visit with Joe."

"Don't think he's home, but maybe he snuck in while I wasn't watching." He wore a slightly shamed expression that threw Shad for a second until he realized Jake felt guilty about being seen with Becka Dudlow at the bonfire. Situations like that could catch up with a man in the light of day.

Shad decided to ignore it, and soon the embarrassed look slid from Jake's face. It occasionally took folks a minute or two to realize they had nothing to feel remorseful about in front of an ex-con.

A chuckle eased from Jake, filled with a certain nastiness but not his own. "Heard about what happened to your friend Zeke Hester. I thought you said you weren't looking to get sent back to the joint."

"I'm not."

"You probably shouldn't have left a good old boy like Griff as a witness then. He hates to talk unless it's about the Normandy Invasion or something that happened out in front of his store."

Left a witness. Like Shad was robbing the place and should've used a shotgun on anybody who saw him. "All that matters is what Zeke said."

"Zeke didn't say anything," Jake told him. "He sure can blubber like a little girl though."

"Throws like one too."

Jake's torso trembled with silent laughter, holding it in where it belonged because one day he might have to make a choice, and Zeke Hester was always going to be his neighbor. The curl flipped over Jake's eye one way, and the breeze hiked it back the other. He acted like he was about to tell secrets again, leaned in, but didn't say anything for a minute. His cooler sat nearby in the hay and he gestured toward it. "Want a beer?"

"No thanks."

"I can't go with whiskey every day and night like the old days."

"Anybody who tries isn't worth much before long."

It was the truth, but having it laid out like that took Jake back a step, as if Shad might suddenly be judging.

Maybe they were all losing their slickness. Christ, you couldn't say any damn thing without offending somebody. He didn't know when everyone in town had gotten so sensitive, and couldn't decide if he'd hardened up too far to simply make regular conversation now. The things you had to worry about.

Jake squinted at him an extra second and broke into a

grin. He still had every tooth in his head, so he hadn't started down the road yet. "Jesus, you haven't lightened up half an inch since the other night. I thought after you were home a while you'd have settled back in."

"I've got too much on my mind," Shad said. "Sorry if it puts me out of sorts. Tell me . . . what do you know about Luppy's wife?"

Chickens squawked and two angry hogs roamed by searching out the fallen corn kernels. Lament whined from the passenger seat, tried to loose a bark but was still too young.

"Callie's sharp, has a nice way about her. Young still, but mature. And I'm not only talking about her body, which is fine, you understand. She can lighten your load just by standing near you. She's smart, and grasps exactly how to keep Joe on his best behavior. He hardly drinks anymore, and you recall what kind of a miscreant he could be when he was tappin' the jug too much."

Luppy used to get drunk and sit naked on the porch with an eleven-gauge pump. He'd fire into the darkness at the smallest noise and claim he was aiming at gophers. He'd wounded two of his employees that way. One lost the tip of his left pinkie, and the other took thirty stitches in the buttocks and wore the flattened shot in a locket around his neck as a kind of good luck charm.

You found providence wherever you could, even if you had to pull it out of your ass.

"You ever see my sister out this way?" Shad asked.

"Here on the farm? Mags? What in the hell would she be doing out this way?"

"Someone said she and this girl Callie were friends."

"Not that I ever noticed."

"They were in Preacher Dudlow's Youth Ministry together."

You couldn't help but come full circle when you were dealing with such a tight circuit. It was no different than when you were making a break for the county line. No matter what back road you took, you eventually hit the river, the gorge, or the highway. You couldn't do ninety across the hollow for more than ten minutes before you had to turn around and go back again.

Jake lit a cigarette. The fumes from the vat caught high above and a blue burst of flame scurried wildly through the air. There were men all over town whose eyebrows would never grow back. "I know Callie used to stop in there on occasion, help Mrs. Swoozie bake pies for the church sales. Go clean out some of the river shacks and sell odd goods at the parking lot flea market."

With a whimper, Lament hopped into the driver's seat, stuck his paws up on the steering wheel like he wanted to drop into fourth gear and rip the hell out of there. Smart dog, all right.

The pigs squealed and circled closer and closer, agitated, noticing something.

His field of vision began to narrow. He blinked but nothing changed, except the night came pushing in, pressing forward as if coming for him. The whole world began to darken. This was new. He took a deep breath and drew a trail of smoke off Jake's cigarette into his face. He felt another presence near him, possibly even watching him from the fields.

Lament pawed the horn twice and Shad's eyes cleared. He snapped to attention as if somebody had pressed a shiv into his kidney.

"Go on in," Jake told him. "You know the way. She ain't the edgy type."

Shad walked across the yard noticing marks in the flattened grass where federal helicopters had landed this week. The other men eyed him and nodded and kept on going about their work, loading the plastic jugs into the backs of pickups, the blockers working on their engines.

If Mags had come around here, what would she have thought of all this? The heat intensified and inched across the back of his neck, and the hinges of his jaw began to ache. Was this where her death had started? Whatever had led her up Gospel Trail?

He stepped to the door of the Anson house and suddenly wanted to talk to his father, put this off for a while and get back to the old man. He didn't know why.

Lament honked again.

Luppy's door was always open. Shad stuck his head in, glanced around.

She was sitting at the kitchen table poring over papers, looking very much like his sister had when Megan was busy doing homework.

Eighteen or so, with willowy blond hair like layered lace adorning her shoulders. She had intense, dark eyes that drew your attention directly to them, even if she wasn't staring at you. They shone like black gems. She wore jeans and a white cable-knit sweater that also reminded him of Mags more than it should have, but perhaps it was good to keep the dead in mind now.

Callie Anson got up and walked across the kitchen carrying a checkbook and bills, frowning as if she didn't like the numbers she kept coming up with. She threw everything down with an aggravated huff of air.

Shad could imagine what Luppy's bank account must look like. For years he'd followed his grandfather's tradition of burying cash in mason jars around the farm. Luppy used to keep intricate maps drawn on graph paper, but one rainy season half his property flooded out, and he lost eighteen grand to the mud. If Luppy Joe was keeping his money in the bank now, he probably had a dozen scattered accounts, funds going in and out of them arbitrarily.

She bustled into the hall, came around toward the living room, and spotted Shad taking up space in the doorway. A breeze washed in around him and her hair whisked about her chin.

Without any show of alarm, she peered over his shoulder and saw Jake still working out there with the wooden slat, the other men crossing the yard to the barn. She was reassured that they'd let Shad through.

She drew to her full height, nearly six foot, as tall as Luppy, and asked, "Who are you?"

"My name's Jenkins. Shad Jenkins." He tried to give a disarming grin but wasn't sure it was coming along the way he hoped.

The dark eyes softened. "Megan's brother?"

"That's right."

"You were in jail."

"Yes."

"And you just got out."

"Yes." So it was going to be like this.

"You're not looking for Joe?" It wasn't really a question, more like a topic of conversation already rejected the instant it was touched on. "You'd like to talk with me."

"Yes."

That sweet girlish voice was pure tallow in the winter,

creamy and thick, smooth and somehow feathery. It reminded him of how young she truly was, and he felt oddly upset with Luppy.

"To speak about her. 'Cause you were away for so long."

You could only nod so many times before you started feeling like a moron, so he just waited until he got an invite to take a step off the welcome mat.

"I don't know what you expect from me."

"Neither do I," he told her.

"Come on inside then."

On the mantel sat a large framed photo of Luppy Joe and Callie on their wedding day. Luppy looked happy but uncomfortable in a short-sleeve shirt and bolo tie. His huge belly hung low over his belt, the button there straining to keep shut. Callie had on a half veil that came midway down the bridge of her nose, obscuring her eyes though you could still discern them under there, black like punctures through the cloth. She wore a long white silk dress, almost antediluvian in style. The kind they wore while strolling their plantations before the War of Northern Aggression. She was at least six months pregnant in the picture.

Shad didn't see any kid's toys around. No crib, no bottles or jars of baby food. He didn't know if maybe her parents were taking care of the child or if she'd lost it. You could never ask certain questions.

"You're the one who bought the Mustang that Joe's cousin died in, aren't you?"

"Yes," he said.

"Way Joe tells it, the guy's hair killed him."

"Chuckie Eagleclaw's mother killed him, though you

could say it was the receding hairline that caused his death."

It nearly brought a smile to her lips, which was enough for the time being. "How's that?"

"He kept checking himself in the rearview and took his eyes off the road."

She grabbed the top of a ladder-back chair and squeezed until the muscles of her neck stood out. Shad tried not to stare at the tightly angled curves packed into the well-fitting clothes, the meaty crook of her throat. It wasn't easy.

"I heard you're scrambling for trouble," she said. "Causing discomfort everywhere you go."

It stopped him cold, the way she put it. "Who's saying that?"

"Everybody knows it. You think hollow folk got something better to talk about than an ex-convict who comes home to find his baby sister dead?"

So much for tiptoeing. It proved she was astute, already in tune with his purpose, and didn't mind laying it out on the line. "I suppose not."

"You're not going to bring any of that distress and annoyance into my house, now are you, Shad Jenkins?"

"I only want to talk."

"All right. Come sit."

Moving across the house was no different than traveling through his own life. He remembered returning here late at night after delivering liquor to the roadhouses and parish bazaars. The guys would be playing poker with their watch fobs and silver dollars in the pot, the same as their fathers and grandfathers. Shad would know he was connected by a real but intangible trail leading back across the dim leagues of his own ancestry.

On the counter sat a jug of moon, a bottle of wine, and a freshly made pot of coffee, but she didn't offer him anything.

"I'm not sure what to ask," he said.

"I'm not sure what I can tell you."

Now that he had someone who might help, every question he came up with sounded faint and weak. "Like you mentioned, I was out of touch for the last couple of years. I missed a big part of her life as she grew from a girl to a woman. I'm trying to find out the kind of things my father wouldn't know."

"Okay."

"What did you do? Where did you go?"

She gave a rough scowl. "What the hell kinds of questions are these?"

She was right, he had to focus. "You were in the Youth Ministry together."

"We went visiting around the county. In the hollow alone there's four Christian churches, including Reverend Sow's room in back of his dry goods shop where he's got a couple pews. Some of them like wine and dancing, some prefer more puritan behavior with the occasional all-night gospel sing. Then there's others who stick to the old ways, around the bottoms. You know how it is. Reverend Dudlow would ask us to talk to them, hand out literature, try to get them to come into town more often and listen to his sermons."

In a movie, the guy playing Shad would've reached out about now. Maybe brushed her on the wrist or the back of the hand, and the audience would've sunk into their seats, feeling the sexual tension building on the screen.

Christ, he was as bad as Zeke, always thinking about a camera going in for a close-up.

It was too easy for your vengeance to blur into something like hope. Shad pawed at his chin some, trying to get a bead. "So you girls went visiting."

"Don't call me a girl, please. You might not mean it to sound offensive, but it is. I'm sensitive to that tone. My mother often gives it to me."

"I apologize. So you both, ah, did what exactly? Knocked on doors?"

"Handing out pamphlets. We sometimes went out as far as Enigma, Poverhoe City, and Waynescross."

A thread of sweat worked down his collar. "Did you go to the Lusk farm?"

"Which one's that?"

"Place out on Route 18 in Waynescross. A sad few acres with a dying cherry orchard and ill children. Two that have flippers instead of arms, another who's hydrocephalic. Kid with a big head, shaped like a pumpkin."

"I know what it means, Shad Jenkins. We had a couple of drop-offs along Route 18. But I don't recall the name Lusk or anything like those children."

"Are you certain?"

She frowned again and a crease appeared between her eyes. "I'd remember a kid with a pumpkin head, don't you think?"

It couldn't be a coincidence, that Megan should be in the area where her own mother lived and not see her.

"Was there ever any trouble? Handing out Preacher Dudlow's brochures? Two young ladies like yourselves?"

"Sometimes we'd get shooed off. Folks aren't very open-minded in praising God some different way than they're used to. Or not at all, as it mostly turns out. A truckful of the Sweetwater haulers give us a hard time once, hootin' and fallin' down in the street and such, but nothing a woman doesn't have to deal with almost every day in this town."

"Zeke Hester?"

"What about him?"

"He ever bother Megan?"

"After she smashed his mouth and you busted him up the way you did? No. He cut a wide path around us."

Lament gave a prolonged honk, and Jake shouted, "I do believe that dog might be asking for a job as a blocker. You boys think we should give him a trial run?"

The flat of Shad's hand began to creep along the table and he realized he was reaching for her, like he had the right. He stood and put his fists in his pockets, leaned against the wall. "Did you ever go up to Gospel Trail Road?"

"No. Nobody needs go up that way."

"There are hill families beyond the ridges. The Johansens. The Taskers. Burnburries and Gabriels."

"I never heard of them before. Besides, it's too far. We usually walked."

"You walked to Waynescross and Enigma?"

"No, Joe gave me his truck on those days, of course."

He caught on at last. An instant wash of regret went through him for being so ignorant, but he didn't let it show. "To make a drop-off. You weren't just handing out church literature; you were delivering moon."

"I was doin' both on certain days. I thought you would've understood that, considering who I'm married to."

"I should've. Did Megan often go with you on runs?"

"She was only trying to get folks involved with the church. If I had a delivery to make, I just brought it along in the truck. The rest of the time, we visited, helped with the bazaars, bake sales, things like that. She was an old soul."

"Preacher Dudlow told me Megan visited him three days before she died."

"Mrs. Swoozie likes a tap of whiskey with her pies. I asked Megan to get the money we were owed."

"She knew it was for moon?"

"She wasn't stupid. Of course she knew. It bothered her on occasion, that so many folks drank, even old church ladies like Mrs. Swoozie. But she never held it against anybody. It's the way of the hollow."

He wanted to ask Callie about the baby, see if there was any story there that would lead him back to his sister. It seemed so foolishly important that it might have some real bearing.

Sex? Underground baby trade? He'd met a couple guys in the slam who'd made big money off that before taking their falls. But Shad couldn't figure out how to go about asking.

"And she didn't have a boyfriend?"

"No."

"Why not? She was beautiful. Didn't any come around?"

"No," Callie whispered, so quiet he almost missed it. "She believed."

"How's that? Believed?"

"Yes."

"In what?" he asked. They were talking at cross angles. "In God?"

Callie Anson looked away for a time, working up to it, as the mood around them grew heavier. With confusion, unspoken tragedies, and general senselessness, like a guy who can die by checking out his hair, a seventeen-year-old girl from a heart attack.

She checked him over to see if he could handle her words, unsure and thinking twice about it, but she decided to press on.

"She thought somebody . . . loved her."

"Who?"

"I was talking about marriage. I told her it was hard sometimes, to curb Luppy and his drinking. I mentioned some of the rough patches we've had. I told her she was lucky not to have to worry on the troubles a wife had all the time. She said, 'I may not be married, but I am loved.'"

"I don't understand."

"I'm probably wrong about this. I might be making more of it than there is."

He shrugged. "It's okay, speak your mind."

The black gems lost some of their shine for a moment, then turned on him, blazing. "Over the last couple of days, when I heard you were back home in the hollow kicking up a fuss, I started to think on it some more. It seemed she might be talking about a man. Like a man wanted her, you understand? And she liked it."

Chapter Ten

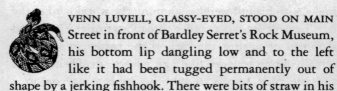VENN LUVELL, GLASSY-EYED, STOOD ON MAIN Street in front of Bardley Serret's Rock Museum, his bottom lip dangling low and to the left like it had been tugged permanently out of shape by a jerking fishhook. There were bits of straw in his hair.

A few years back, he'd been one of the strongest men in Moon Run. He used to tussle with anybody at any time, and his reputation as a grappler grew until guys from all over the county would make official challenges against him.

So they built a ring over in the town square and the gamblers rampaged through the crowd fanning fifties and giving points. The ex–high school football stars and gator wrasslers would try him on for size every Saturday. Venn would end each match by holding his opponent overhead and flinging him over the ropes.

Shad remembered being a kid and looking up to him, hoping one day to be like that.

After a few months of battling and making some money, Venn considered moving to California and becoming a professional wrestler. Sheriff Increase Wintel promised to invest in Venn's career and get him a promotional manager. But before they could gather the gumption to make a real effort, the moonshine got Venn the way it got nearly everybody and it brought him down hard.

The memory gave Shad some pause now as Venn clomped into the street directly in front of the 'Stang and Shad nearly ran him over.

It was close.

The pup yawped. Shad let out a cry and stood on the brake with his full weight, spinning the wheel hard to the left. Lament let out another throaty, terrorized bark and slammed up against the back of the passenger seat. The screech of tires sounded like a girlish scream of frustration, and the blue smoke of burning rubber rose up in a swirling gust. Shad cracked his temple against the window. His head filled with a billowing pain and the ghosts of the two previous owners. You couldn't feel sorry for them, but man, you could feel them.

And unlike the first guy, you didn't even get a chance to die with your hand between a woman's legs, or even the love of one in your heart.

The car lurched to stop sideways in the street, cutting off both lanes like a roadblock.

Venn stepped up like it was nothing, knocked at the window as if he wanted to be let in. Shad glanced over, still stunned, a trickle of blood dribbling through his hairline.

The dead crowded him, and he didn't know if they were

trying to get in or out. Venn blinked and knocked again with that giant fist. The blood-smeared window shattered.

Grunting, Shad threw up an arm to protect his face. The shards rained down into his hair, slithered into his collar. He grappled for the door, swung it wide, and fell into the street. Venn Luvell's arms encircled and lifted him up like a sleepy child.

It took a minute to clear his head, the fog parting and the dead guys withdrawing.

"Would you please let me go?" he asked.

"Y'kay?"

"Yes."

Venn eased him back down until his feet touched ground. Lament snuffed and sneezed, shook up but apparently safe. His tail gingerly flicked twice.

Behind them on the sidewalk, M'am Luvell sat in the wheelchair Shad's father had made her, so covered in blankets that you could only see her small face and the tips of her fingers. Her pipe was packed and the stink of marijuana drifted over and mixed pleasantly with the biting odor of fried rubber.

So, Bardley Serret was the weed supplier that M'am visited upon. Shad had never found it odd before that a Rock Museum could stay open for so long.

M'am said, "Come here."

"No."

"Shad Jenkins, do as I say."

He already felt like a fool, but arguing with an old woman on Main Street was worse than simply obeying. Venn trudged up the sidewalk, and Shad swallowed a curse, tasting copper. The 'Stang had stalled. The pickups and cars still moving on Main Street gave him a wide berth but didn't stop.

He got the Mustang started again and slowly pulled over to the curb. Lament shivered in nervousness and crawled into Shad's lap. He carried the dog as he got out. A few folks on the street stared but no one came close or said anything. They'd be buzzing tonight all over town, and by the morning everybody would know how close Shad Jenkins had come to being another victim of the car.

M'am's voice still had that tinge of mischief to it, as if she was this close to laughing in Shad's face. "You're bleeding." She rummaged under the blankets and held out a rag to him.

"You want to tell me what the hell that was all about?" he asked.

"Walk along with us for a bit."

"Jesus Christ, you people."

"If you're fretting about a little knock on the noggin then you're not ready for what's ahead of you."

"And what's that?"

"Walk along and we'll talk. Give me a few minutes of your time and some words. Won't hurt you and it might help."

It took a great assertion of will not to mention that Venn stepping in front of the car had nearly killed them both, but Shad managed to hold his tongue. He could do it when he had to, he'd done it for two years behind bars. Why was it becoming so difficult to keep his own counsel at home?

She gave a sidelong glance, casual but aware. "You sometimes think you were stronger in prison than you are back in your own birthplace, ain't that so?"

He was giving too much of himself away, but it didn't matter anymore. She was merely showing off now and that said more about her flaws than his own. She nodded at him, eyes closed, her ageless virtue making him feel as if he was the elder. Like this might be no more than an afternoon spent with a child, heading for a picnic.

The oaks grew thick and wide on either side of Main Street. The breeze proved just strong enough to rattle the branches against one another. Crows sat up high without a sound, occasionally dive-bombing for scraps of food in the gutters and behind the diners. The sidewalks, though cracked, were cared for and well swept by the shop owners.

He stepped up beside Venn and saw almost nothing beneath the goliath's perplexed grimace. Maybe a ripple of anxiety. There seemed to be barely enough mental current to keep his limbs moving.

Venn cocked his head at Lament, and went, "Dawg."

M'am's polished, store-bought pipe caught the sun and lit her chin. The craggy features hardly moved even as her expression changed. Only her mouth shifted, from pout to frown to grin. You got more from considering her lips than from watching the blunt angles of her flesh.

"So," Shad said, "what do you ask of me?"

It made her laugh. "My, but you do have brass, boy. It'll serve you well for what you got coming."

"Do you have something to say or are we just going to stand here? I feel like we're doing a drug deal."

"I won't keep you long. Let's head around the town square."

She kept eyeing him impassively. Venn's enormous hands rested lightly on the back of the wheelchair, pressing

M'am along. Lament heeled pretty well for a puppy and never left Shad's ankle.

M'am appeared to be having a difficult time finding a handle on him to pull. She said, "Hoober done saw you out night walkin'."

"It happens on occasion."

She nodded at him, as if listening to someone else close by or watching things occurring around them that he couldn't see.

"You go out of your way to do that?" he asked.

"What's this?"

"You know, being off-putting the way you are, enjoying the unease of others. Or so it looks to me."

She puffed on her pot and showed her brown nubby teeth. "Just sort of happens. My apologies to you, Shad Jenkins."

The lady had a way about her all right, making it seem like he was just being sensitive, weak-minded. He stared at Venn again, took a step closer. Venn apparently didn't recognize him.

Shad's patience was a lot more limited now. The sensation that time was running out was beginning to overcome him.

"I expected you to come see me again," M'am said.

"Why? You didn't tell me anything useful before."

She considered that, then shrugged. "That may be. Even so, it'd behoove you to indulge me a few minutes."

"So you keep telling me. And so I keep doing."

The laughter coming up in her made the bones clatter in her chest. "I been thinkin' about your problem."

"Which one?"

"The one that's gonna send you up into them back hills."

"What if I don't go?"

"You will. I didn't tell you everything about that day my mama was taken."

"I figured not."

M'am began to fidget in her chair, contorting until the toes of one foot popped up through the blankets, then vanished again.

"I already done declared how I used to go up there with my ma and pa on Sunday afternoons after church."

"Yes. When you were dressed in pink with pretty bows in your blond hair, riding up in an ox wagon. You said it might be hard for somebody to picture that now, but it isn't really."

"That's 'cause you see me as a child due to my size. Lots of folks do. They come to ask my advice on matters, and some of them pay me with candy and chocolate. Or with corn-husk dollies and little booties they stitched together. I don't fret it none. We all got our notions and preconceptions. Now let me get on with it."

"Sure."

Something touched him and he looked down to see her tiny fingers plying his wrist. He didn't know what it meant for a second until he thought she must want the rag back. What would a hex woman do with the blood on it? Use it to beguile somebody in his name? Cast a protection spell around him?

He handed the piece of cloth to her and she looked disgusted. "Gah, boy, keep it."

"I thought you wanted it back."

"The hell for? No, I was just patting your hand, the

way your mother probably done, even if you don't remember it none."

"Oh. Sorry."

She didn't hear him, which meant they were into it and already deep. M'am Luvell's teeth ground down on her pipe and her gaze grew faraway, scanning backwards in time and finding horror.

"That ground is scornful and them woods is demented. The wraiths, they come up out of the gorge and across the land like a whirlwind and took my mama." The strength of her emotions made her writhe in the chair as she tried to fight back a groan of distress but finally gave in. Lament keyed in on the old woman's anguish and let loose with a whine. So did Venn. M'am's voice had lost all its force. "It . . . it done things to her first."

"You sure it wasn't just a man?" Shad asked. "A deranged trapper living up there? Or a bear? Mountain lion?"

"I wasn't a toddler nor a fool. I was four years old and I know what happened. Besides, no man would do that to a woman."

A few guys in C-Block had done things with women that had gotten them written up in psychological textbooks. They'd even had psychoses named after them. There was one inmate on death row who'd lived in solitary for six years because of what he'd done to his daughter. He was the subject of a documentary called *The Maniacal House Husband*.

"You see how big Venn is? He gets that from my side of the family, if'n you accept it and even if you don't. My daddy, he was two three inches taller than Venn even. No man ever scairt my daddy, nor bested him neither. My daddy would've folded any trapper in half, lunatic or not. He hunted bear and mountain cat regular, and he had respect for 'em but no fear of any animal."

They made their way around the square, past the Civil War statues and the trim shrubs, the small stone walls where the town trustees and office clerks sometimes sat and took their lunches.

"My daddy...my papa..." The tears spilled freely down her cheeks and slid away in the crevices of her wrinkles. "My papa, he left me there. The ox ran and took off with the cart. Papa ran screaming after them back down Gospel Trail. I ran too, into the woods, didn't know no better. The wraiths clung to me and pretended like they wanted to play. But in time they started to nibble at me, but they was slow after what they done to Mama. They was sated. They eventually let me go on my own way, more or less."

"Why would ghosts do that?"

"I didn't say a damn thing 'bout no ghosts. Ghosts is just dead folks that believe they're still alive. Wraiths is something more. I don't know exactly what, but that's what all abides up in them hills. They part of the sick ground. Took me a full day to get back to town from Jonah Ridge. No one came lookin' for me that night, not even my papa."

"How do I stop it?" he asked, and the seriousness in his tone brought Lament's chin up.

"You ask for help," she said.

"How's that?"

"You know what I mean, boy. You ask for help from those you talk to when you go night walkin'."

It felt like someone had just struck him with a chilled ice pick. "What do you know about it, M'am?"

"I know you got the touch. The resolve to rile them woods even worse than they are. Ah yuh. Maybe you got the strength to put 'em to rest for a time. You call on those you call on, Shad Jenkins. Maybe they'll help."

A weighty silence passed between them, but neither looked away. He stood back and gazed at the dwarf granny witch woman, trying to decide which one of them was crazy, her or himself. He was sort of leaning toward both.

"What did your father say to you?" he asked. "The next day when you got back to town."

"He never said nothin' to me, and after he told some lies to the sheriff, he never spoke to anyone again. Said Mama fell into the gorge on her own. He was scared they'd think he was cracked. He stopped talkin' and stopped workin' and three years later he tried to hang himself in the barn. Hung there an hour or two 'fore Aunt Tilly found him, and he was still alive. He was that strong. They took him away to a hospital in Enigma County. He lived to be eighty-seven 'fore he died there, and never said another word to nobody. Good riddance, I say. My papa died that day on the ridge when he turned tail." She relit her pipe and eased the smoke toward him. "You remember that story up there when you face down the darkness."

"I won't run."

"I believe you. Good luck, boy."

Venn's eyes focused for a moment. He held out his hand to shake, but before Shad could take it Venn appeared to lose the thought and dropped his arm to his side. He started back to his grandmother. His face cleared again and he turned, and said, "Bye, Shad Jenkins," and pushed the old woman away.

WHEN YOU'RE FAVORED, EVEN IF ONLY FOR AN IN-stant, you can sense your fate coming forward at least halfway to meet you. It has no substance or direction, but the brunt of it can set you on your course like deadwood on the river.

Shad got back to the Mustang, cleaned the glass out as best he could, and fired her up. The engine thrummed and sounded as if the accident had given it a hunger, for him or somebody else.

He drew up to his father's place, feeling his pa's sadness like a fog descending. Lament, though, wagged his tail, recognizing home.

Pa was playing chess with himself again, the sunlight bearing down like a mad, golden avalanche. Pa hadn't shaved in three days, which meant he still wasn't sleeping well, but at least the shotgun wasn't in sight. Maybe he no longer feared the menace of Zeke Hester, or had at last been willing to accept the truth that Zeke had never been a real threat at all.

Shad got out and Lament burst from the backseat and raced up the porch.

He took two steps and froze, feeling the hills thinking about him again, distressed and chafing, turning this way to hammer at him.

It was worse this time. The movement beneath the turnings of the world squirmed closer, almost on him be-fore he noticed.

He hadn't been vigilant enough. He'd waited too long.

They were coming for him at the knees, from behind, crawling. Sweat beaded on his face and he had to reach for the rail to steady himself.

Rising now in back of him, knowing he was aware of it, the incomplete figure allowed itself to be observed for a second as it withdrew, hesitantly, like it was almost ready to speak to him.

Shad didn't want to drop where he was and scare his father, but he watched his own hand turn ashen, the veins sticking out as black as if he'd been poisoned. He found himself seated on the bottom porch stair.

Pa came up out of his rocker crying, "Son? You ill? Are you hurt or you just been drinkin' with your friends?"

It gave him an excuse. Shad smiled, hoping he looked abashed. "Must've had one too many with Jake Hapgood."

"That's all right, you earned yourself some good times after what you been through. If you're gonna be sick, turn your chin to the weeds."

Pa's broad, stony face loosened into an expression of care, like he was glad to have somebody left to dote on. His father's strong hands came down and pulled Shad to his feet. Shad went with it for a moment, laying his cheek against Pa's chest, hearing the beat of his powerful heart, that aggressive strength of life within him.

The log house, no less alluring than a tomb, beckoned him inside and he went easily. As they passed through the doorway, he saw Megan's fingers flutter at him from the depths of his darkened old bedroom.

Pa laid him out on the couch, the way he would've years ago when Shad had a fever. Mags would carry a bowl of soup in from the kitchen and feed him while he shivered on the hard cushions. Pa never stuffed enough cotton or feather into them because he liked the feel of the shaved wood against his back.

"Time's coming, isn't it?"

"I think so," Shad said.

"I hear tell you been asking about the back hills. The Pharisee and Jonah Ridge. Been stirring up a lot of folks." Then, with the grin chiseled into his rough features, "But you got the hollow buzzing again."

Shad waited.

"You goin' up there by yourself?" Pa asked.

"Yes."

"Want me to come?"

"No."

"Didn't believe so." It seemed to both rile and sadden the man, the relief showing through. Shad got the sudden but explicit impression that he didn't know his father very well at all, and never would. "I get scared sometimes, son."

"Why?"

"I don't reckon I grasp hold of it exactly. I tend to...to just grow fearful, when I'm sitting on the porch. I worry that I didn't do right by my women, your mother and sister included. That the dead don't rest in the hollow, and they carry their resentment with them. Sounds foolish, I know, but it's the truth. I only hope Megan understands I did my best by her. You think she might not?"

Shad checked his room to see if Mags's hand would give him a sign, either yes or no or perhaps sometimes. It was gone. He turned back and his father was staring at him intently, caring about his response. "You've done your best by all of us, Pa, you've got nothing to regret."

Even as he said it, he knew it was too broad a statement

to make on another man's behalf, even his father. Pa shifted uncomfortably in his seat, as if the frame of the chair wasn't harsh enough against him.

"You ought to get married. Marry Elfie and go someplace else. Out on the coast, go live by the ocean." Pa's smile was nailed in place, as fake as his words. Shad realized his old man was giving him an out, a chance to run from the responsibilities already handed down to him.

There was a serenity in their immediate circumstances that wouldn't last long now. Without meaning to do so, they had somehow reached a discreet balance. Shad couldn't push or pull at his pa. Any pressure would offset the moment. There was so much he wanted to hear his father say, yet Shad was afraid that, in telling them, his father's secrets would prove to be too common to carry any real weight.

Even if the man didn't know it, he would always be part myth to his son—a legend, a desperate fable just as Shad's mother continued to be. The sorcery of tradition and personal history carried down forever.

His father had grown up in the hollow, left at seventeen, and came back when he was thirty-five. You had to let some questions slide, but this was no longer one of them.

"Why'd you leave town? For those eighteen years. You've never said."

Pa, with the dread rising in his eyes. "What's that?"

They all made you repeat yourself. They needed to give themselves an extra second to form their rebuttals, think up their lies, and find a hole to squirrel into.

Shad left his question dangling in the air.

"That's not what you're really asking. You want to know why I come back here."

"Yes."

His father furrowed his brow and stared, first at Shad, then at the dog, and finally back toward Megan's room, as if all the solutions to his life's concerns were lying somewhere between.

"There was no point in me staying anywhere else," Pa said.

"Why?"

" 'Cause I carried the hollow with me wherever I went. It was too deep in my heart and in my way of being. So I come back. That's all there is to it."

Now Shad had no last corner to run into. It was deep in his blood, his domination by this place.

The rage clawed up his back, settled there and twined about his throat. His words came out in a wretched whisper. "Callie Anson told me that Megan might've been in love."

"With who?"

"That's what I'm asking you." His muscles tightened until he snapped out of his seat, every nerve in riot, the near hysteria ripping through him. "You must've seen it!"

"Seen what?"

"Stop making me repeat myself!"

"I didn't see nothing special. There were never any boys around. She never mentioned a word of anything like that to me."

"Did you pay any attention to her in the end?"

"Don't swing on me like that, son."

"Or what?"

His father's powerful hand came up and flattened against Shad's heart. Maybe they were just both after a fight, getting primal here the way it sometimes had to be when your hatred had nowhere to go except into the flesh of your flesh. But Pa's eyes were clear and mournful and affectionate, and the anger quickly drained from Shad.

So close like this—another inch and he'd have been crying in the man's arms, letting everything out that was locked inside.

He broke away and moved to the other end of the room. "Callie said that Mags believed somebody was in love with her. Maybe coming after her."

"It was that Zeke Hester."

"Not according to her. She said Zeke kept his distance."

"You must've argued with her some on that, seeing what you did to him the other day."

"I didn't mind what happened, but I didn't go looking for it either. He came at me and I put him down. But I don't think he caused Megan any more trouble after that first fracas."

"I don't know who it could've been then. You think I wouldn't notice a thing like that if I'd seen it? You believe I'm lying to you?"

His father had played him along, beginning with the phone call in prison. *Your sister's been killed. Come home 'fore you get on with your life.* Pa had needed him to do this thing and follow it to its end, because Karl Jenkins was incapable of doing it himself.

Shad didn't mind much. This had more to do with Pa's devotion to his daughter and belief in his son than any need for vengeance or even resolution. Maybe, in some small way, it was supposed to be a gift.

"Why are you so afraid of that place?" Shad asked. He was a stupid detective. In the end all it came down to was asking the same questions and hoping someone took enough pity to give you a direct answer.

"We always been. Your mama was too. I don't rightly know why, it's just the way it always was."

"M'am Luvell..."

"I can guess what she told you. She thinks ghosts and evil spirits stole her kin. I ain't sayin' she's wrong. The fact is, all you hear about that place, it all might be true as the sunset. It's a bad road. What else are you going to wind up with when you leave poor diseased folks up there to die? There's murder up that way." Pa's gaze drew down on Shad, eyes dark as shale. "You hear me when you want to, so you hear me now. If you got to take a life to save your own, you do it."

Shad pulled his chin back. "Pa?"

"You listen to your father and no more back talk. You make me proud, son. You always have. You handle your load better than I ever endured mine." He stood and drifted into the shadows of the house. "Stay the night in your old room. You got reasons for everything you do, same as any of us. Mine come to me on occasion when I'm asleep. Maybe you'll recollect some of yours tonight too."

AT DAWN, HE ROSE FROM THE PORCH CHAIR. FOR some reason he felt closer to Megan outside, where he could stare into the night sky and look up the road at where she was buried.

Shad found his boots in the closet, remembered what Dave Fox had said about timber rattlers. He heard his father awake in his bedroom but the man didn't come out.

As he drove away Lament loped after the car. It might

be good to have a hound up in the hills, even one that was only a pup, but Shad feared that with this trouble coming the dog might be hurt, and he couldn't bear to be the cause of that. You had to make an effort to save what was close to you, even if it was only a dog.

Shad drew up to the shadow of his mother's tombstone angling down from the hill in the expanding sunlight.

But a compulsion overcame him and he slowed and parked directly in its path.

He turned and looked to the lonely field where the graves of Mama and Mags sat side by side.

Fighting for his calm once again, he shut his eyes and tried to center himself. He had to go with the eddy, find the flourishing current once more. Shad hunted through the blackness for any sign of his sister, struggling to listen for any whisper at the back of his skull.

Blood buffeted in his ears as his heart took on a new cadence, slowing, as if the tide of his pulse grew more idle.

Of course, you dissolve and dissipate this way.

He only barely realized he was holding his breath, with the abundant blue splashes streaked against the dark of his mind. Perspiration flowed and pooled at his collar as he fought to go deeper into himself. The cool coming back on, crafty and honey and invisible. Flux roaring on, towing him down the proper stream.

Suffocating himself until he heard the word.

Jonah.

Shad fell back against the car seat, sucking air. He stuck his head out, letting the wind fill his ears. Pellets of sweat splashed onto the dirt.

Sometimes you had to damn near die to find the next step on the path you had to take.

Nothing ever changed except Mags was dead. Shad reminded himself, feeling the sweet lift that the rage provided him.

He put the 'Stang into drive and headed for Gospel Trail Road, knowing that his enemy—whether the hills or the wraiths or someone hiding up there who also dreamed of blood—was waiting and smirking, urging him forward to meet at last, and mix their bad luck together into a new hellish brew.

PART II

The
Jonah

Chapter Eleven

HE DROVE INTO THE MOUNTAINS ON THE BAD road, past the patch of ground where his sister's body had lain in the darkness.

Heading north to Jonah Ridge and the old train trestle, Shad kept trying to see it the way it had once been. A hundred years ago, in a different life, he might've brought Elfie Danforth up here to go a'courtin', a picnic basket on his arm, with her parents following at a respectful distance behind them.

But other scenes kept pushing in. Imagining how it must've been with the wagons carrying entire families up this way, dying from cholera or yellow fever. The elderly and the children flung onto the back of a cart as they weakly argued for life. Peace officers, doctors, and town fathers dragging their friends and neighbors up the trail. If only they'd trusted themselves enough to even attempt a quarantine, instead of carrying out their duties cold-heartedly. Driving up to the gorge to pitch their own kin off the cliffs.

You knew you were going to a place designed to make you disappear. Even now, if he missed his chance and wound up a casualty in the bramble forest, he hoped Dave would have sense enough not to list it as a "death by misadventure."

Despite the 'Stang's mass and power around him, his chest grew tight and his breath hitched. Already this journey was getting to him and he hadn't even hit the outskirts of town. How the hell was he going to handle it on his own?

He decided to park and take the trail up by foot. He thought maybe he'd spot something—or something might spot him—that could prove to be useful. If he didn't ever come back down, he hoped Tub Gattling would discover the car, get the window fixed and help Pa find another buyer. At least Shad's ghost wouldn't be stuck in the backseat for eternity. You had to take what good fortune you could get.

If he'd planned this pilgrimage through to the end, and if rationality held any small part of it, he would've packed a rucksack. Brought water and provisions, a flashlight, a compass. Shad looked back down the road at the 'Stang and wondered if he should use logic at all. He took a step toward the car and stopped, the chill wind patting him down like the hands of children.

He realized then he could only follow his gut, his mama's call, and Megan's beckoning hand to show him the way. There was a feeling of abstinence to it, where he had to go in wearing only what was on his back. The purity of the act would have to carry him through.

Shad worked his way up the rise toward high ground

dense with oak hammocks and heavy underbrush, the willows bowing in the crosswinds coming over the precipice in the distance. On the other side he saw the squat arch of Scutt's Peak as the sun broke bronzed and crimson around it.

At a bend in the track he looked beyond the dark canopy of scrub and felt his attention being pulled toward the Pharisee. Did it prove that was the direction he should go? Or only that his enemy was much stronger than him and moving Shad blindly to his reckoning?

He should've brought the dog. He felt more alone and uncomfortable here than in lockup after Jeffie O'Rourke got tossed in solitary for killing the warden.

The woods closed in and solidified around him with the wild ash and birch drooping, the briar that could shred a man as badly as razor wire. The land was littered with shards of glass and flattened beer cans. You could see where the lover's lane portion of the road came to an end. Even the horny kids knew not to go beyond a certain point. They cluttered their area and their tire tracks shredded the scrub. As if a line had been toed in the dirt and nobody went past where the fields ended and the thickets began.

The terrain sloped into stands of knotted white and slash pine to the west, and the area diverged into more dirt paths leading into the black groves. Stands of spruce almost appeared blue in the rippling light. He'd traveled over a mile on foot when he finally came to the mold-covered split-rail fence at the top of Gospel Trail.

Sometimes you could feel your life entering through a new door as another closed behind. It was as clear and distinct to him now as it had been when the prison bus had brought him past the gate that first day.

If there was murder waiting for him, it hadn't shown itself yet.

Tushie Kline had never fully understood the need for chapters in a book. It had been one element of reading that Shad had never been able to teach him. Tushie's mind was set up to run from the beginning of a thing straight through to its end. He'd ask Shad at each break, "Where'd the story go?" Always having trouble remembering that you had to turn the next page to find it again.

"Where's my story going now?" Shad said.

He came to the divide and the Pharisee Bridge, the timber trestle that spanned a hundred yards across the gorge to Jonah Ridge.

Bulldozers would've driven up Gospel Trail to push over the trees and clear ground for new track. Men tied by ropes would've dangled over the cliffs to hand-bore holes and set charges, pegged down so they wouldn't blow away in the crosswinds. The pilings on which the trestle rested had been driven deep into the cliff rock on both sides. The rugged walls of the gorge bordered the Chatalaha River for over a mile here, where the waters broke into a series of long, violent rapids directly beneath. Shad looked at the wild forests on the other side of the ravine and felt like he was about to leave something behind forever.

Gnarled firs twined along the path where the railroad ties and tracks had been uprooted. The torn and abandoned rails left behind a wake now heavy with gopher nests. The ties themselves had long since been ripped free and probably recycled farther south. Camps of men would've been strung through the hills, putting it all down, then tearing it back up again two decades later. Maybe the same workers, or their sons.

Shad put his foot on the first rail and got an odd jounce of exhilaration from it.

There were gaps in the tarred planks of the trestle, some only a couple of inches wide. The platform had rotted away by a half foot or more in some spots. You could stand here and imagine the highballing freight coming through at two in the morning, shaking up the mountains. The drunk miners would've come out here to play chicken, stand their ground as long as they could before diving aside. There was about twelve inches of safety space between the rail and the edge of the trestle itself.

There was hardly any embankment at all on either slope, just a sheer drop down to the river and the pilings and support beams driven into the rocky sides of the cliffs.

If you made a misstep now, you wouldn't stop falling for more than half a mile. The hot-air drafts blowing up through the gorge would bounce you end over end and slow you down just enough that you wouldn't croak from shock. You'd be awake and aware the whole ride down, thinking, *holy fuck.*

It must've been a big deal for kids years ago to walk from one side to the other on the rails. They must've known the schedule perfectly and timed the trains coming, then sat on the side posts as the cars crossed. Train speed couldn't have been more than twenty miles an hour, with the mining cars stacked up behind. But the bridge, even in its prime, would've shaken and rattled like the apocalypse. The Pharisee would've felt like it was about to come down at any second.

You had to be aware of the symbols that put you through your paces, so that later on, you didn't sound like an idiot. Crossing a rickety bridge and heading into the backwoods. Taking nothing along, not even a light.

When the men passed this story on, they'd snicker into their beer and shake their heads. Any damn fool knows not to travel up on the ridge without at least a rifle, a canteen, and a bag of trail mix. If you twisted your knee and got stuck outside all night, you could be as good as dead.

Shad kept moving over the trestle, keeping to the rail where he could progress foot over foot like walking a balance beam. He didn't trust those planks at all, staring through the holes and seeing the roiling waters far below.

When he finally made it to the other side he stopped there, a little surprised that he hadn't been ambushed. It seemed like the place for it.

He scanned the forests heavy with pockets of snarled catclaw brambles and briars. The musty scent rose from the matted leaves everywhere. It got you contemplating on who had died in there and who might still be in hiding. Who might be stuck and waiting for your help.

He walked over to the nearest sticker bush and ran his finger over a thorn. With the right equipment, could they tell one scratch from another? If some forensic specialist had examined Megan instead of Doc Bollar, could they have accurately pinpointed where it had happened? Which barb had cut her cheek?

He hiked for over an hour into the backwoods of Jonah

Ridge. A creek wound away in front of him, straggling through the forest on a downslope and careening over rocks worn to a sleek polish. Shad kneeled, washed his face, and wet down his hair in the icy stream. About twenty yards ahead he saw the water break wide over something too white to be a rock. He walked to it, reached into the current, and came up with a dimpled plastic container of moon.

The only people he knew who liked to keep their shine cold were Red and Lottie Sublett. Shad had to be close to their place.

He took a tap of the whiskey and spit it out. It wasn't Luppy Joe's or any of the usual makers. Someone was using an old car radiator as a still, and the lingering fluid tainted the liquor. Red must be making his own.

Shad kept moving along the trail, watching for his sister. Over the next incline, as he parted the drifting branches still wet with dew, he spotted a shack that leaned so far to the left you could reach out the window on that side and touch the ground. Beyond it, a few twisted apple trees and a pumpkin patch took up about a half acre of partially cleared field.

There was a small garden behind the shanty with a couple rows of lettuce and thin, high-growing corn that was mostly dying. To one side sat a rabbit hutch with a skinning knife jabbed into the top of the wooden box.

Lottie Sublett sat on a carpet of pine needles, in the process of diapering four infants. These were the premature quadruplets that had shown up while Shad was in the can. The babies kicked out with stunted legs and held up their deformed fists, fingers missing from nearly every hand. The infants tried to suck their thumbs but only two of them had any.

Five other children clambered and cowered around her, most of them barefoot and dressed only in ragged overalls. The oldest was a boy no more than thirteen.

The November breeze had grown colder but none of Red Sublett's brood looked to be uncomfortable. What did it do to your nervous system, that kind of life? When your parents were brother and sister? Did nature bury your nerve endings so deep in your flesh that you couldn't feel somebody else's sins?

Lottie glanced up and gaped toothlessly at him. She flinched so harshly that the ill child she'd been diapering flipped over like a griddle cake.

The years had forced their raw corruption on her, the trials of such extreme motherhood written in her face. What did you call it when a woman had so many children in so few years? Her body wracked by such burden, day in and out, month after month. She had stretch marks on her neck, along her jawline, and on just about every bald inch of her he could see. What man makes his own sister live this way?

Lottie got to her feet, peered at him, finally tilted her head in recognition. "You," she said. "I know you a bit, don't I? From a few years back."

"That's right. My name is Shad Jenkins."

The infant who'd been flopped like a flapjack sprang over again on his belly. It started creeping and mewling like an animal that had never been given a name. It looked at Shad and started toward him, like it wanted to take a bite out of him.

"Your pa's the carpenter," Lottie said.

"Yes."

"Jenkins. Ah yuh, so you are. What you doing this way? You come to visit on Red? He ain't here right now, and I don't know when he'll be back. Had a red deer out behind the house and Red took a shot but missed the heart. He's out there someplace tracking it so we can have somethin' 'sides hare stew. Or are you meanin' to join them church folk over yonder, eh?"

"I thought I might stop in and talk with them some," Shad admitted.

"You shouldn't."

"No?"

"They got strange ways." She said it with a hint of concern, as if it mattered but not a hell of a lot.

It took Shad back a step. How odd could these people be that a woman with nine inbred kids would call them strange?

"I don't know much about them," Shad said.

"They're snake handlers. They thrill on the venom. Moon ain't strong enough, I suppose. Got a small settlement a few miles off. We don't cotton with them much, but we trade supplies if'n we need to. They ain't bad folks but they got a worshipful way with the snakes. It ain't right, cavorting like that. It ain't a blessed church."

"Did you ever see my sister out on this side of the gorge?"

"Who she?"

"Her name was Megan. She was seventeen, long blond hair."

"Was?"

"She's dead now."

"I'm sorry to hear that. Comfort and condolences to you."

"Thank you."

"I never run into her."

"She might've come up with a boy. Possibly a man."

"Only girls that age I seen up this way are them Gabriel girls. Daughters of the man who runs the church. Lucas Gabriel."

The eldest of her children hobbled over and murmured in her ear, staring at Shad in alarm. She hugged the kid and hummed in his ear for a second, telling him, "No no no. No, Osgood, no."

But the boy had his mind set on something and kept arguing, his gaze shifting back and forth along the tree line.

Shad said, "I'm alone."

"You ain't lyin' now, are you, mister?" Osgood asked.

"No," Shad told him.

So he'd been right. Red had a little still somewhere, the guts of a radiator and copper piping making contaminated liquor. The kid's mind had probably been filled with stories of how the Feds would come around and steal their civil liberties.

You couldn't expect the best social graces from a teenager who probably didn't run into more than ten people a year. Osgood couldn't meet Shad's eyes. His face puckered and went skittering with emotion.

Lottie finally grabbed the boy by the shoulders and shoved him toward the shack, and said, "Go on and start supper."

"He stayin'?"

"Git in there."

"I wanna know if he's stayin' 'round here!"

"Your daddy be back soon and you know he'll be hungry."

"I seen he got a gun tucked in his belt!"

"No, he don't. Yer eyes is bad."

"I see clear 'nough!"

"Hush all this foolishness and git in there and cook supper!"

As the kid trudged off Lottie grinned in embarrassment, showing nothing but gums. "He don't know no better. It ain't his fault. Me and Red really ought to make more of an effort to bring the children into town when we get our supplies. But Red's a'scairt that the city ways might confuse and beguile the family."

Shad had never heard the hollow called a city before. Under different circumstances he might've laughed at that, but the way she said it made him nod in agreement. Her concerns were serious ones.

He wondered how that lesson on the birds and the bees would go in this house.

"Can you give me directions to that village?" Shad asked.

"Ain't rightly a village, I reckon. Just a whole mess of families gathered together within pissin' distance. Their houses is real close together, so they's like one big family. If you visit on them, make sure you're careful on where you step. Those boots go beyond your heel?"

"A little."

"Walk light. They might be doin' a rattler roundup. They beat the fields and collect the vipers." She pointed south, her arm firm and straight and without an ounce of flab. He could almost see the history of her life scrawled in her bones. "Like I says, you be cautious when you get farther on in the forest. You ain't proper dressed for this area. There's lots of thorny woods that way. You get lost in the dark and those thistles will surely trim your hair back for you."

"How far?"

"About five miles or so, but the countryside gets pretty rugged. Don't you have a knapsack or a heavier coat? It gets cold these nights. You didn't bring no water along?"

"I'll be all right."

The children began to mewl, almost in tune with one another, all of them prowling across the yard.

"You already look like you a bit chilled," Lottie said. "You want a tap of the jug?"

"No thanks." He was thirsty but could feel the tension building as she started to stare at him. The tip of her tongue wet those thin lips that buckled in around empty gums.

"Red won't be back for a while."

"You can just tell him I said Hi. Maybe I'll stop back in on my way home again."

"I mean, we got us some time." Her left hand came down over the center of her heavy breasts. Her right came up to fluff at her hair. It gave him a kick in the guts to realize she was trying to be demure. "I hardly get a chance to talk to nobody no more. You can come on inside. We got cards."

"I can't right now, Lottie."

"If'n you wanna, you can come on back anytime. Come visit with us. Come see me."

"Sure," Shad said, taking a step back.

It saved his life. A clutch of rosebay and dogwood exploded about a foot from his head.

"Goddamn!" he screamed.

Osgood stomped off the decrepit porch step holding a double-barrel shotgun. He aimed it at Shad again. He reached for the second trigger and Shad leaped backwards into the brush.

The shit you could get yourself into.

The kid was too eager and reared at the last moment. The shot sheared loose the bark from a nearby oak.

"No!" Lottie cried. "I told you no, child! No no!"

"He's gonna make trouble, Mama!" Osgood shouted. "I seen how he was lookin' at you!"

No wonder the kid was so trigger-happy. Shad saw now that Osgood's index and middle fingers on both hands were fused.

"No, boy, no!"

"He's one of them Federal men Daddy's always talkin' about! They got slick ways. He's tryin' to beguile you, Mama!"

"He's not, he's not! He's your daddy's friend!"

"Undercover lawman! Or a government stool pigeon!"

The other children, the ones that could drag themselves around in circles anyway, moaned and let out agitated grunts. A couple of them were excitedly crabwalking side to side. They flailed and scrambled about in every direction, contorting and wriggling all over the place. It was like an anthill on fire. Leaves and moss flew in the air as they burrowed, caterwauling and braying. Holy Christ. Making more awful sounds, the babies slid and tumbled over one another, dipping into the earth at their mother's feet.

"Yellow G-Man! Don't you never visit around here no more and make eyes at my mama again!"

"Come back, Shad Jenkins," called Lottie Sublett. "It's okay now, he ain't got no more shells. Come on back!"

Shad slid deep into the woods and ran south.

Chapter Twelve

SHE STOOPED AT A STREAM SETTING SHEETS of onionskin paper adrift.

They were so thin they absorbed the water and rode the surface tension of the creek, near invisible unless you knew what you were seeing. There was handwriting on the pages, Shad couldn't make out from here.

He hung back in the trees, watching. The cool burn in his muscles was making him feel as if he'd accomplished something. Sweat swam into his eyes and for an instant the girl shimmered.

How many gorgeous young girls could you see in two days without starting to feel like a dirty old man at twenty-two?

Or did they only become beautiful because you were so lonely? Lust could do serious damage to your vision. Guys in the slam knew all about that.

She let loose with a chuckle as if someone had just spoken, and the laughter reached her eyes, slanted and crinkled them at the corners. So that she squinted like an eager lover about to crawl forward across the floor. Shad checked around to see if she was alone, and he didn't spot anyone else.

"My," he whispered.

This is how it happened in the folk tales and old country songs. The ones they sang around bonfires when they got their banjos out, ready to entertain the little ones. Like a fairy-tale book Tushie Kline once read aloud in a halting rhythm, enjoying it all the more because it had no chapters.

Maybe Shad's story was the same.

A fella wandering along through a strange grove spots a beautiful changeling girl sunning herself in the shallows. They meet, and though she's reluctant to give him attention at first, his charm eventually wins out. She's more lovely than anyone he's ever dreamed of before, so you just knew this couldn't turn out good in the end.

She vanishes into a hole in a stone wall too small for a human to pass through. He can't follow so he slips her notes through the hole, professing his adoration. Her father, the king of goblins, discovers one of the letters. On his right wrist is perched the Killdove and in his left fist is a plague of flies. He locks his daughter in a tower of sapphire and promises obliteration for the fella if she should ever see him again.

The princess weeps so hard that a river of tears flows out the tower window, across the land, and through the hole in the stone wall. The force of her sorrow shifts the rocks far enough apart that the fella can ease past. He follows the flood of tears back to the castle, climbs the thousand steps of the tower while fending off the bloodthirsty Killdove.

He kicks open the door to her chamber and she rushes

into his arms. If they're ever going to be together, she must either renounce her supernatural ways and die like a woman or he must give up his way of life and fade away to some other realm.

Before they can make a choice, the king of goblins prepares to release a plague of flies upon mankind. The fella grapples with the king and leaves his back unprotected as the Killdove strikes him between the shoulders and pecks out his heart.

You didn't get the full moral lesson of a fable unless somebody gave up everything for love and died for his troubles.

When Tushie Kline finished the fairy-tale book, he fingered the knife scar under his chin, and said, "Shit, why can't nobody bust my ass outta jail like that? It was breathtaking, man!"

Shad watched the girl slip another piece of paper into the creek, humming as it drifted along the stream. It really did sound like she was talking to somebody else. He looked around again, saw nothing, and took a step forward.

She gave a half turn and grinned over her shoulder as if she knew he was there but didn't want to look at him. She pressed another page into the water and her finger urged it along downstream. The paper was so thin and delicate that it split apart before it had gone twenty feet, torn by the soft current. Shreds hung on stones and dead willow switches jutting from the mud.

He said, "Hello."

Startled, she wheeled and nearly fell into the brook. She took two halting steps, stumbled over the slick rock, and went in up to her knees. It was cold water and she showed her teeth, hissing through them.

Okay, he thought, *so here it comes.*

She gave him a withering glare, and shouted, "The goddamn hell are you looking at!"

He sighed. He was starting to realize that he didn't possess as much natural charm as he'd always thought he did. He sure wasn't bringing out the best in the people on either side of the Pharisee Bridge.

Nobody in prison ever hated him at first sight the way people at home did.

"Can't you be civil?" he asked.

She had an aloof but still-compassionate face, with soft lines at the corners of her mouth like afterimages from smiling too much. She was young, late teens or early twenties maybe, and it gave her an extra touch of humanity.

Her bare shoulders were freckled and dappled with gooseflesh. The air grew heavy with the smell of rain. Disheveled blond bangs framed her heart-shaped face, and she swung her hair off her forehead with the back of her hand, pursing lavish, bee-stung lips.

Shad's breathing grew rapid. Had he been this horny for years and only just now noticed?

"Well, what do you want then?" she said. "And why you creepin' up behind me like that for?"

"I didn't mean to frighten you. I'm just—ah—"

How did you explain yourself, about why you were here? Or why you were glancing left and right looking for your dead sister's hand to give you some sign?

"You're just what?"

"Looking for the church," he told her.

"Why?"

"I want to learn more about it."

It softened her face, and she said, "Not many strangers are interested in our ways. Who are you?"

"Shad Jenkins." As if his name held its own meaning and had nothing to do with him at all. "Were you waiting on someone?"

"I was hoping to see him today."

"Who?"

"Not you. I surely wasn't expecting you. I don't think, anyhow."

Shad couldn't argue with that so he just stood there. She did the same. The seconds ticked off like the passing of ice ages. You could waste half your life standing around wishing that somebody else would make the first move.

The princess of goblins held firm to her stoic pride, unafraid but expecting him to do something terrible. It got to him after a minute and he backed away and started to walk south again.

"I'm Jerilyn Gabriel."

"Lucas Gabriel's daughter?"

"Yes."

He stepped to her and saw that her eyes were green with flecks of gold in them catching the light. She crumpled the remaining pages into a ball and threw them into the water, picked up a stick, and poked them down until they sank into the mud.

Letters to an unrequited love? Diary entries containing the secrets of her tribe? Some words counted for more if you released them into the world, even if they went unread.

"Can you show me the way to your, ah, settlement?" he

asked. He didn't know if the community even had a name. What did you call it? A community? A colony?

"You from town?"

"Yes."

"I hardly ever go there into the hollow."

"Why?"

"They'd call me a witch."

"Would they? Why do you think that?"

"We handle snakes. That scares a lot of townsfolk."

Shad couldn't see it. There were enough granny women still sticking to the old ways that nobody in the hollow would give her any trouble. As he was discovering, the folks he'd known all his life were a superstitious lot that ran on fears they couldn't even name. No one would bother her except the men at Dober's Roadhouse catcalling from the alleyways.

"Don't it worry you none? That I might call a rain of rattlers down on you?"

"No."

"Maybe I'll just do so. Teach you a lesson for sneaking up on people."

She eased closer to him, studying his face. As if he might be someone she knew but didn't fully recognize. She shifted to one side and checked his profile, reached out like she might ruffle his hair. He was hoping, but she didn't. She was a girl of many half-completed movements.

"What are you examining me for?" he asked.

"Nothing, just considerin'."

"Okay. Considering what?"

"You ain't him, are you?" she said, and her voice was suffused with both hope and regret.

"Who?"

"*Him.*"

"I don't think so."

"Then you're not."

"I suppose you're right."

"You want to come for supper?"

Ten minutes ago she'd looked at him like he'd escaped from a chain gang, and now he was being invited home to dinner. "Maybe your family wouldn't take kindly to having another place set beside them. I just want to talk to some of your congregation for a few minutes."

"Come eat and talk with them all," she said. "They look forward to sharing with strangers."

"Really? Why?" Shad asked, genuinely interested. "I thought you people stuck together because you didn't want outsiders coming around and inconveniencing you."

"Nah, the hollow folk are always welcome. But hardly any come round."

"Hardly any?"

"Some come to sit with my daddy."

He kept thinking of her father being the Goblin King with two handfuls of destruction.

She led him downstream, over embankments that sloped to marshy areas that reminded him of the river bottoms, even though they were three or four thousand feet above the Chatalaha by now.

The wind blew harsher, carrying with it leaves and moans through the boles. Jerilyn shivered and leaned over to take Shad's hand. She tugged him closer, insistent but also obliging. Self-assured and sexy but somehow also critical, as if testing the structure of his fingers, reading his scars, appraising the bones. She used her thumb to gently rub across his knuckles, the same way Elfie used to do, like, *Baby, baby, all will be fine, go sleep now.*

They walked in silence, listening to the complaints of the deepening forest. The sun spun down through the branches laced overhead, skewering the ground with golden spearlike shafts. The woods closed in here, briars knotting into a grove of thorn and thistle anchored by oak and drifting boughs of slash pine. The cedar below was matted and wet with dew and heavy November sap.

Shad scanned the bark and didn't see any buckshot or bullet holes nearby, but the trunks were scarred with thin chop marks. They probably used machetes to cut through the catclaw thickets.

When they broke into a clearing, Shad heard wild giggling.

"There," Jerilyn said, pointing. "That's where we live."

They had their children out gathering the snakes.

SHE STARTED FORWARD IN A RUSH, AND THE TAWDRY color of the trees reared around her. Shad got his bearings and found himself stumbling into a bedlam of activity, as the brush rustled and parted with laughing kids and rattlers.

Two diamondbacks slithered over his boots. He leaped back with a startled grunt and almost dropped over on his ass.

What would have happened then? Would they have sprung for his face, latched on to his cheeks?

"Goddamn," he whispered. Revulsion nearly overpowered him. Two girls no more than ten years old bumped into his leg, looked up at him, and smiled. He had to fight the urge to run.

So this was how they had fun up here past Jonah Ridge. Roundups.

He watched the parents carrying their croker sacks, drinking beer, and encouraging their children. They cheered and gave advice, pointing out the snakes in the deep grasses. No one wore gloves. Several Plexiglas containers hung open, with their lids unlatched. Someone sang a hymn Shad didn't recognize. Adults stood in small groups here and there holding crooked metal rods, pouring gasoline in small amounts and setting fires to drive the snakes from their holes.

Pubescent boys leaped over the flames and dove into the undergrowth.

Nobody showed the slightest bit of apprehension. Kids carried snakes back in their arms, thrown over their shoulders. Holding two or three in each hand. They were playing with the things.

Once their sacks were full the folks emptied them into the containers.

He knew the original intent of roundups was to rid certain areas of rattler overpopulation. Gather and destroy as many snakes as possible. In some states, dealers harvested the skins.

An old-timer with a sunburned pate and a Mount Sinai voice ambled by, and said, "Hey there, how you today?"

Shad couldn't even bring himself to nod in acknowledgment. The guy used a metal rod to trap a diamondback against the earth, hook it up, and draw it closer. The snake opened wide and bared its dripping fangs as the old man stuffed it into his sack. The muscles in Shad's jaw ached from clenching his teeth.

He recognized most of the different species from books he'd read in the can. Seeing them all in one place surprised him. He didn't think so many different species could live together in such a small area: garter, cottonmouth, ring-neck, hognose, diamondback, indigo, and yellow rat snake.

Jesus, they couldn't all be indigenous to this patch of woods, could they? Were these church folks bringing them in and breeding them? Penning them up and letting them loose again for their children to chase.

Could you train rattlers? Would they go only so far, then turn around and come on back home again?

Clouds drifted over the sun. The threat of rain grew stronger. The wind rose, carrying the flames higher until smoke and the smell of burning scrub wafted into Shad's face. Trees swooned and the heady clack of thick oak limbs battering together resounded through the clearing. The oncoming storm seemed to make the folks even more excited. Their Plexiglas bins were filling.

Jerilyn reappeared. One last shaft of sun angled down toward her feet as she approached, then snuffed out as she reached him. Her bangs swept back and forth in the breeze, and he watched her bare shoulders and tried hard not to be entranced by the glimmer of raindrops on her skin. He couldn't help it. The way the scene had been set, it appeared to have been directed especially for him. She very nearly managed to draw his attention away from the snakes boiling over in her path.

So maybe some of the hollow folks would've called her a witch.

"You ever see a roundup before?" she asked.

"Christ, no."

"You said you wanted to learn about our church."

"Yes," he told her. "I did say that."

Listening to the hisses coming from off to the left, the right, mothers calling their kids to them because they had to get out of the rain. They'd finish catching the rattlers tomorrow, if it was nice out.

There was a different kind of friction working in the air now. A new energy coming toward him, a presence quickly homing in on him. He spun and lifted his hands in case he had to fight. Jerilyn's face closed up. Her lips pressed together and the fine, soft chin scrunched into wrinkles of annoyance.

"Mr. Shad Jenkins," she said, "I'd like to introduce you to my sister, Rebi."

He watched the grasses part, and the storm was on him.

You couldn't look at her without a list of all the biblical seductresses flashing through your mind. She was perhaps a year or two younger than Jerilyn. Long dark hair framed by the gathered darkness, rain coming down on her and bearing through the bramble patches. An expression of insolence or petulance on that face. She was compact and had graceful curves that crowded her outfit until the seams wanted to split.

She gripped a ringneck in each hand, casually holding them out before her. She struck a provocative pose, hip out, the snakes adding some indefinable wanton abandon. It was bestial in its own way. When she came at him again, it was with a slow, big-cat walk, predatory with a hint of violence.

Doom didn't always sneak up on you, sometimes it sashayed.

"Hello," he said.

There was meat and jiggle to her. A light blue skirt sheathed her fine hip, and she wore a loose black top cinched at the waist by a thick belt. He should've spotted her from twenty yards off but he hadn't until she was on top of him. Her breasts moved vigorously beneath her blouse. A dab of crimson touched the cheeks in her round face, the lips equally red. Her hair coiled and clung against the sides of her neck. A flicker in her black eyes made him think of Callie Anson for an instant.

He hadn't seen a woman—any woman—during the two years he was in the slam, and now they were coming out of the weeds to find him.

"A pleasure to meet you, Mr. Jenkins."

It took him a second to find his voice. "You too, Rebi."

Jerilyn's eyes narrowed and he saw the anger move through her like an iron smoothing out creases. It had nothing to do with him. His presence served as a catalyst for some dispute that had started a long time ago.

"You're a little wide-eyed, Mr. Jenkins. Never handle snakes before?"

"No."

"You a'scairt?"

Everybody always asking him that, like they were waiting for him to fall apart. You say yes, and they have something to hang over you. If you say no, they shove the fucking thing right in your face. Better to sound like an urban hippie who'd never set foot in a field before.

He said, "I know enough to respect them."

"Don't you be worried none. If'n you get bit, we got plenty of that there antivenom serum."

Just the thing to set his mind at ease. There was something sly about her that he both liked and hated.

"He won't be bit, so long as you turn those ringnecks aside, Rebi," Jerilyn told her. "You angered them some."

"Oh, these is just babies. They wouldn't likely break the skin."

"Come on," Jerilyn said. "It's time for supper."

Rebi looked at Shad, let her tongue out to moisten her top lip. "You eatin' with us?"

"Yes, he is," Jerilyn answered for him.

"That's fine then. Daddy's gonna enjoy meetin' him."

Rebi held the snakes up before him, opened her mouth wide, and brought the reptiles closer and closer and closer until all their tongues were flicking wildly together.

It made him sick to his stomach, and hard.

Chapter Thirteen

THEY LED HIM BACK UP OVER THE EMBANK-
ments and down to a trail that ran through a
tract of catclaw briar. The rain came down and
brought a cold that somehow became despair. It
reminded Shad of the evenings when he was a kid and he
and Pa would walk out to his mother's grave and blunder
their way through prayers. Six or seven years old, sometimes Mags would come along and say the proper words
for them.

Rebi eventually let the two snakes she'd been carrying
go free, and the girls began to walk faster. Rain cascaded
off the slash pine, and oak branches snapped in the winds.
The temperature dropped quickly until they could see
their breath. Rebi began to laugh quietly.

He heard the other snake handlers up ahead on the
trail, the children still giggling and chattering excitedly,
parents giving sharp commands to watch for stickers.
Jerilyn pressed a hand to Shad's elbow, helping to guide
him over the rough path.

When they broke from beneath the heavy brush, the trail sloped to a hamlet he hadn't been expecting.

The community proved to be much larger than Shad had imagined. He'd been thinking it might be like the shantytown quarter in Poverhoe City, but it was much more formalized than that. Lottie Sublett had been right. Houses and cabins sat close together, porches bunched up to form plank walkways.

There was some money here in the settlement. But the men had done the work themselves and they hadn't had the skills or craftsmanship to do an impeccable job. His father would've been appalled. Foundations had shifted and the walls inclined at bad angles. Rain would cause doors and window frames to stick or jam shut. They had sunk their own wells and septic tanks and the area had unnatural grades to it.

Now folks returned to their homes carrying their containers of snakes, the kids asking questions about church services, men talking about their hunger.

In the center of the small colony stood a two-story farmhouse with a wide veranda. It was much larger and better constructed than the surrounding buildings, erected on rocky, thorn-choked land that could never be properly farmed. It showed that these people either believed in miracles or had an insane amount of faith in themselves.

Unlike the other homes, which looked to have been built within the last couple of years, the farmhouse had been around for decades.

"That's our place," Jerilyn said. "It doubles as a communal center for the congregation."

"A church?"

"We don't really have a proper chapel," Rebi told him, and when she spoke she turned and moved against him. He had a hard time listening even with her talking in his ear. "Just a big room in back of the house with seats."

"Is your father the preacher?"

"I reckon you could say that, though anybody can give witness if they like. The rest of the congregation, well, they're more than just neighbors. A lot of them are cousins, family now through marriage. More every year."

"Was your whole village out there this afternoon?"

Jerilyn let out a smile at that, and said, "Mama and a couple of the other women stayed out of the roundup so they could prepare supper."

One question led to another. He was starting to grow annoyed by the inquiring tone of his own voice, but pressed on. "Is this considered a holiday for you? A holy day?"

"Every month or so we do the snake hunt. No particular day, really, just whenever Daddy and the rest of them get in the mood for the celebration."

"And what do you do with them all? The snakes."

Rebi slid up into his face again. The girl had no idea what personal space might mean. Ferociously sexy as she was, it still got on your nerves. "Daddy does some preaching and everybody bears witness and they handle the rattlers during services. Afterward, we set 'em free, then round 'em up again." She drew her hair aside and cocked her head so he could see. There were puncture scars along the edge of her throat.

"Jesus Christ," he said. "Why the hell are they on your neck?"

" 'Cause I like to dance with snakes in my hair and draped over my shoulders, that's why."

Glowering, Jerilyn pulled her sister roughly away. "It's not like we let the snakes bite us on purpose. We're not fools, and we don't believe that God will protect us from the poison because our souls are pure. It's just another way to pay tribute to the Lord. We've all built up a resistance over the years, so it's not as dire as you might think. Like I said before, townsfolk would think that witchy."

Rebi's blouse had been soaked through and when she moved beside him she gave it an extra nudge so he could feel the weight of her chest pressing in close and pay attention. He did. Her hair flowed across the left side of his face and Jerilyn's flailed against the right.

Still, you had to pretend that you weren't aware when your life took on the pattern of a tale you'd heard before. How many guys in prison had talked about fucking two sisters back to back, back to forward, right to left, and the catfights that came afterward? The crews on C-Block would be drunk on pruno listening to how the cops would come in and bust up a brawl between two razor-wielding ladies. A rookie getting slashed in the face and screaming while he bled all over the place. The nightsticks and cuffs coming out, paramedics in the hallway, and the guy stoned and just lying there on the bed watching it all. The C-Block crews would laugh their asses off, and they never got tired of sister stories.

Rebi gripped his arm and pulled Shad up the veranda stairs. "We're late getting back. It sounds like they're about to start."

"It'll be all right," Jerilyn said. "They'll be glad to see we've brought a new friend."

They marched to the front door and Shad stopped in his tracks and stared into the foyer ahead. Prison was closing in on him again. Both Gabriel girls tugged at him harder, but he didn't budge.

Megan's hand beckoned him from the hall and he finally stepped forward.

It wasn't dark inside the home at all. He even had to shield his eyes, moving from the gloom of the storm to an abruptly illuminated room. He was suddenly surrounded by clamor: voices, a clatter of silverware, and the rattling of windows as the rain throbbed against the glass.

Rebi brought him a towel, and said, "Come sit."

"The whole settlement sits down and takes meals together?"

"On certain days. The babies and real young'uns are put down for naps after a roundup."

"You sure no one will be upset?"

"You got no sense about you at all."

"There's plenty who'd say you were right."

"You're thinking it's a big fuss, Shad Jenkins," Jerilyn said. "It's not. You got no call to be distressed. Nobody's going to hurt you."

"Sorry, it's been a long time since I've sat down and had dinner with any family."

"Even your own?"

"I don't have much of one anymore."

With a casual grace, she led him down the corridor into the depths of the house. They moved side by side as if they were a long-enduring couple who'd been together so many years that they balanced each other out. It somehow felt more natural now that it ever had with Elfie. It was such a disturbing thought that it put a hitch in his stride.

Jerilyn reacted with subtle adjustments, slowing to match his pace. He dried himself but couldn't shake the chill. Falling behind him, Rebi slid herself against his back and urged him along.

Okay, he thought, *so where does the game go from here?*

When do I get to wrangle the rattlers and prove myself a servant of the lord?

Folks were already seated for dinner and the first plates were being served when Shad stepped into the room. He sat between the sisters and his introduction into the fold hardly made a ripple. He counted twenty-five people and none of the children were in sight. A few of them reached over and shook his hand, clapped him on the back. A couple knew his name already and said they'd met his father years ago.

A woman flitted over, hugged him, and made a comment he didn't catch. He heard various names spoken at him, but few he could remember. Taskers. Johansens. Burnburries. It was the first time he'd had a meal with another person since the prison cafeteria.

Up on the wall they'd nailed Hellfire Christ, and he didn't want your sympathy. He didn't even want your love. He just scowled at you from his agony and wrath and let you know he was up there for the sole purpose of making you come face-to-face with your own crimes and weaknesses. Hellfire Christ was damn near smiling. He wanted to see you go down.

Shad was a tad surprised. He'd thought only the Catholics went in for crucifixes. If these folks were going to have one, then he expected snakes to be wreathed around the gaunt figure. Snapping at the Messiah's feet, twined at the bottom of the cross.

But there weren't any other idols or paintings of serpents anywhere in view. Did snake handlers believe that Saint Patrick was a good man for casting the vipers out of Ireland or did they consider his actions disgraceful?

The shit you had to think about.

Shad ate beside the snake handlers, giving short precise answers whenever he was asked a question. The old-timer with the sunburned crown looked over and said it again. "Hey there, how you today?"

"Fine, thanks."

"Good taters!"

"Yes."

It felt exactly like it did in the can. Your first view of the new world's hierarchy happened in the cafeteria. You learned how the place was organized, who ran the show. Where you were allowed to sit, how the power structure worked. You started with the guy at the head of the table. All the others would fall into line eventually.

There he was. Leader of the nameless church, master of vipers, King of the Goblins, Jerilyn and Rebi's father, Lucas Gabriel.

A bull of a man dressed all in white except for the carefully knotted narrow black bow tie that had been fashionable before Atlanta burned. The tie told Shad something about Gabriel but he didn't know what. He was bald, his skull knobby and creased, with a fringe of kinky brown hair above each ear. His shirtsleeves were rolled up to reveal powerful forearms covered with purplish snakebite scars. He showed them off the way cons advertised their jailhouse tats. It proved you didn't care about the surface of your flesh. Only what was in your blood really mattered.

There was an element about Lucas Gabriel that reminded Shad of Pa. Maybe the tightly compressed potential of force waiting for the chance to escape.

The patriarch. Shad knew the man had a hell of a story, and he wished he'd asked Dave Fox or somebody else what it was.

Gabriel watched Shad with washed-out eyes the color of gravel. There was no suspicion in them. Only an impish sparkle of authority that let you know he was in charge and never to cross him. It was the same gleam the warden's gaze had held until Jeffie O'Rourke rammed a paintbrush through his eye.

"He came here on his own, Daddy," Jerilyn said. "This is Mr. Shad Jenkins."

"There's always room at our table for one more," Gabriel told her. "If someone wants to share our bread with us." His voice had a laugh to it, but the laugh didn't come out.

No direct acknowledgment or real welcome from the man, which put another spin on the situation.

"He ain't never handled snakes before," Rebi put in. Almost mocking but having fun with it, pushing a little. Shad figured these people did a lot of that, honing their social skills against one another like sharpening knives.

"Folks from the hollow, or most towns anywhere, don't truck much with snakes except to kill 'em." Gabriel's smile showed off his small, even, white teeth. "Must've been quite a sight for him to come upon, seeing as how we were rounding up so many for services."

"Yes, it was."

Shad figured the hard sell was about to start, and they were going to talk about the burgeoning ranks of God's saved people now. He began to draw his thoughts together and gather his words, but then Gabriel asked somebody to pass him the potatoes. The whole group fell to talking among themselves again even louder than before. Most of them were garrulous, chuckling noisily, leaning toward him to welcome him into their long-winded jokes and conversations. No one addressed him specifically.

He checked around to see who might be keeping to themselves.

Those were the ones you had to watch for. The hitters. The muscle.

They weren't hard to spot. Two toughs, brothers by the look of it, with feral eyes and fixed dull faces covered with patchy beards. Shirts buttoned up to the collars, thick hair parted at the side and combed over into ridiculous juvenile waves and curls. Perhaps they were Gabriel blood, but Shad didn't see any of the same poise in them. They sat obediently like dogs.

It took a while but eventually he heard their names. Hart and Howell Wegg.

They ate silently and with good manners, wiping their mouths a lot. They kept their elbows off the table, cut the ribs off the bone, and sliced their meat into small pieces. Whenever someone spoke to them they smiled dutifully but hardly said a word. They appeared so docile that Shad could feel himself gearing up for impending grief. He hoped he was being paranoid but really didn't think it would be that easy.

The meal seemed to be a carefully rehearsed performance put on for his benefit, and he paid no serious attention to it. He tuned out most of it and found that even Jerilyn wasn't saying anything of importance though she kept whispering to him. He could feel how keyed up they all were, holding back but edgy and raring. Was it due to his entrance or because this was one of their holy days? He sat and waited and knew it wouldn't be too much longer.

It took another twenty minutes. As the ladies began to clear the table, he started to stand and Rebi shoved him back down. She told him, "It's not anything sexist, it's just our turn to clean up. You sit and relax, talk to Daddy for a bit."

Gabriel held his chin up in Shad's direction. That proved to be the only gesture he needed to make for everyone to quiet down. Some folks had already left, others didn't seem certain of where they should go or what they should be doing.

"Not many men from town would share a plate of food from our table."

"Why's that?" Shad asked.

"There was talk a hundred years ago that my forefathers were cannibals."

So now things were going to be silly.

Shad got the feeling that Gabriel was testing him, but he'd expected as much. Cannibals though? He guessed everybody had to play out their dark secret, no matter how goofy it sounded.

Rebi brought him a slice of cranberry pie for dessert. He couldn't put it past these folks to have tossed in a fingernail or a couple strands of hair to get a reaction.

"Anybody remember that talk besides you?" Shad asked.

"Some, I suspect."

"I never heard it." He spooned in a mouthful of pie and swallowed without tasting. Sometimes you pushed back, and sometimes you just played along and considered the angles. Shad stared at the man.

Hart and Howell Wegg ate their dessert too, without any hint that they understood what was going on. Rebi and Jerilyn returned and took up their seats beside him again, but didn't eat.

"You want to know about us, don't you?" Lucas Gabriel said. His voice had a sigh to it, but the sigh didn't come out either.

"Yes."

"Why's that? Not because you're lookin' for the Lord."

The man was right, but you couldn't give anything away this early in the game. "It's presumptuous for you to say that, Mr. Gabriel."

"I reckon that's true. I got no defense for such boldness."

"We all have our reasons."

"So then, name some of yours, Mr. Jenkins. Why have you come to us?"

"I'm not certain," Shad said. If you straddled the line, no one could trouble you for being on one side or the other.

"Good, I can appreciate a man in agitation who's not afraid to admit it."

Shad didn't think he'd admitted to any such thing, but the man's assuming nature was something to keep notice of. "My sister recently died."

Murmurs went around the table, the usual kind words and sympathies. The Wegg brothers kept staring, vacuous but amenable. Rebi licked her lips, a gesture of sex and girlish fidgeting.

Gabriel began to paw at his chin, the scars on his arms twisting in the light like snakes themselves. "So then, perhaps you do seek to ease your burden."

"Everyone seeks that, don't they?"

"I do believe you're right."

"She was part of the Youth Ministry in Preacher Dudlow's church down in the hollow."

"A fine man. I've met the reverend in town on occasion, and at some of the Christian tent gatherings when traveling ministers come to visit."

"I was wondering if you'd ever seen her up this way. She was seventeen, long blond hair?" He couldn't believe that this was the only way he could describe his sister, and he wasn't even sure if she'd still had long hair. "Her name was Megan."

"No," Gabriel said. "We have few visitors, and I recall each of them well." He glanced around the table and others shook their heads and agreed they'd never met her. "Was there something we could have done for her?"

"I don't know. I was away for a time. I'm sad to say I didn't know her well anymore."

Lucas Gabriel grunted loudly. "Loss of a family member is one of our most painful trials. It's made so much worse if there are regrets or unresolved circumstances."

Time to divert the course of the conversation, allow the man to have his say. Shad could see that Gabriel was beginning to get a touch antsy, waiting to cut loose. "Does your sect have a name?"

The man caught on to the word—sect, sounding so much like cult—and the glimmer in his eyes seemed to flare. "No, we believe that the denomination of churches and religions has more to do with man's hubris than his following the Lord. Shall I tell you about us? Our history?"

"Sure."

"Are you familiar with Mark 16:18?"

"No," Shad said, though he realized it had to be the verse about snakes. Something about laying hands on. If you couldn't quote the passage word for word, then you couldn't say you actually knew it. That's how it had been back in Becka Dudlow's Bible class.

"It's the central passage that forms the core of our faith. *They shall take up serpents; and if they drink any deadly thing, it shall not hurt them; they shall lay hands on the sick, and they shall recover.'* From that verse came the original belief of the snake handlers."

"Everybody's got to have their own blessing," Shad said. "Makes them feel like God's giving them extra attention."

"Well, I'd say you're probably right about that, much of the time. We want to earn our consideration. My great-grandpa Saul was one of the founders of the Holiness Church in eastern Tennessee. Used to bring the serpents with him to the camps and down into the mines."

"How'd that go over with the other men?"

"Not well, at first."

"I'd guess not."

The others at the table had heard the tale before, but expectation and curiosity still grew in the air, the mood fluctuating, as if they had never heard the end of the story.

"At the close of the nineteenth century, the industrialization and factories of Moloch were spreading down through the South. The rich owners began to turn their backs on God and praise only silver. They replaced our farming and our way of life. They paid poor wages for unskilled labor, offered only high-priced rental properties and unsanitary conditions. The bitterness of men took hold and they became violent."

"Tell what happened, Daddy," Rebi said. Jerilyn let out a soft snort that only Shad could hear.

"The snakes saved us," Gabriel said. "God gave us the signs of his power. We followed his will. We bore witness and struggled with the serpents, and sometimes managed to heal the dying with the venom."

Shad had talked to a couple of drug dealers in the slam who'd come out of the river bottoms and whose fathers had mined those same mountains. On the outside they drove Mercedes and Porsches, had houses in Miami, and yet they still fucked around with snake handling. It wasn't poverty that pushed them. It was the primitive urge to try yourself against the hand of fate.

The glass of the windows vibrated with a gentle staccato.

"Thing was, all of them were actually afraid of snakes," Lucas Gabriel said. He shifted in his seat until he was aimed entirely at Shad. "Saul most of all. Rattlers terrified him. His baby brother had died in the crib after being bitten. They knew firsthand the kind of agony one would go through. All of them had seen congregation members die. They went to church and were visited by the spirit of the Lord, and yet they never knew if they were going to get back out the door alive. If not, at least they died in service."

That was about as old-school as you could get. "Where's the cannibalism come in?"

"One summer the green timbers of a mine gave way and there was a cave-in. They got most of the men out safely, but it took rescuers seven days to dig Saul free. He was trapped alone there in a far chamber, except for the snakes. When he was rescued, the lower half of Saul's left leg was gone. People figured that he got so hungry he actually ate it."

There was an even more subtle analysis going on now. Shad allowed himself to be set up, and said, "He was driven to that extreme in only a week?"

"No, a'course not, but that's the way legends get started. Saul's leg had been crushed and gangrene had set in. He surely would've died from his wounds, but he claimed the snakes fed off his rotting leg and saved him."

"Maybe it's true."

"Maybe it is, at that." Shad knew he was expected to grin but not laugh at the miraculous twist, so he did. Gabriel joined in for a moment. "After that, Saul came out here with his wife and sons, my grandfather among them, and together they built this house. This hamlet grew up around the faith."

Looking down to take another bite of pie, Shad saw that it had been cleared along with all the other plates. Only a few folks remained around the table, and some were talking and appeared to have been deep in conversation much of the time. He'd been focused too sharply on Gabriel.

It was dark outside and a weariness began to settle on

him. He'd been up since dawn with almost no sleep and had covered at least fifteen miles of rugged terrain on foot. Jerilyn's shoulder pressed him from one side and Rebi sort of nuzzled him on the other. They both smelled faintly of jasmine, which he hadn't noticed before.

Gabriel pursed his lips and appeared to be considering his words. "Will you stay the night? You appear to be exhausted, and I doubt you'll find your way back to Jonah Ridge in the dark. Pardon my saying so but you don't seem to be an expert mountain traveler."

"I'm not."

"One misstep on the Pharisee and you'll meet the Lord earlier than I presume you're expecting."

"Aren't you holding your services tonight?"

"No, that'll be tomorrow afternoon. The roundup and the storm have agitated the snakes. I want to give them a chance to calm down some."

All right, now it wasn't a fairy tale anymore, but the beginning of a dirty joke. Traveling salesman staying overnight with the farmer's two luscious young daughters. There were so many punch lines he couldn't decide on any one of them.

"So, you'll stay?" Gabriel asked.

"Yes, if you'll have me." Where else would he go?

"Of course we will. Jerilyn will make up one of the guest rooms for you. Although the house seconds as a communal center of sorts there's still plenty of free space. We'll talk more in the morning about your sister if you like."

This huge home just for Gabriel's family and the snakes. Shad could hear them thumping and knocking about in their containers somewhere deeper in the house. "Thank you."

The sisters looked at him and he looked back, wondering how far into perdition he'd already fallen and how much further he had left to go.

Chapter Fourteen

IN THE MIDDLE OF THE NIGHT SHAD AWOKE naked on his feet, standing at the side of the bed. Jerilyn sat next to him, her open hand on his slick back. The room was filled with a muted pink light from where she'd thrown her slip over the small nightstand lamp. He was breathless and his chest hair was heavy with sweat.

He was aware of the nearness of her beautiful body, and the pattern of drying salt on her belly and between her breasts. A fine mist of perspiration still coated her flesh. That heady scent of jasmine wafted through the room. Shad's breath came in bites. There was a remote sense of satisfaction within him—no, it was satiation. He struggled to remember their lovemaking and couldn't. Your own mind was sometimes the worst gyp of all.

She grinned and her teeth were bright in the shadows. "You're not him, but it's okay, we still had fun together." Jerilyn leaned back upon the pillows, spread herself over the sheets. "You're a nice-looking boy. I like your body. And those streaks of white hair."

He'd missed so much of what had happened that he felt dispossessed and displaced before her. He should be flattering her or cooing other soft words, but the proper time had already passed by.

"Who are you waiting for?" he asked.

"It's not for you to know."

Shad tried to search out the truth in Jerilyn's eyes, but saw only a glistening of love that wasn't for him. "You really write him letters and send them off on the creek?"

"Yes."

"Aren't you upset that he doesn't get to read them?"

"He does read them. He quotes from them when he comes to me."

"But you said you thought I was him. Don't you know who he is?"

She kissed him.

A storm now shrieked outside, blustery winds tearing at the clapboards and tossing shingles. The rafters groaned and creaked furiously. When he'd moved Tushie Kline up to reading poems, Shad had to explain about metaphor and symbolism. How what happened in a man was paralleled in the heavens. As above, so below.

Tushie Kline marveled at that, and asked, "Like the depletion of the ozone could be a symbol for man's spiritual bankruptcy? Ain't that some fucked-up shit right there?"

"Mags," Shad whispered, and scanned the corners of the room searching for her. "I'm losing you."

"Who's that?" Jerilyn asked. "A girl? Mags?"

"My sister."

"Losing her? Now? But didn't you say she was dead?"

"Yes."

"How'd she die?"

"I don't know."

Staring at him in the darkness, Jerilyn stirred and crept across the bed, reaching for him. She took his hand and tried to pull him to her, but he wouldn't go.

"Why are you here, Shad Jenkins?"

"Tell me everything your father didn't."

She curled and twined among the blankets, and her breasts swayed and her eyes lit and he wanted to fall on her. He drew back a step.

"I don't understand," she said. "Like what?"

"About what goes on here."

"He told you the truth . . . well, except for about the snakes drawing out the poison in Great-great Grandpa Saul's leg. That's not so. After a few days trapped down in the mine he ate the snakes. His leg was crushed and taken off by the cave-in so he ate his leg too. If you can call eating bits of yourself being a cannibal, then he was one."

"Goddamn."

She turned over in the pink light, and the glow worked itself against her skin and Shad started to sweat again. "But Daddy was right, the snakes did help save Saul. From starvation and thirst anyways."

He couldn't stand it anymore. He moved to her and she drew him down on the bed, wrapping her arms around his back as he kissed her. In a minute it became much rougher, and her laughter grew harsh and dizzying.

"My, you're a feisty one, Mr. Jenkins," she said. "I didn't think you'd have the energy for another go, considering the day you've had."

Something broke deep within the center of his chest and a small moan escaped him. He champed it short for fear he wouldn't stop until he was wailing. He bent her to his will and buried his face in her throat and her unstoppable pulse snapped savagely against his tongue.

Grappling sticker bushes pivoted wildly outside the window, scratching at the glass like manic children wanting in. The heavy rain sheeted and lapped across the pane. It formed peering liquid faces that glowered and sneered from all angles, looking in at him, scrutinizing, hating.

WHEN HE AWOKE NEXT HE WAS ON HIS FEET AGAIN, with dawn inching through the wet branches framed in the morning light. Rebi was naked and creeping closer on all fours.

She rose up like a rattler, arms at her sides, and touched his belly once with her lips.

She looked up from under a fan of dark hair hanging in her eyes, and she kissed him harder, raked him with her teeth. Her expression remained the same as the first moment he'd met her. Insolent, petulant. He didn't mind it as much now since there was a cunning in there hidden among wayward promises.

The rain had eased back to a drizzle. She reached up and gripped his wrists, casually holding them the way she'd held the ringnecks in her hands. She bit deeper, trying to draw blood but hadn't managed to yet.

The room was now filled with a sullen blue light from where she'd thrown her skirt over the lamp. She glanced up at him, released his skin, and said, "So, you're a night walker, are you?"

"Yes." You couldn't really play coy when you were wandering around in somebody else's house with your goodies hanging loose.

"I smell my sister on you. You have at her?"

"We were together. Where is she?"

"Not here. I knew she'd be along quick. That's fine. You ain't him but you can have me too, if you want."

The living fire of his rage carried him across the room and back again to her until she was staggering in his embrace. He tightened his hold on her until she let out a heated grunt of pain. "Who? Who the hell are you girls waiting for?"

"You're gonna hurt me."

"You might be right."

"Do it. You can if you want. Hurt me, it's all right."

"Tell me his name."

"He ain't got a name that matters, not one worth saying. We're here together and I want you right now."

His temper could only save him for so much longer. In another minute he wouldn't be able to talk. "I want to know about him. Why he's so special. Why you won't say his name."

"What's it any of your concern? Why do you care so much?"

"It might have something to do with my sister," he told her, feeling farther away from Mags than ever.

"How can that be?" Rebi asked. "You surely are out of your head."

"Do you write to him too?"

"Nah, I ain't much good with pen and letters like Jerilyn.

'Sides, all I need do is talk into the southern wind, and he hears me."

Shad let out a bark of derisive laughter. "And you think I'm cracked, eh?"

"More than most, I'd venture. But that's all right. I'll take some of your pain away for a time." She slid against his bare flesh, smoothing her breasts into him, using her nails on his skin.

"What the hell do you want with me?"

She reared as if he'd just backhanded her across the nose. "I'd think that was pretty damn clear."

"No," he said. "It's not."

"Are you afflicted? I got my own pains too."

He checked the corners of the room, searching for his departed mother or his lost sister. It was distressing to learn that you couldn't make your way through the world without somebody dead to show you the way.

The seeping, dour blue light only made Rebi appear more alive to him, full of grim and intense charms. He looked down and saw fine traces in the dust on the floor on the far side of the bed. He hadn't stepped there.

Grabbing the footboard, he pulled the bed aside.

Jerilyn's body lay on the floor, as if she were only sleeping, with a slight smile on her lips.

Shad whimpered, "God no."

He kneeled and brought his hand to her throat, where he'd buried his face only hours before. He was so cold that for a moment she felt much warmer than him. Her icy blue flesh turned a terrible red where he touched her.

"Did you do that?" Rebi whispered with an animal excitement. No sadness or fear, just her breath quickly becoming a rapid panting. "You kill her?"

"No."

"You must've."

"I'm telling you no," he said, wondering and despairing.

"You sure about that, Shad Jenkins?" Her mouth pressed against his ear, and she licked him.

"For Christ's sake, Rebi, shut up."

"Don't boss me. I don't take guff from killers."

He dragged the bed aside even farther, seeing that the dust had other trails in it, spelling out words.

Run
Now

"Is that from him?" Shad asked. "The one you were expecting?"

"I don't know. He don't write me ever. Sounds like it's for you though. Maybe you wrote it yourself."

He checked his fingers to see if they were dirty. He couldn't tell in the dim light. Not even after he'd tore her skirt from the lamp and held his hands out in front.

Rebi moved on the bed, waggled the backs of her fingers against his naked ass. He nearly jumped into the wall. She tried to get her mouth on him again. He gripped her by the shoulders and pushed her away, but she only hauled him to her again.

"I want you," she said.

"Oh Jesus Christ."

He had to get control, had to focus. Get C-Block solid again. Tighten up his guts before he got sick all over the floor. He forced himself to calm down. You had to deal with one thing at a time.

Like you couldn't have two gorgeous girls coming after you any other damn day. No, had to be now like this, with a corpse under the bed and your dried spit dappling the body.

But the rage had its own will. It rose and ran inside him, moved him along until he'd grabbed Rebi and flung her across the bed. She let out a sharp laugh, part burlesque and part accommodating, as she twisted and tried to yank him down into her.

You learned to pay heed to the dead breath on your neck.

Shad clutched his pants and started to get dressed. He heard doors opening around the house and abruptly he knew that his life was in danger. The hills were being cute, playing him like this.

He grabbed his boots. He wanted to make sure he had something on his feet in case he had to run. He unlocked the window and opened it, thinking, *Yeah, this really is a punch line.* Traveling salesman nails the farmer's daughters and then has to hop out the window with his pants half on. Except the wooden track of the frame had warped over the years and the window wouldn't go all the way up.

"Someone's comin'," Rebi said. "You better jump."

Lucas Gabriel burst through the doorway wearing only white long johns and heavy cotton socks, looking like he hadn't slept a minute during the night. He rushed inside and barely glanced at Jerilyn's corpse. His hand rested on the butt of an old army .45 that smelled like the ass end of Da Nang.

"I wasn't sure if you were him or not," Gabriel said. "Him with another face on."

"What's that mean?" Shad said. "What's all this about faces?"

"But you're not him, are you?"

"I told you who I am, Mr. Gabriel."

"You're just another moon-running townie bastard poisoning our people!"

Shad didn't know why that annoyed him so much, but it did. He started to growl a curse but thought better of it. The man's daughter had been murdered, even if he didn't seem to care much at the moment.

A peculiar situation that just kept getting worse, begetting more and more strange things.

Gabriel hunched as if to charge forward with his knobby hairless skull. He was letting the compressed force within him free, and it wasn't going to stop rushing out until more blood spilled. Shad saw that Gabriel's throat, without the collar and tie to cover it, was also covered with snakebite scars.

Those washed-out eyes of grit and rubble gazed at him in confusion and pain.

"I haven't done anything, Mr. Gabriel."

"Yes you have. You don't even know what it is you've done."

"Call the sheriff's office. Get Increase Wintel or Dave Fox up here. We need this looked into."

"I don't know them, and we don't want any more hollow outsiders. I'll handle this myself."

That had the nuance of a threat but no will behind it. Shad thought he could cover the distance between them before Gabriel could pull his gun, but the man didn't seem to want to draw.

You could be cornered in a room with an open door and a

half-opened window. Shad couldn't defuse the situation. Couldn't truly even make the attempt. Not with both Gabriel daughters in the room, one on the bed, one under it.

Gabriel's eyes narrowed and he worked his lips, staring at Rebi naked between the messy sheets. She reached over for her blouse and put it on. She moved to stand beside Shad and sort of slumped against his shoulder. Her skin still burned. Was she baiting Shad or her old man, and for what purpose?

"She isn't for you," Gabriel said.

"That so?" Shad asked. "Who then? Tell me his name."

There it was, coming around to the same question, sounding like an owl. Unable to do anything except go *who who who fucking who.*

"He'll show you no mercy." Gabriel's voice took on a plaintive note.

"Who won't?"

"He'll drag you down into the gorge with the other doomed."

"Fairly vicious talk for a man of God."

"Would you expect any more from a snake handler?"

"Yes."

Whatever was going on in this house had started a long time ago. Shad knew he was the catalyst that had forced someone else's hand, and Jerilyn had paid the price. He wanted to ask the man why he wasn't crying. Why the bastard wasn't showing any regret or true anger. What he was really afraid of. And *who who who fucking who.*

But Shad didn't want to shock Gabriel from his paralysis. He turned to Rebi, hoping she'd say something calming and reassuring, take the edge off, but she only let out a slow grin that was pure backwoods jezebel. Any other time it would've made him hum, but now he could only groan.

The man took another step, angling sideways to show off the handle of the pistol. He flexed his fingers, inched his hand closer to the butt of the gun.

"Don't do that," Shad said. "I can't smell a trace of oil. You haven't cleaned that .45 in years. It'll take off your hand. Or your damn head."

"Why are you here?"

"I told you."

"You said nothing of consequence! What are you doing in my house? You're no friend. You don't hear the word."

Like it was all in playfulness, Gabriel actually put his hand on the gun and began to tug it loose.

As if you were just supposed to stand there and wait for it to clear leather.

"Don't!"

If they were mouthy, you let them run with their talk. It gave you a wedge while they went along posturing. But when they were quiet and slow you knew they were already disconnected.

Shad slapped out with his left hand and smacked the .45 to the ground, swung around with his right, and drove a fist into Gabriel's face. The man fell back into the door and the wood tore loose from the top hinge. His mouth spurted and a streak of blood curved down the wall.

Rebi coiled beside Shad, her arms writhing over him, and said, "Kill him. Kill my daddy."

Their Jesus had hellfire in his eyes. You couldn't forget it.

A scream resounded in the corridor. It had to be Mrs. Gabriel. He didn't remember her features and couldn't see her now in the shadowed recesses of the house. There are some people who are in your story but not of it.

"I was right," Gabriel said. "You didn't come here with an open heart lookin' for the Lord."

"You're a real contrary bastard, you know that? Why don't you tend to your own house?"

"He'll find you eventually."

"Will he?" Shad would ask one final time and then let it go. "Who's the serpent stalking your garden, Gabriel?"

He saw a blur of black motion in the trees, coming toward the house from the shack next door. He knew it would be the Wegg brothers with more guns. Shad pushed past Gabriel but Rebi reached around from in back and hugged him. "No need for fussin'. You got no reason to fear ordinary fool men."

He shoved her off and started for the door again, but Hart and Howell Wegg were already inside, keyed up by the scream. Hart held a rifle. Howell carried one of the Plexiglas containers filled with snakes.

These people and their snakes, like bringing over a crumb cake.

There was no animosity in their faces. Nothing like when Little Pepe had lumbered closer, intent on doing the job.

The Plexiglas canister opened and the rattlers came pouring out in heaps, twining and slithering among each other, spreading across the floor.

They uncoiled and several flowed directly for Shad as if they'd always hated him.

Hart lifted the rifle, took a step forward, and swung it around.

Gabriel shouted, "No!"

So, Shad thought, *here it is again.*

They had called him a jonah in the slam because violence circled him without ever quite touching down on his shoulder. Instead, it would miss him and hit somebody else close by.

The rifle blast struck Rebi in the left side of the chest. A broken cry that almost sounded like Shad's name erupted from her mouth. Blood and viscera washed across his neck in a wave of warm brutality. Wet hair whisked across his face as she flopped sideways into his arms, slid from him, and draped dead over the bed.

Every man wanted to be a hero for a woman, even when it was too late. It gave him a reason to stand tall. The rage made him roar. Snakes hissed and lunged. Two bit into Shad's boots and hung on. Hart and Howell Wegg, still without expression, continued to stare. The woman in the house screamed again.

Shad caught Lucas Gabriel's eye and the moment lengthened further than it ever should have. He fought back a twinge, gave a huff that wasn't quite a sigh as Gabriel, with great remorse, grimaced and started to lift his gun. The rattlers rose and closed in, slithering over Jerilyn's body and blotting the smile from her lips.

The rifle swung. Shad crossed his arms over his face and went barreling out the mostly shut window, where Mags's hand was waving to him.

Chapter Fifteen

 IN THE FEDERAL PEN THE OLD MOB GUYS SUP-
posedly had 812 channels of cable and sat around
watching porno movies and *The Godfather* trilogy
all day long.

But on C-Block, the warden only let them have
two hours of TV time in the afternoon. Nothing that
might incite violence, suicide, depression, or sexual excitement—no action pictures, no Jerry Springer, no MTV,
no Ah-nuld, not even Oprah. The Aryans used to lose
their shit when the O was on, they'd start flinging their
chairs, chase the homeboys down in the shower stalls.
No O.

But every once in a while the TV guide would get
their programming wrong and you could catch the last
half hour of some trash hit. The ones about the regular
guy pushed to his limits and having to get revenge on
the criminals: the sadistic sheriff, the terrorists, his
evil twin brother, his cheating wife who faked her
own death and framed him for the murder. He'd cut loose

and tape a hand grenade in some fucker's mouth and toss off a quip while brains flew. He'd be bashed to hell by the end but still limping along saying funny shit, and if he heard a gun cock or a rocket launcher hum, he'd always be able to dive out of the way at the last second.

It looked easy in the flicks. The guy goes through a barroom window and the wood and glass just explode away in a shower of tiny bits like sugar candy. He does a cool diving roll, snaps onto his feet, and does a zig and a zag, breezing through the woods. Maybe one or two wild gunshots behind him, little puffs of smoke on the breeze. You couldn't laugh too loudly or else the bulls would know somebody screwed up and there was something good on the tube.

Jeffie O'Rourke once looked at him while they watched five minutes of some seventies Southern sadism film, an innocent guy trying to escape from the chain gang. Jeffie said, "This is the only kind of movie where the hero dies or goes to prison for life but still manages to win something."

"Win what?" Shad asked.

Like that, like a Greek chorus expounding on morality, like the Stage Manager in *Our Town* coming out to narrate the closing scene and put some polish on the whole thing. Maybe Jeffie had answered him, Shad couldn't remember.

His nose poured blood and it felt like every muscle in his body had been stabbed with an awl. His forearms were covered with deep lacerations, and the briars tore at him as he came through the scrub. His face had been whipped by thistle branches and thorns still stuck out from his fore-head and cheeks.

He ran.

It only took a minute before he was so turned around that he didn't know what direction he was going. Gray clouds hung heavily in the sky and he couldn't spot the sun. All he could see was the same smeared vermilion haze up there behind the ashen billowing stratus.

He tried not to put a sound track to it but couldn't help himself. He heard the silly banjos and redneck mouth harps. The washboard slaps and scratches as he rolled down the embankments head over ass. The catclaws dug in deeper every second.

If he was heading back toward the ridge, all he had to do was make it across the trestle and back to his car. If he was heading farther south, he'd have to climb down the whole damn mountain before he got to the river. Maybe he could find one of the old logging or hogback trails that led to town. Otherwise, he'd either hit the cliffs or the bramble forest, both impassable.

Rebi's blood dried slowly on him, and she glazed his tongue.

THE WOODS CONTINUED TO SOLIDIFY WITH OAK, ASH, stands of spruce and slash pine. Carpets of cedar, leaves, needles, and moss tore wide in his wake as he struggled to keep his feet. It was slippery as hell and he kept going down, tripping over concealed roots and logs. He sprawled on his face a couple of times and crawled past jagged tree trunks and broad-headed skinks.

He didn't know how close the Wegg brothers were, but he knew they'd be coming.

Thickets swarmed around him, branches lurching in the breeze and swatting at his hair. Shad could hear the churning of water nearby and made for it.

Looking down, he saw that he'd picked up a dirt-filled beer bottle someplace and for some reason still held on to it. It felt important to keep it with him. You didn't question your right hand at a time like this.

He slid down a muddy embankment and came to a creek that had become violently swollen with the rain. He had no idea if this was the same place where he'd first met Jerilyn and watched her pressing the onionskin pages into the stream, but he stared at the fast-moving brook and instantly hated it.

Okay, so now maybe he had a reason for the bottle. The ripped, worn label peeled off with almost no prodding. He used his filthy index finger to scrawl on the back of it

Who R U, Fucker?

He pressed the label into the bottle and threw it in the creek. Let the bastard read that, if he could. Wherever he was.

Shad crossed the brook and had just drifted behind some Catawba and dogwood when he heard the harsh clatter of tree limbs scraping back and forth against each other. Someone pushing through.

He went to his knees and hit the mat of spongy cedar, turned, and peered through the bushes.

So here came Hart and Howell Wegg—capable, efficient, and moving with deadly competence through the

woods. Hart still had the rifle and Howell had stopped off
to pick up his shotgun. They checked the ground for
markings like they were tracking wild boar. Shad saw just
how clear a trail he'd left behind him. Mauled chunks
of ground, busted sticks, and bent saplings leading right
to him.

Where did that leave Lucas Gabriel? The man might
think Shad had killed Jerilyn, but he'd seen Rebi die at
the hands of his own thugs. Would the entire settlement
keep quiet about this? Would any of them go for the
sheriff?

He kept thinking that a last-minute rescue from Dave
Fox was about the best he could hope for.

The Weggs murmured to one another as they hunted,
appearing casual and even aloof. Frigid-blooded sons of
bitches. How could they have lived so close to the Gabriel
girls and not fallen in love?

They had Shad cut off on this side of the creek channel,
so he couldn't circle back and return to the snake town
even if he wanted to. Find that old-timer who kept asking
him how his day was, pop the geezer in the chin and ran-
sack his closet until he found a revolver.

No, Shad was on his own.

They saw the bottle floating away in the brook and
didn't know what to make of it. Shad was a touch surprised when he heard their clipped, formal conversation.
They were discussing soil degradation, water erosion, or-
ganic content, and nutrient cycling in the area. All this
just looking at the ground. Pointing here and there, seeing footprints, coming on slow and relentless.

Last night, he'd thought they'd been polite but a little
ignorant, but they were much sharper than that. Worse,

they were proving they were patient and in no hurry to make a mistake. Shad wasn't going to last long out here with them following, and he couldn't outrun them. He had to make a play and do it fast.

Those movies he'd watched with Jeffie O'Rourke always had the Southern boy checking all the angles, knowing where the perfect spot for an ambush would be. He'd tie a handful of leaves to his back with a vine and become invisible, maybe walk backwards in his own tracks to fake out the cops. All these little tricks to show how much smarter he was than them.

Shad had never felt so stupid in his life. He thought about what his father had told him. How if he had to take a life to save his own, he should.

For a guy who'd survived two years in the can, and being out here with a couple of huckleberries ready to shoot him for something he didn't do, you would've thought it would be easy, killing somebody.

He used to see the faces of murderers on C-Block, the way their eyes would roll back in their heads with delight when they plunged the shiv in. One inch, two, then even farther, and still shoving deeper until it nicked bone and got stuck in the muscles and they couldn't pull it out again.

They made it seem so effortless and fun, like it meant nothing more than a quick, fierce lay. But he wasn't built like that. The very idea of it, even now, made him snort with fear.

When you couldn't run away, you had to run forward.

The only chance he had was to wait here for the Weggs to step up the embankment, and when they got to the top, he'd launch himself. He didn't know how to take down two men with weapons, but there wasn't any choice any-more. He had to make the suicide play.

They were talking about the beer bottle now, wonder-ing where it had come from, what it meant, if this was further proof of a widening sphere of pollution. They moved up the hill toward where Shad waited beneath the brush.

His vision flared red and black. He felt the hills think-ing about him again, agitated and somehow even fidget-ing, wheeling toward him. But it was different now. The anxiety of the land had a loving quality to it, he sensed, like a parent pacing around the kitchen at midnight, wait-ing for a teenager to come home. The undercurrent of the world reached for him, apologetic in a steely inflexible way, as if sorry for the trials it forced others to endure and remorseful for its needs.

The Weggs reached the top of the slope and Shad stood up from behind the bushes and pounced. You didn't get much dumber than this.

He clamped one hand around Howell Wegg's throat. Swung wide with his other arm and knocked the shotgun aside, pointing it down toward Hart's crotch.

The plan—such as it was—depended on whether Hart Wegg flinched at having a shotgun aimed at his nuts. If he did, Shad had another second to work on things. If not, Hart would just fire his rifle into Shad's head and that would be the end of it.

Adept and effective, but only a man like any other, Hart Wegg tightened up, did a little hop, and twisted aside to save his dick. Shad let go of the shotgun but not Howell's throat, reached out and put his free hand on Hart's chest and shoved. Off-balance like that, Hart Wegg teetered on the rim of the embankment for an instant before he went over backwards and rolled down through the cedar and brush until he was out of sight.

Strangling a man was goddamn tough, but using your thumbs to press in on the Adam's apple made it a lot easier. None of that trying to choke a guy where the muscles and tendons were rigid and well developed. Shad got in close, leaned his hip forward tying up Howell so he couldn't move or drop. Howell brought the shotgun around once more, trying to slam the barrel of it hard against Shad's arms and break his grip, but Shad wouldn't let go.

Jesus, he thought, *this is it, I'm actually going to kill a man now.*

"Win what?" Shad asked, because his thoughts were all over the fucking place.

Howell's terrified eyes spurted tears that ran into his patchy beard. Hart would be along any second. Shad didn't have much time, he had to get the shotgun. He let loose with a shout and exerted himself even more, wondering what price would be on him now for doing this thing with his own hands.

He felt the cartilage beginning to slip beneath the pressure. Howell felt it too and his eyes lit with an anguished, living panic as he realized he was seconds away from having his windpipe crushed. He tried to slip the shotgun barrel closer to Shad's face, on a poor angle, hoping to get a shot off. Shad pushed harder and Howell Wegg's throat collapsed.

Hart must've had a pretty good view of it all because he let out a shriek from below. He couldn't fire the rifle because Shad had Howell's slumping body propped up in front of him. A final wheezing rustle passed into the November air and Shad took the shotgun from Howell's dying hand, turned, and ran.

HART WEGG WOULDN'T COME UP THE SAME EMBANK-ment. He'd circle tight, probably around the Catawba and slip through the woods on Shad's left, keep no more than twenty or thirty yards off. Maybe. It didn't matter. You couldn't fake your way through something like this. Shad didn't have the know-how to set an ambush or build a roost and dig in to wait. He was back to running his ass off.

Shit, extra shells. He should've checked Howell's pockets. Why is it you're so smart ten seconds too late for it to do you any good?

Somber, writhing clouds covered the sky, and the sun cowered behind the hills. Crimson light spurted distantly and leaked off in an arcing swirl like a cut carotid.

Rain started to come down again and he kept his stride as best as he could over the rough landscape. The pain slowed him some but he was working past it. He wasn't graceful but holding the shotgun somehow helped. Carrying it gave him a subtle reassurance, the heft and weight of it connecting him to the world.

Shad continued stumbling through the woods, branches clawing at his forehead and adding to his gashes. He wouldn't go easy, and that resistance might help keep him from going at all.

Just as Dave Fox had predicted, Shad had done little besides cause himself a lot of pain.

Soon the hitch in his side got worse and the rage deserted him, leaving only a void in the center of his chest. He bounced into jagged, rotting maple tree trunks, snarled bramble vines, red chokeberry, and wild indigo. He didn't know how many miles he'd covered or where he might be, or whether he'd done anything besides go in one absurd loop back to where he'd started.

Whenever he came to a bank of rock that he couldn't see over, he had to pause and check, for fear of going right over Jonah Ridge. At least then he'd die closer to home.

And as he came around through another grove of cat-claw and sticker bushes the land broke wide in a series of hillocks, with the thick and menacing stands of virgin pine leading into a bleak forest of darkness that spread for miles. He slowed, stopped, and slid to his knees.

As he threw his head back gasping for air he saw Hart Wegg standing high above on a craggy bluff about a quarter mile off, sighting on him.

Shad had played it all wrong. He could see it very clearly now.

Right after killing Howell, Shad should've just sat down and tried to hide behind a bush. He would've been much better off. Now he had a shotgun that was worthless beyond twenty-five feet and Hart Wegg, the slick hunter, had a rifle good up to a thousand yards.

He wouldn't need that much. The childishly chaotic curls of his thick hair flipped back and forth in the wind. He appeared only slightly less docile than before.

Shad knew it was already too late.

He ran for the pine, hurled himself over the rim of the slope, and saw how it eased away beneath him for dozens of feet before disappearing into shadows.

The bullet took him low in the back. He glided through

the saturated air as thin wisps of mist rose from the dense, black floor of the woods and burst against his face. He watched the spray of his own blood precede him on the breeze, as he sailed for a vague and burdened eternity that ended much too soon yet not at all.

Chapter Sixteen

 YOU DIDN'T MEET DEATH ALONE AND ALL AT once. You met your death a little at a time over the course of years, through the loss of your family and friends, the dead pets. The death of all the Laments.

You've been here many times before, you just didn't know it then because you hadn't gone quite far enough.

Not like this.

You hold your breath for two minutes and you're swimming and having fun. You hold it for four and you're drowning and about to be a corpse. You can't hold it for six. If you've been turning blue that long, then take a good look around, see the saints and the martyrs and all the other turquoise-colored spooks milling about, the short-diapered fat guys with tiny wings playing the harp behind you.

Shad staggered on. He'd lost the shotgun and felt a touch lonely without it. He was in shock and knew it in a remote, uncaring way. If Mags were coming she'd be here soon—first one hand, then the other, then finally she'd be whole again and standing there with her arms out to him.

He tried to hold on to himself but kept wafting off, passing out on his feet and waking up a moment later. Sometimes he found that he was crawling or propped against a tree with his blood slathered against the bark. This wasn't good.

"Oh Mama," he said, because that's the sort of thing you say when you're dying and you know it. You always want your mama before the end, even if you've never met her.

From his waist down he was completely drenched in blood. The rain didn't wash any of it off the way it would've if this had been a sixteenth-century morality play. If he was getting close to God and cleansing his worldly sins from his soul. He'd be on his deathbed but redeemed, and ultimately filled with insight.

Since Shad was still tremendously stupid, he hoped he had a while left to go yet.

The bullet had entered above his left buttock and gone right through. The exit wound was the size of a child's fist, punched out the right side of his belly, slightly over his hip. He tried to remember what organs were there. He thought that most of the major shit was on the left. He couldn't remember.

It was almost a straight line through because Shad had been diving at the moment of impact. If he'd been an instant slower, he would've been standing upright when the bullet hit. The angle of the shot would have taken out his entire groin. Cut his femoral artery, and ended the game a whole lot quicker.

Bad enough to die, but really, did you have to go without your nuts?

He'd read a first-aid manual in the slam, toward the end of his sentence, because he'd read everything else in the prison library by then. He saw the pages of the book in his mind now, much nearer than his own pain.

He was in shock. Made you think you were wide-eyed and surprised, in your pajamas with the back door open, looking outside in the gloom and a cat springs out. "Oh!"

Like how his father must've felt when he found out his third wife, Tandy Mae Lusk, had skipped town with her own first cousin. Oh!

The definition had something to do with blood circulation being seriously disturbed. Symptoms included restlessness and apprehension, followed by apathy. Check. His breathing was rapid and labored. His eyes were probably glassy and dull, with dilated pupils. A person in shock is usually very pale, but may have an olive or reddish color to the skin. He glanced down at the back of his hand and saw only shadow.

Treatment included maintaining an open airway. Preventing loss of body heat. Control all bleeding by direct pressure.

Oh, the bleeding. Oh Mama.

Shad shivered uncontrollably with the cold. He had to stop the bleeding. Okay. Glancing left and right, he checked to see if Megan were drawing near. Or the elusive contradictory presence of the hills. Or Hart Wegg. Nothing yet.

He started talking to himself, hoping it would focus him, but his voice was a reedy, manic whisper. He sounded even more crazy so shut the hell up. On C-Block, guys with anxious wired voices like his didn't last long.

Besides, the more of your voice you gave away, the more power you consigned to your foe.

He reached up and tore off his shirtsleeves, knotted them together, and looped the rags around his belly. He put a finger in the new hole in his ass and couldn't stick it in past the first knuckle. It didn't hurt. His muscle and tendon and fat and whatever else was in there had shifted and sort of plugged the gap. There was hardly any blood coming from the spot, and he didn't know what it meant. You took what luck you got and tried to be thankful. Sometimes you could only shake your head.

His stomach was still seeping badly. The patch job barely covered the exit wound but maybe it would be good enough. When he drew the knot tight he heard his own scream from a distant place. He was surprised at how high a pitch he hit, almost girlish until he let out a coughing cry. It proved to be more manly, the way the tough guys died in old Westerns.

What next?

Elevating the lower extremities. Transport to a medical center as soon as possible.

Get out of the fucking woods. A good hunter didn't let his injured prey wander around long before making sure of the kill. Hart Wegg would be coming.

Shad took two steps and leaned against a pine. He pressed himself on, got a few feet farther along, drifted to another tree.

This was going to take a while.

His feet went numb and his skin crawled. The pain got closer and finally descended. He lurched and limped through the forest. Another burst of panic filled him, and he gritted his teeth against it.

The storm rose and the wind grew stronger, driving rain hard as rock salt against him. Branches heaved and struck out, the howling becoming louder. As above, so below. He could imagine Tushie Kline sitting there reading from *A Century of the World's Best Poetry*, the book in his lap, pulling apart symbols like tearing legs off spiders.

Shad was talking again, low but quite intelligently, as if he was back in the prison library with Tush and explaining the grandeur of literature. Shad listened to himself and thought he should shut up but realized he couldn't stop. "A morality play is essentially an allegory in dramatic form. It shares the key features of allegorical prose and verse narratives. It's intended to be understood on more than one level at a time."

Shad wasn't completely sure if he agreed with what he was saying, but decided not to argue. "Its main purpose is pedantic as well as dogmatic, and the characters are personified abstractions with aptronyms."

He didn't remember the word, and said, "What's that?"

"A label name," he answered. "The nondramatic precursors to the morality play are to be found in medieval sermon literature."

"That's right."

"Homilies, fables, parables, and other works of moral edification."

"Sure," he said.

The agony took him over until he cried out once more, then it receded and his mind cleared.

He turned and saw his body on the ground with his face

screwed up in pain, sucking air heavily as he slept. Trickles of rain ran in and out of his open mouth.

Above him stood his mother and Hellfire Christ.

"Oh Mama," he said, and wondered if this was it.

The Jesus before him wasn't the Christ in Mrs. Rhyerson's paint-by-numbers portrait. Nor Old Lady Hester's picture either. You had trouble visualizing this Christ shaking hands with Conway Twitty or sitting on a cloud with Elvis.

Hellfire Christ's fists were much larger and the wrists thicker than the gaunt icons you saw hanging on dining room walls. He was a stonemason who walked three miles from his village to the cosmopolitan city of Sepherus, where the Romans were constructing along the Sea of Galilee. He worked to the point of exhaustion because the Romans took one-fourth of his pay in taxes. If it was a bad week, they came to Nazareth and forced the two hundred peasant villagers to cough up their tribute in produce and farm animals. He's learned a great deal about Plato and Aristotle from the Greek artisans laboring on the floor mosaics.

His features were plain, grim, and heavily wrinkled from the desert sun. The corners of his eyes were crusted with grime and dust. About five-eight and slightly balding. With no easy access to a daily bath he had a repugnant odor that nobody in the Middle East would ever notice. Even Shad's mother was making a face, sniffing the air.

Jesus, whose voice might or might not have been the voice of Shad's father, whispered something too low to hear.

You come all this way to meet God and the guy mumbles.

"Shad?"

"Yes, Mama."

"You . . . are you hurt?"

"Yes."

"Will you come see me now? Are we going to be together again?" Her face brightened.

"No, Mama. Not just yet. You have to help me."

"I do?"

"Yes, you have to show me the way out."

He saw himself now, coughing on the ground. Speckled black phlegm coated his lips. He'd read somewhere that it indicated liver damage. You might survive for a while, but it pretty much meant you were through. Maybe the liver wasn't on the left side the way he'd thought. Terror seized him again and he looked at Jesus.

No chance at mercy there. Hellfire Christ had a lot on his mind, his burning eyes glancing side to side as he paced around the woods like a prowling animal. He didn't want sympathy and wouldn't give any either.

He was as bad as Barabbas, wanting to kill tyrants, cut the throats of soldiers. He stared down at Shad's body and glowered. Hellfire Christ wasn't smiling and looked like he'd forgotten how to.

"Shad?"

"Mama, you have to help me!"

He didn't know which was worse—the fear of dying or the humiliation he felt hearing the squeak in his voice. He gritted his teeth and the frustration yanked at his belly and became something much more awful. He just didn't want to die up here without getting the answers he was after. He didn't want to die.

"You should've brought Lament," she said. "The hound might've helped."

Even the ghosts had to get in potshots when they could, say that they told you so.

"Son?"

"I'm here, Mama."

"Son?"

"I'm still next to you."

Tears dripped down her cheeks. He'd never seen his mother cry before. She held her hand out to him but he couldn't touch her.

"I said you should listen to me, son."

"I know. You were right."

Her gaze skittered past, then fell on him once more. "The harlot. He lay with the harlot. I still had skin, the earth wasn't cold, and he sanded his stone and cleaved to another."

"Enough about Pa. Tell me how to get back to the road."

"There's bad will on the road."

"Just guide me back to it."

"You can't return that way. You've come too far. You can't go back. You've got to go on. To the harlot."

Hellfire Christ, his eyes brimming with vengeance, whispered to Shad's mother again.

She said, "I don't want to tell him that."

Oh, Jesus.

Hellfire Christ actually put his hand on Mama, gave her a little shove forward. She said, "No. Please, no."

"What?" Shad asked.

"Behind you," she told him. "There."

Shad had been wrong. Hellfire Christ still knew how to smile. His teeth were tiny and sharp and his leer kept getting wider until you knew for sure he was insane. He must've given it to them that way when he was on the cross, spitting down on them, smiling in his scorn. In his last moments, Christ took a piss and really let them know what he thought.

Shad turned.

He didn't see anything for a second because he was scanning too far ahead. He took a step and hit something at his feet.

Hart Wegg's corpse had been laid out before him like an offering.

Without a scratch on him, and with his lips tugged into a scant grin.

Hart was twined around the rifle the same way a sleeping child might hold on to a beloved toy. Like the snakes that should have been wreathed around the figure of Hellfire Christ on the Gabriels' cross.

"But he was your man," Shad said to the mountains. "And Jerilyn was your woman, she loved you. They died smiling." And then hissing, so much louder than any of the rattlers. "But not my sister! She wasn't yours!"

He spun back and his mother was gone. Hellfire Christ stood a yard away, and then a foot, and then an inch until they were nose to nose, and this Messiah stared into Shad's eyes. His rage was no different than what Shad felt himself. It had nothing to do with fighting for freedom or redemption or heaven's love. You were simply crazy with hate.

They both reached for each other's throat, and when he touched God, Shad woke in agony and retched black blood across his own chest.

SOMETIMES HE STOOD OUTSIDE THE MISERY AND watched his body lurch and crawl through the woods.

It had stopped raining. The rags around his belly were gummy with red mud and stuck with foliage and moss, which helped to seal the wound.

His sister's hand appeared only once, on an incline as he began to flounder downhill. She waved him upward through the brush and he turned and followed and kept stumbling on.

Where'd the story go? he thought, having trouble remembering how to find his next page. He might have already reached the end of it but was just too foolish to realize it. Like those people who sit in the movie theater watching the end credits roll and say to one another, *Is that it? Is it over? No, can't be.* Looking around at the rest of the audience, checking the faces of strangers as they proceeded by. *It is? That's all? The movie's over? Huh? Well...that sucked ass!*

His tenacity proved more powerful than his dread. The fear that had overwhelmed him earlier had slowly been replaced by the understanding that death had already dipped down for him but had chosen not take him. He wasn't finished yet with what he had to do.

Why had Hart Wegg been killed? Or Jerilyn? Or Megan? What purpose did it serve to keep Shad alive in the face of so much murder?

The woods thinned and shifted into a sparse cherry orchard. A note of memory chimed at the back of his mind and he began to move faster. Everywhere he touched the diseased bark of the spindly trees his hands came away covered with runny purple sap. The fruit was dying.

A surge of strength filled him and he pushed on until he broke into a clearing. He heard the truck horns nearby, wailing on Route 18.

Shad went to his knees for a minute, panting heavily, tried to get back to his feet, and couldn't make it. He rolled over onto his back and let out a gurgling cry. He had nothing left and hoped he'd come far enough for them to find him.

It took a while but eventually the pumpkin-headed kid appeared, staring down into Shad's face. The boy made a flat wheezing sound like calling an animal. It brought out another child, this one with arms like flippers and no bones in his legs, who hopped and crept closer, mewling. The distant corners of the yard stirred. A spineless kid with slashes for nostrils came squirming through the high grass.

Megan had led him back to Tandy Mae Lusk's farm, to the ill children, to her own mother.

PART III

December Preys

Chapter Seventeen

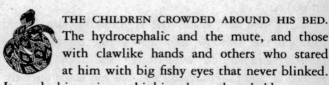THE CHILDREN CROWDED AROUND HIS BED. The hydrocephalic and the mute, and those with clawlike hands and others who stared at him with big fishy eyes that never blinked. It made him wince, thinking how close he'd come to being kin to these kids. Tandy Mae and her cousin had been damn busy out here in Waynescross, building their family.

Shad lay on a thick goose-feather mattress under heavy blankets. The warmth and comfort drove him down toward sleep. He tried to stay awake but kept fading, his mind tumbling, until a strong male voice he recognized came into the room.

There were three hypodermics first, two in his belly and one in his upper leg. An IV kept popping out of his arm until the fourth try. Then the sewing needle went in and out of his flesh, in and out, all over the place. First his side, then his chest, and now, hell, he was being turned over and they were sewing up his ass.

He felt the splashing of his own blood as it spattered in one direction then dribbled away in another. The stains would never come out of the sheets or the pillows but he knew they wouldn't throw anything away.

Shad drifted forward and back, and the pain was bad but not nearly as bad as before. He was no longer consumed by despair. The tranquilizers helped. His nerves had tightened. His hands formed into fists and he drove them against the bruised meat of his legs.

He angled aside in bed and saw Doc Bollar sleeping in a chair beside him, his doctor's bag and a pot of coffee on the floor, the ceiling light on but three of the four bulbs burned out.

Night had fallen and the shimmering sky lapped through the window and across the blankets. The pumpkin-headed kid walked past the open doorway, peeked in, and caught Shad's eye. The boy eased open the tiny jaws beneath the behemoth skull, and said, "You should sleep."

Shad did.

He woke with a heavy aching deep in his belly but was mostly numb everywhere else. He tried to move and managed to roll up on one shoulder about three inches. That was it. Craning his neck, he could look over the edge of the bed and see bloody towels and rags on the floor. Unstrung catgut and rubber gloves. Clots of dried mud and moss, shards of glass, thorns and wood splinters.

Doc Bollar had a couple days of white whiskers on his face, and his heavily seamed face was clenched with tension. He hung himself awkwardly in the ladder-back chair as if he was uncomfortable and had piles from sitting in the Lusk outhouse to do his business.

Shad had never seen the man where he didn't look like he'd just woken up five minutes before and had dressed without a mirror. His thin hair ran into one wild tuft that flapped backwards off his skull like the lid of a silver creamer flipping open. Doc was small and getting smaller every year, hunched with excruciatingly sharp shoulder blades jabbing up at his shirt. Thin except for his feet, which were so large you kept waiting for him to take off his brown clown shoes and show you it was all a joke. It made you think that without those big feet he'd go spiraling out the window like a stuck balloon.

His eyes opened, spun for a second, then immediately focused into a glare. "You know where you are, Shad Jenkins?"

"Yes. How long's it been?"

"Three days."

You couldn't get away from symbolism no matter what you did to yourself.

"Who else is here?" he asked.

"Just Tandy Mae and her kids. I don't have to tell you about them, do I?"

"No. What about her husband?"

"He run off a few months back." Doc let out a groan as he shifted in his seat, slumped forward but didn't stand. "Stop asking fool questions. You need a hospital."

"What's the damage?"

"You want to tell me what the hell happened to you first?"

"No."

It got the old man pissy, made him look around like he

wanted to pick up a hammer and smack Shad in the head with it. Instead, he grabbed the cold coffee and let out an exasperated sigh. The smell of curdling milk made Shad wince, and he could feel the thread pull in different spots of his face.

"I stitched you up okay, but your wounds are bad. I can say that you're probably the luckiest son of a bitch I've ever seen. By all rights you should be dead from the blood loss alone. Bullet passed through a lot of soft tissue, missed your vitals. He must've been a fair distance off, whoever done it." He waited for Shad to respond, and after a minute went on. "Any closer and you'd have been disemboweled. I'm going to have you transferred to Poverhoe City General."

"No, Doc."

"I should inform the sheriff—"

"It's been three days. Tandy Mae didn't do it already?"

"Apparently you told her not to. You were adamant, slid out of bed and scared her pretty bad. She probably thinks you were running moon and got shot by the federal law."

"Good."

"That's not what happened though?"

"No."

"You have trouble with those snake people?"

No reason to lie about it at this point. "Yes."

"They might come after you."

"No, they won't."

Doc was a little startled, and now the worry entered his face. "Did you . . . ?" Leaving a nice dramatic pause, like he was on a dinner theater stage practicing a scene out of *Who's Afraid of Virginia Woolf?* "Did you—"

"What?"

"Did you kill them all?"

"Stop talking crazy, Doc. Why didn't you call Increase Wintel when you first saw me?"

An expression of shame contorted Doc's features. He jutted his clown feet out and stared down at them. "From what I can gather, you went up Gospel Trail Road. If it had been my sister, I might've done the same. I had no answers for your father when I examined Megan's body. Neither did the sheriff. That rankles me. I was raised here in the hollow same as you. I know about them hills."

Doc stopped as if that explained everything. Shad frowned but let it slide because it served his own purpose. This is what the advance of science and medicine had come to in this county?

Maybe Doc was cutting him a break because he felt guilty for botching Megan's cause of death. Or maybe he was just sick of the hollow and of Shad and of the ill babies he kept bringing into the world.

"Now that you've . . . finished your business with that road, I have to report this, Shad Jenkins."

"I'm not quite finished yet, Doc."

"Son—"

When they wouldn't listen to you when you were on your back, you reminded them of when they'd been in the same spot. "Do you remember when I'd come across you out cold on the lower banks with your feet in the water? I'd stop and pick you up and drive you home before you floated off. Your wife always tried to pay me forty dollars. I'm not sure how she arrived at that price."

"It's all the money she ever had at one time," Doc said. "I kept her on a strict allowance 'cause she'd go all over the damn county looking for garage sales and bring home the most ugly piece of useless furniture you've ever seen. Wicker. All this goddamn wicker. Folks who make wicker seats are inhuman and ought to be torched at the stake."

Doc had some issues. "Can't say I blame you then."

"You're putting me in a bind."

"Maybe three days ago you were in a bind. Now it's more or less an afterthought."

Doc considered that. "All right, I won't go to the police. I'll also deny that I was ever here. I got enough trouble in my life."

"We all do. Thanks."

"You mind telling me why you won't go? That's a bad rifle wound. You've got internal injuries. Even if you do heal up you'll be bedridden for months. You're always going to have a limp."

"I've passed through the fire, Doc. God doesn't want me. If he did, he would've taken me."

"You're raving."

"You think so?"

Doc Bollar stepped back, his shoulders slouched, defeated long before he ever came to this house. In a confessional whisper, he asked, "What happened up there in those briar woods, Shad Jenkins?"

Jerilyn dead. Rebi dead.

Hart and Howell Wegg dead, one by Shad's own hand.

How did you frame the overwhelming nature of it all, the crimes of his search? The enormity of the chasm he had crossed from one side to the other?

He wet his lips and kept at it for another minute, trying to find the right words to explain himself, and looking just as foolish and discouraged as the old man. Some questions you could never answer aloud. He finally managed to say, "So tell me, how's your bunions, Doc?"

TANDY MAE LUSK, MEGAN'S MOTHER, THE THIRD WIFE of Karl Jenkins, had always been a little bowlegged. But in the past twenty years she'd gained some weight and birthed so many babies that her knees were now perpetually bent.

She had to sort of swing her way into the room as if her pelvis was cracked or her legs had been broken in the past. Some of the ill children huddled around her, others trailing behind and hanging back in the dark hall.

Shad had driven past the Lusk farm on occasion, pulled over on Route 18 to stare over at the house, wondering what it would've been like to have Tandy Mae for a stepmother for longer than the couple of years she'd shared with Pa. If he would've wound up stronger or simply been derailed even faster. And how Megan would've fared through her times of need if she'd had her mother's care always on hand.

There are sorrows that can gut you a millimeter at a time, for years without you knowing it, until you wake up one day emptied out and completely hollow with no idea of how it happened.

That's the kind of expression Tandy Mae Lusk wore now. She sent the kids from the room to do chores. They hobbled and rolled and cantered off, wriggling and creeping in a chaos of half-finished bodies. She didn't address any of them by name.

Only the pumpkin-headed boy stayed close. Just outside

the doorway but occasionally peeking in. Shad raised his hand and waved. The kid flapped his fingers back. He only had four.

Tandy Mae's face was as closed as a fist, stony but not exactly angry. She still had a certain youthful appearance to her, as if she hadn't quite grown old naturally but instead had the decades imposed on her all at once. Maybe it's how she felt too.

What did it to you? Bearing this many ill children for whatever reason, unable to stop? Shad could see Tandy Mae's husband forcing her to stay pregnant year in and out, hoping for the one normal son to finally show up. A boy to play baseball with and teach how to drive a car. After this many kids what finally made him leave?

She sat on the edge of the bed and stared at the floor as if expecting to be beaten. It gave Shad another view on what had gone on inside this house.

"Thank you for taking me in," he said.

"I had no choice," she told him with no hostility.

"You could've phoned the sheriff."

"I think you would've killed me. You were about as close to dying without being dead as any man or animal I've ever seen. But you told me not to call, so I didn't."

He didn't remember. "Or my father."

It didn't jolt her in the least. She seemed unaware that she'd once been married to the man. That this sort of situation might be considered uncomfortable by some. "I figured he knew what you were up to and had already made his peace with it. That's the way your pa is."

"You haven't seen him for a long time."

"Folks don't change."

"I suppose I have to agree."

The pumpkin-headed boy shifted outside the room, and the floorboards creaked. "You want to talk about Megan now, don't you?"

"Yes. Did she ever visit you, Tandy Mae?"

"A couple'a times over the last few months. She would stop by on occasion. She and that Callie Anson."

"To drop off moon."

She nodded. "My husband Jimmy Ray had a taste for it, though he didn't indulge like some of them in the hollow."

"Callie told me she didn't know the farm."

"You asked if she'd seen my children, didn't you? She never saw them."

"She didn't know the name Lusk."

"We had to sell the farm ten years back. We been tenants ever since, working for the man who bought it. His name is Cyril Patchee. This is the Patchee Place. When we put in an order for moon, we use Cyril's name."

"I never knew."

"No reason why you should."

"How was it? Seeing Megan again for the first time in years?"

Tandy Mae looked in his eyes for the first time. "It settled some of my heart. We didn't talk much like mother and daughter. We chatted like a couple of old town nellies. She'd come on her own too and help me with the babies. She liked taking them down by the river and spending time there on the wet mornings. We got along fine, and she never took me to task for making the choices I made."

Shad got the impression she was truly sorry for all the

lost years. He tried to put a hand on her elbow, but he couldn't make it without the stitches pulling.

"How'd she get here on those days when she was alone?" he asked. "It's too far to walk. She couldn't have taken Pa's pickup without him knowing."

"I don't know. She'd just show up. I figured Callie was dropping her off down the road."

"No," Shad said. "Not Callie."

"Well, someone then."

That's right, someone. "Did she ever talk about anyone? A boy or a man in her life?"

"No. But toward the end...the last one or two times I saw her...she seemed excited about something. Happy, the way a young girl should be."

"A girl in love?"

Tandy Mae, who'd left his father to take up with her own cousin, forging a life from a leased hardscrabble farm and dying cherry trees, who perhaps knew a good deal about love, said, "Maybe. She had this new glow to her. She sometimes went down to the river after the kids were quieted and spent some time with a pad and pen. I think she wrote poetry."

"Or letters."

"Maybe so. The water trails past the edge of our property here, way out back, farther east than where you came down from. It wasn't my place to act motherly. She was a girl who knew her own mind. Maybe she was meeting a boy there. I don't rightly know."

The rage woke inside him and he wanted to take Tandy Mae by the shoulders and shake her and ask why she let the girl go down there alone. After so much time had passed, why not ask questions and get to the truth instead of putting her to work watching over an ever-increasing band of ill children.

Mags had gone down to the river and tossed her letters out on the current and sent them to her new love. To someone who would be able to quote from them when he met her later on, in the night, on the bad road.

IT TOOK THREE WEEKS BEFORE HE FELT STRONG enough to take a step outside. Shad hadn't spoken to his father in all that time and wondered if the man was worried. Or if Pa had made do cutting and polishing Megan's headstone.

The December air had a heaviness to it, crisp and hard. It hadn't snowed in the hollow for almost twelve years, but he wouldn't be surprised if the sky cracked wide and heaved down a blizzard. As above, so below. He was getting colder but still fighting for his cool.

When he thought he could handle it, he walked across the property, headed down to the river, and sat at the shore. He wondered if the snake handlers might still be after him. Lucas Gabriel hadn't wanted to involve the police, but had he eventually done it? Were Increase Wintel and Dave Fox after him?

He bent, put his hands in the icy river, and splashed his face. No, his thinking was still a little foggy. Dave wouldn't have gone three weeks before checking on Tandy Mae's farm. Either nobody gave a damn or he was considered lost up on Jonah Ridge or Dave had been around and knew exactly where Shad was but was giving him time to recuperate.

The pumpkin-headed kid stood a few yards off,

sort of hiding behind a small copse of cottonwood. Shad waved and the kid fluttered his four fingers, beckoning.

"Daddy," the boy said, with a heavy thrum of sorrow. His strange voice carried in the woods and echoed above the sound of the water surging over rocks. For a moment Shad thought the kid was calling him his daddy. But no, that wasn't it.

Oh Mama, what now.

Shad stood, walked over to the boy, and saw that a pile of wildflowers had been laid out on a patch of washed-out ground.

The grave had been shallow to begin with. It looked like a runoff of rain edged down the grade toward the river and had eroded a wide track of soil.

The forehead and eyes of the man were still covered with dirt, but his nose and chin were now exposed. A few plumes of hair stuck up like brown weeds. Most of the flesh was gone and his jaws had been pried open by animals going after the tongue.

So, there's Jimmy Ray Lusk.

Shad turned to say something but the kid had vanished into the brush. From the corner of his eye he spotted Tandy Mae, carrying one of her brood, coming straight for him. Was he supposed to run? Was she going to shoot him in the head for discovering the body?

He stood his ground for no other reason than inertia. Where was he going to go?

The baby was wrapped tightly in a blanket and from what Shad could see, it only had two small holes where its ears should be.

Glancing down, Tandy Mae said, "I killed him."

"I figured that part."

"With his own gun. Then I tossed him in the truck and drove him down here."

"I see. Any particular reason why you did it?" Not that anybody needed one.

That closed-up face opened just a little. "He wanted to stop."

His thoughts were ahead of him. He knew what she meant but couldn't help but repeat the word. "Stop?"

"Stop giving me children," she explained.

You didn't have a dialogue with someone like this, he knew, about things like this, but he couldn't quit so far in. He sounded a touch more weary than he actually felt. "Why did you want even more?"

"You didn't notice, did you?"

"I guess not."

"They're boys," she said. "All my babies. They're boys. I wanted another girl. I wouldn't let him stop until he gave me a girl."

"But why did you want a girl so badly?"

She frowned and touched her forehead with her free hand, like somebody was knocking from the other side of her skull. "I needed to make up for leaving Megan behind."

It made no sense. "But you were talking to her again, after all those years."

"I'd already done it by then."

The infant threw the bottle on the ground. Shad stooped with a grunt, picked it up, and the cutting, familiar smell hit him. He squirted a few drops of the bottle's contents into his palm and saw that the liquid was clear. He dipped the tip of his tongue into it.

She was giving the babies moon.

He stared at her with a mix of regret, hopelessness, and indifference.

"It's the only thing that will get them quiet," she told him. "This child I'm holding is deaf and mute and got no knees. You think you could live like that without some make-liquor to hold you over?"

"No," he whispered.

"You gonna tell the police about this?"

"No," he said. If Sheriff Increase Wintel put her in jail, who in the hell would take care of all the ill children?

"I didn't think so. You don't even sound upset. Do me a favor then and cover up Jimmy Ray's nose. He always had such a big goddamn nose, I should've cut it off first."

Tandy Mae trudged off with the kid in her arms. The pumpkin-headed boy slipped out of the brush and started kicking flowers and leaves over his dead father's nose. Shad stood there in silence for a while, then wandered off, trembling. The little tap of moon he'd taken had given him a bad thirst for it.

There were sticker bushes on the shore. Where a young girl might scratch her cheek before lying back to sleep or to daydream, to cry or fret or hum to herself. Where she could be with a man, perhaps for the first time, perhaps for the last.

His toe scuffed over a hump in the dirt.

The things you went and tripped over. You never knew what you were going to find.

It was a beer bottle, half-buried in the mud.

He pulled it out and saw a piece of paper stuffed inside.

Shad smashed the glass against a rock, plucked through the shards and found that the paper had been perfectly folded into quarters.

He opened it and read:

Glad to see you're okay

Chapter Eighteen

TANDY MAE PACKED UP THE WHOLE BROOD OF ill children in her truck and drove Shad back to Mrs. Rhyerson's boardinghouse. He lay on his back, in his room, waiting for the end to find him.

It wouldn't be long. He'd pulled at all the threads he could find, and gone into the hills, and now whatever was up there had to come down to town. He knew it would happen but he was getting sick of waiting.

With moonlight tracked across his brow, Shad awoke naked on his feet, standing at the side of the bed with a woman seated next to him, her open hand on his back. For an instant he thought it was Jerilyn. And then her sister. Even as he stared and shook off the feeling, he nearly spoke Rebi's name. He was still panting, and his sweat plied down across the vivid partially healed wounds on his belly.

She leaned up on her knees and embraced him from behind, shimmering in the silver radiance of the room. The glass pane was coated with a trace of ice, and the shadows of frosted patterns wheeled against the far wall.

There was a remote sense of dissatisfaction within him. As if he had not yet completed the chore set before him. It was the kind of feeling you got used to after a while.

Elfie Danforth nodded down at him, gave him a flicker of that devastating smile, and Shad felt himself curl up and roll over inside. That rough tickle started working through his chest.

"What are you doing here, Elf?"

"The hell kind of question is that to ask me?"

A foolish one. You had to work with what was given to you.

Her shoulder-length blond hair caught in the breeze and came after him in a tangle. He wanted to run his palms along the angle of her nose, around the sharp jut of her chin. She grinned and it crinkled her eyes.

"I told you," she said, joking, trying to play around some, "that you were a stupid man."

"As I recall, I didn't argue with you."

"I'm glad you're talking to me again. I hate when you're silent. You're such a difficult person to love."

And here he was thinking he was so easy to get along with.

"I don't mean to be," he said.

"I know that." She took his face in her hands and drew him to her and she held him like that for a time. "Did you find out what happened up on Gospel Trail? Do you know how Megan died?"

"No."

"So you're going to keep looking."

"No, I think I've done about all I can do."

"Are you leaving?"

"No, I'm going to stay."

"For a while?"

She tried to keep some hope lit inside, believing that he would achieve something in this world, manage to take her with him despite their past, the baby, everything else.

"Yes, only for a while."

And there it was, the smile that opened him wide.

She entwined herself around him as tightly as she could and forced him inside her, pulling him deeper, holding him there and clinging even tighter, until some of his wounds began to open. This wasn't for pleasure or even love. She wanted a child to make up for the one they'd lost. The same way Tandy Mae had wanted a girl to make up for losing Megan. His blood spattered between them.

Afterwards, when she finally released him, Shad fell back on the mattress and wondered if he could've gotten away from the hollow if only his father hadn't called him in prison.

Elfie rubbed her thumb over his knuckles—the nail a heavy cream color in the darkness, and filed very smooth—back and forth just like all the times before, patting him like, *Baby, baby, all will be fine, go sleep now.*

She leaned in to kiss him and her lips were cold, but no colder than his own.

AT DAWN, SHAD HEARD DRUNKEN LAUGHTER OUT IN the brush behind the house and followed the sound. Jake Hapgood squatted beside Becka Dudlow on a tree stump with his hand inside her blouse, stoned out of his mind on meth and moon.

Becka turned her angry teeth on him and started nibbling at his chin, raising tiny welts on his skin. Jake didn't notice. His hair hung down in his eyes and he tilted his head at Shad without focusing on him. A loose, malicious titter eased from Jake's throat and kept going on and on, as if he couldn't stop laughing at himself, couldn't fully believe he was here. All the slickness was gone.

Shad grabbed Jake by the chin and squeezed hard enough to feel the loose teeth inside his friend's jaw about to give way in their sick gums. It didn't surprise him much. The moon gets us all in the end.

He moved a step off and felt a gun barrel pressing into his back.

Preacher Dudlow stood behind him, one hand over his mammoth belly and the other holding the .38 very firmly. No gloves this time, but the man was still sucking at the edges of his mustache.

Well now, Shad thought.

He figured the reverend wasn't there for him, so he just slid out of the way to the left a little until the barrel was pointing at Becka on the stump. Jake's hand continued to work vigorously at one breast.

Dudlow didn't have a coat on but still wore his bright red hunter's cap with the flaps down over his ears. The knitted scarf his mother had made remained wrapped twice around his throat and trailing over his shoulders, down to his ankles. The aroma of Mrs. Swoozie's boysenberry pie wafted off Dudlow's chin.

"We all have our temptations," Shad said, referencing their last conversation at Megan's and Mama's graves. When you threw somebody's own words back at them they hit much harder than anything you could come up with on your own.

"So true," Dudlow answered.

Shad tried to remember how it went. "So human of us. It's a divine test. We're fated to quarrel with our flaws."

"I've quit fighting," Dudlow said. "Are you going to try to stop me from what I'm about to do?"

"No," Shad said, a little surprised at himself. But it was the truth.

"You know where she goes? What she's been doing?"

"Yes."

Dudlow pulled a face, showing his purple tongue. "It's disgraceful. Disgusting. All my fault. I didn't keep to my own house!"

"Then you can't blame her completely."

"No, no, you're right. You're quite right about that, yes indeed."

He handled the gun too easily, without any respect. He turned it one way and the other, as if he was going to hold it up to his eye, peer into it, start thumbing the hammer back—click, click, click . . . bang! Turn this all into a stupid gag from a French farce. Like he'd wind up with ash on his face, a little cut on his nose, everybody giggling.

Dudlow shifted from foot to foot, sometimes catching the ends of the scarf under his heels.

Shad said, "You told me you weren't a fool. You said you took your responsibilities in safeguarding your congregation very seriously."

"I do. I thought—" His mouth worked impotently, and he started bending his knees like a child about to break into a wail.

When it got bad, you always wanted to drop and call for Mama.

"What did you think, Reverend?"

"I thought it would be you."

"Me?"

"That you were the one primed and set to go off, Shad Jenkins. That you were going to kill and take some of us to hell with you."

"The only one I want is whoever killed my sister."

"So you say."

"We all have our frustrations. Maybe you just need to be a touch more forgiving."

"Actually, I believe I may prefer being a martyr too much. I've known about this for a time, but—I was trapped by my own pride. By the burden of my cross. Of her, my wife."

"That's why it's called a burden, because you have to carry it."

Jake must've pinched a serious amount of Becka's flesh because she let out a bizarre little yeep noise at that moment and her eyes cleared for an instant. She saw her husband standing there, the pistol trained on her, and an expression of solace filled her face. Dudlow saw it and let loose with a whimper and held the .38 out straight at her face.

"Stop me," he begged.

"No."

"I beseech you."

"No."

If Shad made a snatch for the gun Dudlow would have the excuse he needed to give himself up to his pain and squeeze the trigger. He wouldn't feel the pressure of guilt because he'd always be able to throw the blame on Shad's involvement.

So they had to wait. It didn't take long. Jake and Becka passed out after a couple of minutes, their heads clunking forward together into something like a maimed kiss. They fell off the tree stump.

Morning mist rose from the ground and plied between their bodies, pressed into a swirl by their ragged breathing and snorting. Dudlow threw down the pistol, let out a manic cry, whirled around, and ran from the thicket.

Shad picked up the .38 and started back to the house, then thought better of it. He should get rid of the pistol, maybe hide it somewhere, but couldn't think of a proper spot. Peel up floorboards in Mrs. Rhyerson's attic? Under the porch?

He considered burying it or carrying it down to the river and hurling it in. He'd never even held a handgun before and the compact nature of its power kept drawing his attention.

He turned it one way and the other, as if he was going to hold it up to his eye, peer into it, start thumbing the hammer back—click, click, click . . .

Finally, he walked back to Jake and Becka and tossed the gun in the same place Dudlow had.

You didn't always have to have the answers. It was hard enough just keeping the bullet out of your brain.

ELFIE TOOK HIM INTO TOWN AND DROPPED HIM OFF at the end of the road leading to Pa's house. He leaned over to kiss her good-bye. Although their mouths met with some passion, he couldn't shake the feeling that she'd gotten whatever she might need from him and there was nothing left. He shut the door and she stomped the pedal getting away. The tires spit dirt across his knees.

Shad slowly walked home. Pa wasn't there. Wherever he'd gone, he'd taken Lament with him. The 'Stang sat out in front, freshly waxed. Dave Fox must've found it weeks ago and had it brought over to Tub Gattling's shop. This time, Tub hadn't been able to control himself. The car now had an enhanced carriage and augmented suspension. Tub must've been certain that Shad was running moon again. The window had been fixed and Tub's bill sat on the dashboard. It was reasonable.

The keys were in the 'Stang and he started the engine, listening to it thrum until some of his strength and calm seemed to be returning to him.

Shad shut off the car and moved from it with a heaviness he hadn't felt when leaving Elfie. On the porch, he was surprised to see that Pa's chessboard was missing. He stepped into the house. The always loaded shotgun rested in the corner.

He stood in Megan's empty room for a while before telling her, "I'm sorry."

Everything he'd done since getting out of the can had been botched right down the line. The snakes were loose. There was blood on his hands. The hollow was getting crazier, and so was he.

Shad looked through Megan's bedroom again, hunting for any clue. Her clothes, magazines, schoolbooks. Dave Fox had done all this as well. Searched through her things wearing a pair of latex gloves. Inspecting different parts of the house, looking around the yard some. If Dave had found nothing suspicious, what chance did Shad have?

There wasn't any choice. When you hit the wall you backed up a few steps and ran at it again. Shad checked the floorboards, the back of the closet for secret panels, and the molding around the doors. Teenage girls would have their hiding spots, their special places to keep their treasures.

He searched for the pad she'd used down at Tandy Mae's farm, where she wrote her love poems and notes and set them loose on the river.

He was so careful that it took over two hours to cover every inch of the entire room. He turned up nothing.

A knock at the front door spun him around as if he'd been mule-kicked. The silence of the house had gotten so deeply inside him that he barked Megan's name. You didn't know how far you'd gone until something pulled you back a half inch.

Shad opened the door and there stood Dave Fox, dressed as always in his sharply creased gray uniform, with his massive arms hanging at his sides.

"Been looking for you."

"You already found me, though, didn't you?"

"I ran into Doc Bollar a week or so ago passed out with his feet in the river. He's going to get hypothermia that way, you just wait. Frostbite, and he'll need his feet amputated. Anyway, I prodded him a touch, and in his stupor he mentioned you were at the Patchee place."

Of course, Dave would know it wasn't really called the Lusk farm like Shad had always thought. "Were you skulking around up there?"

"A little. Peeked in the windows some. Since he didn't know anything except that you'd been shot, and since you weren't going anywhere and appeared to be recovering, I let it go."

Dave Fox drew his line in the sand and kicked the shit out of everybody to one side and let everyone on the other side slide. "Thanks."

"He kept calling you the luckiest son of a bitch ever, the

way the bullet missed all your internal goodies. I figured you'd show up at Mrs. Rhyerson's when you were ready."

"So you watched her place and spotted me there last night."

"On my night patrol. I didn't want to ruin your reunion with Elfie Dansforth, so I didn't bother you then."

"You waited until now. Don't you ever sleep?"

"No." Dave shifted, and the porch slats creaked beneath his weight. "I thought we could chat."

"Come in and pull up a chair."

Dave didn't sit. Shad felt compelled to stand and face the deputy despite the weariness settled heavily in Shad's shoulders. Dave saw the exhaustion in him and put a wide hand on Shad's chest and pressed him back until he was seated on the couch.

"Goddamn Doc," Dave said. "He should have insisted you go to a hospital."

"He did."

"Then he should've come got me or the sheriff."

"Doc wanted to."

"And you're the damn fool who talked him out of it."

"You're going to hurt my feelings soon."

"To hell with that. Red and Lottie Sublett suffered through a couple of weeks of guilt, then came down into town. They thought their eldest boy had shot you and you crawled off into the woods to die. That weirdo kid had them half-convinced you were an FBI agent and the bureau was planning a full-scale attack on Red's still. That what happened?"

"No, I'm not an undercover Fed," Shad said.

"I mean about him shooting you."

"No, Osgood missed."

With the gun belt rasping, Dave did a slow turn, his gaze steely, making sure Shad realized this was a serious moment. "We're not going to play it this way. None of this going around in circles showing how cute and witty you are. Out with it. The snake handlers do this?"

"No."

"All of them up there, they live the same way. They're disassociated. They think killing a man is no different than skinning a hare."

"It wasn't like that."

Not exactly, but how was he going to explain it? You could only go so far with the truth before you had to talk about Hellfire Christ. And the ghost of your mother. And the fact that you had killed a man with your bare hands.

"I think you're lying to me," Dave said. "And I haven't heard a whisper of what actually happened."

"You going to take me in for getting shot?"

"It's a crime not to report it."

But Dave wouldn't play it that way, dragging Shad into Increase Wintel's office for something so crappy. Not the guy who'd broken up the Boxcars ring in Okra County in two hours, all on his own. Killing three men and the madam, shot twice in the thigh by a .22, and not slowing up a step.

"Was she smiling?" Shad asked.

It almost made Dave frown. "What's this?"

Maybe it was Shad's enunciation. He was always repeating himself, so maybe he wasn't speaking clearly enough. Right now, his tongue felt too large and sharp for his mouth. He had to sound the words out slow and carefully, the way he used to make Tushie Kline do it. "Was . . . she . . . smiling?"

"Are you talking about Megan?"

"I want to see her."

"Shad Jenkins, she's been buried for—"

"Don't be ridiculous. I want to see a picture. You cops must've taken plenty of photos, even if it was a death by misadventure. I need to know if she was smiling."

Turning his back, Dave Fox shambled across the room for the door. "You can live without knowing something like that. I'm going to pay my respects to Megan and your ma. I'll be back in a few minutes. Use the time to reflect on how you want this to play out."

"Sure."

Shad got up and watched Dave walk down the road and up the knoll toward the graves. Pa would have Megan's unfinished headstone somewhere out back, where he poured his pain and misgivings and loneliness into each blow of the chisel. If you cut your grief and anguish into something from the earth, would it be taken away? Or did it just taint the world around you with human weakness?

Maybe both.

Shad moved to his old bedroom, sat on the bed ready to stretch out, and heard an odd crinkling beneath the sheets. His breath caught.

He drew back the comforter and there, laid out on his pillow, was a sheet of lined paper.

He recognized Megan's handwriting and suddenly the sweat rose and began writhing across his face.

I love you but I can't have you. I will not give this letter to the wind or the water. You won't have it. I'll take it home and hide it where you'll never find it. If you take me into darkness, I'll still love you, but you know you'll pay a price. This letter is my heart, and my heart will remain mine, no matter what happens next.

Oh Mags.

He was trembling so hard that the page tore down the middle.

Jesus Christ, she left it here for me on my own bed, and I never even checked.

That's all she'd wanted him to do since he'd come back home. Just to look in his room.

He had to hold the two sections of paper back together.

We're not what we choose to be, David. We're chosen. You by God, and I by you.

David.

Oh.

So look at that, he was here all the time.

Of course he was. And he's behind you right now. His breath is colder than the flesh of your sister, and the shotgun's in the other room.

Shad didn't even have the one small chance he'd been banking on. He would turn and throw everything he had into one swing aimed directly for the point of Dave's chin, and Dave would be a step ahead of him and watch the fist approach much too slowly, and he would catch Shad's wrist in his huge hand, pull him close into the crook of his powerful arm, and put a hammerlock on Shad's throat until the blood squeezed out from the indent of his eyes. He wasn't going to make it but there was nothing left to do.

"Don't try it," Dave said softly, so very far ahead of him.

Shad turned around and Dave Fox was there, staring at the note in his hand. This was it, the final act he'd been waiting for, and it wasn't going to play out anything like he'd been hoping. He dropped the two pieces of paper and they dipped and twirled to the floor.

Always a mile behind. He stared at Dave's chest and imagined Megan in those arms, leaning up to kiss the deputy's lips and catching her cheek against the curved edge of the badge pinned there.

That's where the scratch came from.

"What happened, Dave?" Shad asked. All the rage had fled now that he needed it most. His voice was hardly more than a whine. He had to lean on the corner post of the headboard to keep from going over. "Why did you kill my baby sister?"

"I didn't. But I couldn't save her either," Dave admitted casually. "The hills use my body on occasion, to take what they want."

"Then why do you look so guilty, Dave, if it's not your fault?"

Dave didn't look guilty in the slightest and he knew it. "I fight but I fail. This is who I am, the purpose given to me. I was chosen."

"By what?"

"I don't know."

Shad's knees were ready to give and he had to lean more heavily on the perfectly sanded wood of the bed his father had made. It was so smooth it felt like he might fall through it like fog.

"And you chose Mags. Why?"

Rising to his full height, Dave crossed his arms across his broad chest and seemed to fill the entire room with his power and righteousness. Through his tears, Shad had trouble seeing him. It was like staring into the sun.

"Because she was special," Dave told him. "She had to be taken back to the land. She'll return again soon. They all will."

"All of them?" Shad asked. "How many?"

But Dave Fox wouldn't answer.

"So that means you're a wraith? Something that comes out of the gorge and plays with the little girls, then bites into them."

"It's not like that. I'm a part of the current, the same as all hollow folk. I'm just different." Then, dropping his voice, and giving Shad the killer eye. "Even from you."

"You knew I was going up Gospel Trail Road. Were you there when I met the Gabriels?"

"Yes."

"You're the one they were waiting for."

"Yes."

"The one Jerilyn was writing to, sending letters on the creek."

"I can read them that way. I was in the woods, watching the snake gathering."

"Why?"

"I thought I could help you," Dave said.

"Help me to do what? All I wanted was to find my sister's killer!"

Still with the questions. Trying to find your way from one end of the bitter confusion to the other. Shad hated himself for even talking. He should be fighting, running for the shotgun. Take another bullet in the back if need be, but he should be doing *something*.

"Help you to finish walking the road." Dave paused,

finding the right words to use, like he was talking to an ill child. "You're already different than when you first got back to town, Shad. You must know that. We're all in a state of . . . incompletion. Every one of us except the dead."

So now it was about resurrection.

"Why didn't you let the Weggs kill me off? If it's all about sacrificing our lives to the hollow?"

"It's not. Only favored folk, at certain times. If I'd let them kill you, it would've been murder, and why would I go and do a fool thing like that? You're my friend."

Shad let out a little chuckle of malice. "Who've you got your eyes on next? Who's the next special person?"

"You need to stop asking questions if you don't want the answers. Don't be in a rush to judge. You've got blood on your hands now too."

"You think it's the same?" Shad shouted. "Murdering teenage girls and taking out some guy coming at you with a shotgun?" Thinking about Howell Wegg's throat made Shad even more ill. Now, when he needed it, the fire in his skull had deserted him. "I should've figured it out. You told me you'd met with some of those snake church folks."

"Yes."

"I mentioned your name to Lucas Gabriel. I asked him to call the sheriff's office and get you and Increase Wintel up there. I mentioned your name. He said he had no need for Moon Run Hollow outsiders. He told me he didn't know you."

"He doesn't. Not with this face."

"I mean, I should've realized it then."

Dave's expression grew more disappointed. "You're a terrible detective, you know that, Shad Jenkins? I said that I'd run into a couple of them snake handlers now and

again. I never said I'd met Lucas Gabriel. You didn't catch
me in a lie. I don't lie."

Shad grimaced and let out a groan. Okay, he already
knew he wasn't cut out for this private investigator shit.

"That day you searched Megan's room wearing your little
latex gloves. You were looking for this letter, weren't you?"

"Yes," Dave said. "She didn't send it to me but she read
it aloud. I heard her."

It was kind of a relief knowing you weren't the only lunatic in the room.

"You looked high and low and didn't check my room?"

"It was an oversight."

So Dave Fox did make mistakes. He did have a weakness. He wasn't infallible.

"I don't lie, Shad. Once you accept that, you'll begin
embracing the truth about yourself."

"You terrified Lucas Gabriel. He actually wanted you to
have his daughters."

"And so I took one. But I didn't frighten him. He loved
me. He still does even now. The same way he loves the rattlers. I came to him crawling on my belly through the
thorns, with the face of a snake."

"Oh Jesus."

"Because a serpent is as much a part of Eden and man's
nature as anything else. Through our pain and forbearance
we grow closer to paradise."

It made Shad snarl with impotence. How many people
would be alive if only he'd spent his first night in the hollow back in his own bed? He counted three, and who
knew how many others were lying out in the woods?

"How do you kill them? Hold your hand over their

faces? Suffocate them? Did you press your mouth over theirs so they couldn't breathe?"

"You'll understand eventually."

"Is that why their lips are always screwed into a smile and there wasn't a mark on them?"

"They smile because they're happy. Fulfilled."

"You stole Jerilyn right out from beneath me."

"No, Shad," Dave Fox said, and his voice was filled with as much honesty as you'd ever heard in one man before. "You let me have her."

"What?"

"You helped me. Then you wrote yourself a note in the dust."

"That's not true."

"It is. You've probably written yourself other messages too, thinking they were from someone else. The hollow uses your body as well, to give them whatever they want."

"Like hell!"

But you couldn't argue when you were starting to believe a little. It was no more insane than talking to your dead Mama or seeing your murdered sister's hand wherever you went. Chatting it up with the devil dressed in the warden's finest suit and silk tie. Finding old beer bottles with notes in them written for you. Really, even at a moment like this, you couldn't be that much of a hypocrite.

His mother had told him that they would take him.

She'd said there was someone in the hills who could demonstrate his belief on his belly. Who manifested nothing but poison. One of Mama's prophecies had finally come true. Or perhaps Shad had suspected Dave all along, because they were so much like alike. Was that the joke here? Were they simply two schizophrenics trying to find common ground?

Dave Fox didn't think he was human. Just another ill child with a sick brain, born or made into something that wasn't quite right. Another damned part of the hollow like all the plague victims they'd brought up Gospel Trail and left there to become dust sifting into the river. The earth and water had gone bad. The flesh had gone wild.

You had to keep them talking. In the morality plays this was the scene where all the revelations were made right before the clouds parted and God came down in his wicker basket on a rope and solved all your problems.

"Why is it you've never shown yourself before, Dave? The real you."

"I have many faces. Some are unfinished."

"You've only got one, Dave. I've only seen you with one."

"The one I wear now I show only to you. Nobody else but you."

"You're cracked. It's the moon. The moon's done it to us. It's poisoned us. We're all brain-damaged from it."

"We're changing on the road. It's the way the hollow needs it to be."

He tried to raise his voice above Dave's but he didn't have the strength. "That's why there's so many ill children being born. The dying gene pool. The diseased bodies thrown into the river and sinking into the ground. Into our food. Into the corn and the mash. We're all monstrosities. But everything you did, you did on your own. You chose Megan."

"She was favored."

With his vision swimming, Shad bent and retrieved the sheet of paper and held it out before him. "She said you chose her, David. *You*. You think you're a slave to the woods? To the road?"

"To my nature," Dave admitted. "Same as you are to your own. That's why you lay with both the Gabriel girls. Because it's natural to perpetuate with your own kind. You're no less a hostage than me or anyone. You gave Jerilyn to me, Shad. She was mine and Rebi was yours."

"I didn't kill Rebi."

"Didn't you?"

Being a jonah didn't make you a murderer, but Dave was so damn sure of himself. "Ever think you've just gone insane?"

Dave Fox, for the first time since Shad had known him, hesitated. His mouth worked and formed a word or two, and a subtle ripple passed over his face. "No."

"I've got to stop you," Shad said.

"Don't you think I've already tried to end it?"

He grabbed Shad by the throat, hauled him off the floor, and pinned him to the wall without any effort. Shad let out a cry and struggled vainly. Dave wasn't even straining and Shad couldn't breathe. "I don't want it to be this way, but this is our world. You think I like doing this? The hollow won't let me die."

You could never beat someone as powerful as this.

Using all his strength, he tried to pry Dave's fingers from his neck but couldn't move him an inch. He was suffocating and in his terror strained even more, kicking out now, trying to scream. Nothing helped. Dave pulled Shad's body forward and thrust him into the wall. Battering him once, twice, and again until the crossbeams splintered and Shad gave up any resistance.

Oh Mama. Oh Megan. He's gonna plant one on me and I'm going to the grave a grinning idiot.

"Your eyes are closed," Dave said. "Open them."

Shad did, the blood flowing from his nose and mouth, down the back of his throat. There was smashed plaster on his face, in his hair, all over the floor. Dave really had put him through the wall, then yanked him out again. This wasn't going to be like the other times. They were going to know he'd been in a fight.

Then, with an extraordinary amount of gentleness, Dave Fox laid Shad on the bed.

"I told you," he said. "You're my friend."

That rasp of leather filled the room as Dave drew his .38 from the holster and held it to his own temple. "No matter what I do it never stops. I tried to kill myself for years before I understood and accepted my purpose. I'm theirs, same as you are. I get by all right bearing my sins, and you will too."

Look at this, look at what you have to do now. You've got to try to stop the guy.

Shad reached out but there was a hideous tearing in his stomach as the opened wound ripped wider. His voice was barely a whisper. "No. Listen—"

"Watch and learn, Shad Jenkins."

Dave Fox, slave to the hollow and all the back hills, derailed by corn mash moonshine and mutated plagues deep inside his chromosomes, and maybe something more, gave the same smile that had branded the lips of his victims, pulled the trigger, and blasted the top third of his head off.

Chapter Nineteen

ON BOGAN ROAD, THE BULLFROGS CRAWLED out of the pond and tried to make it over the wire grass. It cut them to pieces but they kept staggering and hopping forward until their bellies were sliced open. They roared and staggered on with their guts dangling loose. Some turned back but they couldn't make it to the water.

Pa was building coffins. One of the four Luvell shacks covered in crow shit had been torn down, and Shad's father had carefully stacked the lumber up in the yard. He'd used the wood to complete one coffin already and was busy at work on a second. Lament sat nearby, sluggishly wagging his tail.

Mags's hand was on Pa's neck. Now she was reaching up to stroke his face.

You weren't finished yet and might never be.

When you learned so much all at once, it was worse than never knowing anything at all. And you had no one left to blame except for yourself.

Glide moved about the area, working the vats of bubbling gruel, wearing heavier clothing and checking the sky. She wouldn't remember the last time it had snowed in Moon Run, and you could tell she was a little frightened. She circled the steaming drums with a lot less wriggle today, and her cheeks were red with windburn.

As he watched, Glide slipped over to his father and gave the old man a peck on the chin. They embraced and kissed and his pa said something that made her laugh.

Shad thought, *Well, there's something.*

When Glide returned to the vats, Shad straggled forward. It felt like something had given way in the small of his back. His stitches were loose but the bleeding seemed to have stopped. He limped toward Glide. He had to admit, the smell of the boiling whiskey made him feel a bit better.

"Haven't seen you for a spell," she said. "You hurt? Why you walking so odd? Is that blood in your hair?"

Shad tried to form a response but could only stare.

"What's this look on your face? You didn't know about me and your pa?"

"No."

"What's that?"

He coughed and spit bloody phlegm. His throat burned badly and his voice had a rough, grating squeak to it. "I said no."

"You sound funny. I would've thought he'd have told you about that by now. He asked me to marry him."

Yes, you might've thought your father would tell you something like that. That you had a seventeen-year-old new mom. It might make for a good topic of conversation. "When did he propose?"

"A day or two after the last time you was here."

Before he'd gone up Gospel Trail Road.

"Did you agree?"

"A 'course," she said, like she found it odd he was even asking.

"Why's my father making coffins?"

"Well, Venn's dead. That's who the big one is for. I'm not sure about the others. Maybe he's going to sell them."

So that's the way it was getting now, when you could just drop the fact that your own brother was dead without even a note of sorrow. "What happened to Venn?"

"Dunno. Think his brain just rusted in place until it stopped telling his heart and lungs to work. He didn't suffer none."

It made Shad think about the scene this morning again, with Jake and Becka Dudlow on the stump out back of Mrs. Rhyerson's. "Where's Hoober?"

"Don't know that either. Ain't nobody seen him in over a month. Maybe he left the hollow."

"I don't think so."

"You might be right at that."

Karl Jenkins crouched near M'am's front door, hammering at the lumber. His craggy features were fixed with intent, and his deep-set eyes had glazed a bit, the melancholia sort of just rattling around in there. The terrible grace and brutal force within him was barely constrained, and Pa's lips were scabbed from where he'd been chewing them. Or from where Glide had been gnawing on him.

His father didn't look up at him.

"Hello, Pa."

"Hello, son."

"Dave Fox is dead in our house."

Pa didn't appear to be surprised, and kept working with the wood.

"You already knew that, didn't you? Is that who you're building this coffin for?"

His father said, "Venn passed on a few days back. They got his body wrapped in the barn. Nobody's seen Hoober in so long that they're fearing he's come to an awful end too."

But Shad was certain that his father already knew Dave was lying spattered across the bedroom, a few feet from Mags's last love letter to him.

"Who told you about Dave Fox? Was it Megan? Or did you find a note scuffed in the dirt?"

"You're talking foolish now, Shad. I'll hear no more a'that."

"Or was it Dave himself, Pa? Did Dave come by and tell you he blew his brains out in front of me?"

But Dave wasn't dead. You didn't live in the hollow, and you couldn't die in it either.

"Shad, you've gone a little sick, son. That's what happens when you head up the bad road into them woods. You need to go inside and talk with M'am. She's gonna help you."

"Will she?"

"Go on now."

His father dismissing him was both comforting and insulting. He wanted to shout at Pa and explain how he'd committed murder with his own hands. But Tandy Mae had been right. Once his father had made his peace with Shad going up into the hills, he'd considered his son lost to him. It was an act of will. The same way it took incredible resolve for Pa to ignore Megan's hand pressing across his cheek.

"I've still got more to say to you."

"I don't wanna talk no more right now, son. Go on inside."

Shad realized his father was silently sobbing, the man's shoulders quivering. It should have startled him but somehow it didn't. "You were right, Pa. That the dead don't rest in the hollow."

His father's strong palm came up and flattened against Shad's belly. It came away red and wet. Tears tracked his cheeks. "You're bleeding, son. Please go on inside now, she'll help with that too."

"Sure. Congratulations on the new bride."

You couldn't do anything except follow the course laid out in front of you. Megan had been right. You didn't choose, you were chosen.

Shad stepped to M'am Luvell's ramshackle pineboard door and tapped as the walls creaked and scraped together, tilting worse than before. His knuckles came away stained with wet moss. If the shack went over, it would crush his father.

The dying bullfrogs continued to roar and scream.

M'am's voice, dangerous and without the quaint mischief, slid out through the slats like a fishing blade. "Shad Jenkins, you just—"

He didn't like her tone and walked in without waiting to hear her bidding. The place had lost the hallowed essence that he'd sensed before. The stink of marijuana filled the room.. His skin grew clammy and he began to cough uncontrollably. After a minute he checked the window and saw the first patterns of snow emerging in the sky.

Huddled in her chair, M'am Luvell sat wearing only a silk slip, smoking her pipe. The hex woman was sweating even as the temperature dropped. It made him giggle and shake his head. You couldn't get away from the backass contradictions of this town.

Beside her, set on a table his father had built, stood the old man's chessboard. They were in midgame, which might have taken days or weeks.

Uncovered from all her sweaters and blankets, M'am's dwarf body still showed that timeless quality she had. She looked as much like a girl as she did a hag, and the ambiguity struck him as something curious and creepy and very funny.

"You see more of my bare flesh and you get the giggles, boy? Another lady would be shamed and disgraced."

"But not you."

It made her cackle. Threads of smoke clung to her teeth. "Take a sight more than that, I reckon."

"So do I, especially since I wasn't laughing at you."

"But you were. At the fact that I get me the sweats in weather like this. I guess it is a sight."

Like there was nothing else to talk about than how fascinating a seminude dwarf witchy woman might be.

"You made it back alive," she said. "You should be proud of that. Not many people go up the bad road and come back again. People like us, that is."

"And who are the people like us?" he asked.

"Those who got special consideration under the Lord."

"Is that what you call it?"

"Sit on the bed. I'm gonna care for your wounds."

She clambered down from her seat and moved about the shack, so small and familiar with the place that even at her age she somehow managed to scurry. More like a small animal skittering around the place, like something you'd chase after with a broom and set traps for.

He lay back on the bed and watched her brew tea. For a few minutes he slept, and when he woke she had cleaned his belly and the cuts on his scalp. She'd wrapped a cloth around his neck soaked in a cooling fluid. The tea tasted worse than he would've guessed but he immediately felt more alert.

After he sat up, she immediately returned to her seat and began smoking again.

"I heard what you said outside," she told him. "Don't you worry none on the death of your friend. It's December. It's a time meant for dying."

"So why didn't I?"

"Considering the size of the bruises on your throat and the hole in your guts, you're lucky you didn't. Then again, December ain't over just yet." She let out a spurt of cackling that went on for too long.

"I thought you were supposed to ease my mind."

"I can only do so much."

"Well, feel free to start whenever you like."

"She's with child," M'am Luvell said, her forehead misted with perspiration. "Your woman, if that's who she be. That Elfie Danforth."

It got the heat flowing back through his veins again, and the rage that had abandoned him bucked once, like an engine trying to turn over.

Was this all he was good for? Being baited and toyed

with? To what goddamn end? "And you learned that when I was with her only last night?"

M'am sucked on the pipe loudly, holding the smoke in her lungs until her lips fluttered, then letting it out. "Oh, the baby ain't yours. She been with a lot of other fellas since you been away. I don't rightly think she knows who the daddy is. But her mama come in here to get some Black Haw jam, and that takes the morning sickness off."

Now Elfie and her Ma could sit back together on their Uninterrupted Airflow Pillows late at night and order off the shopping channel. Painless Nostril Hair Waxer. A four-gallon tub of Dissolve'a'Grit.

"Even if it's true, why are you telling me?"

"You mentioned her while you slept. It weighs on your mind that you might have a child born in the hollow. But that baby, it's a girl, she won't be yours."

He let out a long sigh and drew the chill rag from around his neck. "Did you really think that would make me feel better?"

"Boy, it's my aim to get you on to where you need to go, not to make you spin cartwheels for joy. Did you find what you were after on Gospel Trail Road?"

"No."

"Then you ain't done with what you got to do."

"I know that."

"You might never be."

Shad stared at her. "Old woman, are you ever going to tell me anything helpful?"

M'am Luvell tilted her chin and considered on that for a while, nodding as the smoke writhed in the air. "I reckon not."

"Then shut the hell up!"

"It's only gonna get worse for you now."

"You're as crazy as the rest of them."

She broke into that wild laughter again that sounded like bones clashing and crushing together, and even after he walked from the shack past his father and the girl, with Lament now loping beside him, the noise followed and managed to drown out the shrieking croaks of the deranged, dying bullfrogs.

THE 'STANG WAS ALL YOU COULD COUNT ON.

He drove into the mountains with Lament in the passenger seat, past the patch of ground where his sister's body had lain in the darkness. Where Dave Fox had gingerly placed it after killing her, leaving Megan there alone for hours while he drove around the town as if searching for her.

It began to snow.

He could feel the breath of the two dead guys in the backseat on his hackles. Lament felt it too and started giving sidelong glances, snapping at emptiness.

When Shad parked, Lament hopped out and gazed north along the trail. It took a while for Shad to limp that far. They hiked up and stood where the wagons had unloaded families dying from cholera and yellow fever. The elderly and the children flung from the back of a cart as they weakly argued for life.

You knew you were going to a place designed to make you disappear.

The dead knew something about life that the living didn't. They knew how it ended.

Lament chased the snowflakes and rolled happily in the mud. He kept trying to get Shad to chase him. Slowly they worked up the rise toward the dense oak and slash pine, with the willows bowing to the ground, beaten in the crosswinds coming across the precipice.

The woods continued to close in as they walked. They finally came to the mold-covered split-rail fence at the top of Gospel Trail Road.

Thousands of feet below, the Chatalaha River boiled at the bottom of the gorge.

Sometimes you could feel your life entering through a new door as another closed behind. You did what you could to stay sane and strong from one moment to the next, but it was never quite enough.

"Where's my story going now?" Shad asked, and Lament began to whine and nervously turn in circles.

The movement beneath the turnings of the world climbed toward him. Something reached for Shad's ankle, tightened on him, and began to yank him down. He wondered if he was strong enough to resist. He held for a moment, then started to slide over the edge. It felt powerful enough to be Dave's fist.

The suicides didn't sleep. Lament barked and lunged and squealed. Shad grabbed for the dog. We have to save our Laments, they're the only ones alive who still care for us. Wraiths bit into his legs. His lower back gave way again and the pain made him cry out. He slid farther to the rim, went to one knee, and the wind brought a burst of snow up into his face.

Lament's howling made a sob break from his chest, and he nearly went over. *The moon,* he thought, *this might only be the moon and the sickness in your mind.* Behind him, Megan's hand appeared and flashed out to grip his wrist, trying to pull him back up, as the snow thrashed and outlined the rising, reaching forms all around, and he waited to see where the fight would go from here.

TOM PICCIRILLI is the author of thirteen novels, including *A Choir of Ill Children*, *The Night Class*, *A Lower Deep*, *Coffin Blues*, and the forthcoming *Headstone City*. He's had over 150 stories published, and his short fiction spans multiple genres and demonstrates his wide-ranging narrative skills. He has been a World Fantasy Award finalist and a three-time Bram Stoker Award winner. Visit Tom's official website, Epitaphs, at www.tompiccirilli.com. Tom welcomes email at PicSelf1@aol.com.

If you enjoyed

November Mourns

you won't want to miss any of

Tom Piccirilli's

acclaimed novels from Bantam Spectra.

Read on for an exclusive sneak peek at

Headstone City

coming in March 2006.

Look for your copy at
your favorite bookseller.

Headstone City
by
Tom Piccirilli

On sale March 2006

THEY CAME AFTER DANE IN THE SHOWERS while he had soap in his eyes.

It was pretty much how he'd expected the hit to go down during his first six months in the can, but by the end of the year he'd dropped his guard and started to grow a little comfortable. You'd think it was impossible, getting used to a place like this, but it had slowly crept over him until now he nearly enjoyed the joint. The crazy sounds in the middle of the night, the constant action, and the consoling security of having bars and walls on every side.

He'd gotten some of his edge back after the fire, but it hadn't lasted long enough. The Monticelli family had such a low regard for Dane that they contracted outside their usual channels and hired one of the Aryans. A guy called Sig who whistled old Broadway tunes only Dane recognized. Usually from *South Pacific*, *Fiorello*, and *Oh, Kay!* It got your foot tapping. Sig had a self-made brand of Josef

Mengele's profile burned into his chest. He used matches to singe away his body hair, the black char marks standing out and cross-hatching his body. This Sig, he was a masochistic pyro who'd hooked up with the skinheads because you could get away with searing yourself to pieces with them. In the name of racial purification.

Dane was in his cell reading when Sig walked down the D-Block aisle holding a little plastic bottle of gasoline he'd filched from the workshop. Unable to contain himself, Sig let out a squeal of wild joy and Dane looked up to see a liquid arc flashing through the air. He rolled over and yanked his mattress on top of him as Sig lit a match and tossed it, his eyes full of love and awe. The cell burst into flames and Dane squeezed himself behind the toilet, pressed his face into the bowl so his hair was soaked, and used his hands to cup water and splash himself down.

This Sig, though, he had some issues. He cherished the fire so much that, standing there, he grew jealous of Dane being in the middle of the flames. Tugging at his crotch, he stepped into the cell spritzing gas from his bottle left and right. It was a good thing the mental institutions were even more overpacked than the prisons, or maybe the Monti family wouldn't have wound up with such a schiz.

The fire bucked and toppled over Sig as he flailed, spun, and took a running leap off the second floor D-Block tier.

Dane sat with toilet water dripping down his face while he tried to take in the whole moronic situation. The bulls worked fast with their extinguishers.

When they found him he was laughing on the shitter, thinking about how Vinny would react to the news when it got back to him.

It had been more funny than anything, so he got complacent again. He kept waiting for the family to pay off a pro hitter who would do the job right. There were at least five guys on D-Block that Dane would never be able to take on his best day. But instead of doing him in, they let him read his books, play chess with the old-timers, and even spotted him when he worked the heavy weights in the gym.

Dane had grown especially sloppy these last few weeks, with his grandmother and the dead girl always on his mind. He should've known the hit would happen today since it was their last chance to make a play while he was still on the inside.

But he'd been worried about getting presentable and smelling fresh for when he saw his Grandma Lucia this afternoon. He thought about her slapping him in the back of the head, telling him that just because he was in prison didn't mean he couldn't still look nice.

Dane thumbed the suds off his face and tried to clear his vision as they came at him from the front, standing shoulder to shoulder. They weren't pros and had the jitters, hands trembling as they held out poorly sharpened shanks.

Mako stood about 5'1" and suffered from short guy syndrome. Always getting into everybody's face and tackling the biggest cons just to show them he wasn't afraid. He loved to scrap but never went in for anything much heavier than that. Put a weapon in his hand and he didn't know what the hell to do with it. He held the shank wrong, high and aimed back toward his own belly, so it would be easy to twist his wrist and get him to fall onto the blade. He looked like he was either going to scream or cry, and Dane felt a sudden wash of pity for him.

Kremitz was an insurance investigator who'd sign off on almost any suspicious claim so long as he got a kickback from it. He did all right for himself for a couple of years but finally got nabbed in a sting run by the fire marshal. Kremitz was muscular but gangly, with an ambiguous temperament. He'd used a shiv on his Aryan cell mate a while back but only after being sodomized for about a year. He was known as a wild card on the block. You never knew which way Kremitz might jump.

Dane had never gotten used to being naked in front of other men. Not in the high school showers, not in the army, and especially not here in the slam. And now he had to stare down these two with his crank hanging out.

They gaped at his scars, the way they wove up and twisted around to the back of his neck. Dane could brush his hair to hide most of the metal plates securing his scull, but under the showerhead they came up polished and gleaming. The shiv started to really dance in Mako's hand.

"How'd they get to you two?" Dane asked, genuinely curious.

"The same way they get everybody," Kremitz said. "They want something done, they put the pressure on until it's done. Me, they reeled me in through my brother. He owes twelve grand to their book. Likes to think he's going to get off the docks by winning on college basketball. He used to get out from under before by jacking a few crates, but this time, he gets caught. The other longshoremen kick the shit out of him because he hasn't given anybody a taste. He's got no other way to pay off. So it falls to me to save his worthless neck."

"Sorry to cause you trouble."

"It's not your fault. Just bad luck all around. Except for my brother. He's just an asshole."

Turning to Mako, you could see the little guy had no other excuse except he was scared.

Water swirled madly down the drains. Dane could see a shadow moving at the front of the showers, where someone was standing guard to keep others out. At least one bull would've been paid off, possibly more.

Dane touched the scars and felt some of the tension leave him. There was power in your own history, in the stupid traumas you'd endured.

"I ain't got nothin' against you," Mako told him.

Defensively, as if apologizing for not saying it first, Kremitz agreed. "Me neither. Really."

"I know it," Dane said. He just kept shaking his head, thinking how ridiculous it would be to buy it now, only a couple of hours from being on the street again. "I'll be out of here this afternoon. When I'm gone, the heat'll be off you."

"Lis—listen—" Mako had to cough the quiver out of his throat. "The Monticelli family won't forget us if we foul this up."

"Yeah, they will." It was true. This wasn't Vinny's serious play anyhow. It was him having fun, breaking balls, keeping Dane on his toes.

"Those bunch of goomba pricks don't forget nothin' about nobody," Mako whined, shuffling his feet so they squeaked. "If they did, they'd have let you ride out of here."

"It's a different situation."

"And I'm supposed to trust what you say? That they'll fade back?"

"Yeah."

"I get told I got a visitor. First visitor I've had my entire nickel in the joint. My Pa don't come, my old lady, not even my kid, the little bastard. He's seventeen and into meth now. Steals cars and drives 'em out to Kansas, writes me letters from the road, what a good time he's having with some chick working his nob. Anyway, I got a visitor. A big guy in an Armani suit, one eyebrow, hands like he goes around slugging brick walls for fun."

That'd be Roberto Monticelli. It took Dane back some, wondering why 'Berto had come himself instead of one of the family capos or lieutenants.

"Guy tells me I do this to you or I get it done to me. Goes into all this bullshit about blowtorches and pliers and meat grinders, how he's gonna mail me to six cities all over New Jersey. Except with him, I know it's not bullshit."

Dane couldn't really help but argue the point. "Most of it is."

"It's the part that's not that worries me."

"Maybe I can help."

"The hell you gonna do that?" Mako groused, trying to make himself angry. Thinking about 'Berto had gotten him all wired up, given him the shakes. The point of the shiv danced against his T-shirt. "Even if you get out the front gate you'll be dead before you hit the corner."

"Don't believe it."

"We got no choice."

Kremitz started to steel himself. Jaws clenched, leaning forward on his toes, he was jazzing himself up to attack.

Dane had been a pretty poor soldier on the overall, but he'd liked the hand-to-hand combat training. His drill instructor would use him all the time as a practice dummy, flipping Dane over his hip and throwing him in the dirt. Kicking his feet out from under him over and over. The D.I. would show how to drive the knife in, how to keep the blade from getting stuck in bone.

Without fully realizing it, Dane had absorbed a lot, and would pull the moves when he got drunk, beating on the loud-mouthed Irish officers who called him a greasy guinea. He never got used to the stockade the way he did the slam, and couldn't figure out why.

They weren't going to be too tough so long as he didn't slip on the wet tile. Mako and Kremitz didn't know how to work as a team, standing too far away from each other. They swept out clumsily with their shanks and both of them tightened up, lurching, wanting to end it fast. Faces growing more grim, but with a hint of pleading in their eyes.

The drill instructor would call Dane and another guy over, tell them to charge at him. He had this one maneuver where he'd slip past Dane, grab hold of him by the elbows, and use his body like a shield to block the other soldier's attack. Dane would be standing there like a bag of potatoes getting the crap beat out of him while the D.I. let out a brash chuckle.

Dane had never tried it and decided this might be

a good time. He dodged past Kremitz, hooked him by the elbows, and swung him around into Mako's face. Mako let out a grunt of surprise and jumped backward under the steaming force of the shower. Dane kneed Kremitz in the thigh from behind, brought him low and shoved. The soundtrack from a Stooges short couldn't have made it any more perfect. Kremitz and Mako clunked heads and dropped their shivs, went to all fours sliding in the soapy water.

Dane couldn't help himself and let out a brash chuckle. He hated the sound of it, but there it was. You were nothing but an amalgam of your influences. He grabbed one of the shivs and stabbed both men in their upper legs, in the thick meat of the muscle where it wouldn't do a lot of damage. He twisted the blades just enough to make the wounds look especially ugly. Mako and Kremitz both started to scream and Dane said, "I'm doing you a favor so shut the hell up."

While they writhed on the shower floor Dane ducked back under the showerhead and got the rest of the soap off of him. Blood swirled near his feet and he had to sidestep away. When he was finished he toweled off and got dressed, listening to them groan through their teeth trying to swallow down the pain. They rolled and squirmed across the tiles.

"Sheezus shheee–it!" Kremitz hissed. "Y–you crippled us!"

Moaning, Mako stuck his face in the drain, blowing bubbles as he gripped his leg to hold in the spurting blood.

"You're both going to be fine. Say that you got into a fight with each other."

"Jeezus!"

"You'll be in the infirmary for three or four weeks. You're not hurt bad but they'll want to keep an eye on you for infection. After that, the bulls will toss you into solitary for at least another month. By the end of your run, I'll either be dead or this shit with the Monticelli family will be cleared up."

"You sure...about that, Johnny?" Mako whimpered.

"Even if I'm not, you're better off than I would've been, right?" Dane let out a slow smile. A part of him wanted him to end it now, do it the way it should be done. Cut their throats, finish it the right way. You don't injure the enemy, you eradicate him. His fingers twitched. A small, sharp fury nearly broke free from the center of his chest, but as he felt himself about to take a step forward, it receded. He almost wished it hadn't gone. "Don't fuckin' complain."

Mako grabbed him by the ankle and squeezed once, as a sign of thanks. Dane combed his hair back, checked himself in the mirror to make certain his grandmother wouldn't give him a rough time.

He walked out past the guard on the Monti payroll, gave him a grin and a little salute. He felt good, stronger than earlier in the day, much more settled. He'd been half wondering if he'd had a death wish, and now the answer seemed to be no. Still, it was the kind of thing you couldn't be a hundred percent about.

When he got back to his cell, the girl he'd sort of killed, Angelina Monticelli, was sitting on his cot.

"Oh Christ," he said, his scars suddenly burning.

She wavered for a second, fading and reappearing, then vanishing until an old man sat where she'd been. It was Aaron Fielding, a neighborhood grocer and fish seller buried a couple of rows from her in Wisewood cemetery. The guy always smiling and letting the kids steal cheap candy bars from the wire racks at the front of the store. He'd let out this heavy, booming laugh whenever something hit him just right.

But now, old man Fielding had a wild and desperate look to him, colorless eyes flitting all over the place, hinges of his jaws pulsing. He raised a hand to Dane in a gesture of pleading. "Johnny, I need—"

"I can't talk to you right now, Mr. Fielding. Later."

His dimly gray face filled with terror. There was none of the joy and peace the nuns taught you about when you were a kid, what you were hoping for when you hit the other side. "Please!"

"No."

"Just for a little while."

"No, Mr. Fielding."

"A minute. Only one moment more!"

"No!"

Angie snapped back into focus. She let out a soft laugh, like it was funny the shit she had to go through to talk to Dane. Or what he had to do to bring her in.

She told him, "'Berto says they're going to let you go home and visit your grandmother first and then they'll clip you on your second or third week out."

"I guess he's not as eager as I thought he was."

"He wants to build up tension, make it spectacular."

"He doesn't have the imagination or style for that."

"I know, but it's what he tells his crew."

"Does the Don agree with all this?"

"No, but Daddy doesn't really stand up to Roberto anymore. He's old and in a lot of pain."

"What about Vinny?"

"He's waiting for you."

Fifteen years old when she'd bought it two years ago, but still appearing so full of life, with that overwhelming hipness of youth. She was dressed the way she was the day she OD'ed: oversized black sweater and blue jeans, no make-up, with her dark hair falling straight back over her ears, showing the slightest curl of bangs up front.

The old heat flooded his stomach and got his skin dancing. He started breathing heavily, and when his breath reached her she closed her eyes and lifted her face to meet it. Her bangs stirred and wafted as if in a strong breeze. She smiled and he swallowed thickly, again and again.

Jesus. He realized he still wanted her. What the hell did that say about you, when you were aroused by the dead? Or was it only because she looked so much like her older sister, Maria?

"Angie—"

"You don't have to be embarrassed with me, Johnny."

"I'm not."

"There's no shame in it. You keep me sane in hell."

It made him chew his lips, hearing that. He sat on the floor across from his bunk, staring at her. If only he'd driven faster, or hadn't run over the cop.

But why stop there? If you're going to go back, go further. If he hadn't given in to her and taken her to Bed-Stuy in the first place. She'd talked circles around him until he'd cracked, and it hadn't been difficult. If only he'd cared a little more and been a lot smarter. He shouldn't have been so listless, but that's what the familiar streets had done to him. What he'd allowed them to do. What they were still doing, even in here.

"Will you visit me in Headstone City?" she asked.

"I don't think so. It's best if I'm not seen there."

"You live there."

"I mean at your grave."

"Nobody visits. They act like they miss me so much, but nobody takes the time to say a prayer or bring a shitty plastic flower."

"I'm sorry, Angie."

"Johnny, I need you."

Something began to soften in his belly then, and he felt himself going with it. A weakness that had always been there but was now broadening, intensifying. Maybe he was about to cut loose with a sob. Twenty minutes ago he was almost ready to cut throats, and now this fragility and brittleness. He wanted to ask her if she held him responsible the way her family did. It was a question he'd never asked her before. She didn't appear to want to make him feel guilty, didn't try to get her claws into him, the way she had in life.

Dane heard the bull coming for him, turned to watch as the guard stepped up to the cell door. "Danetello. Let's go."

He got up and was escorted down the tier, through

the gen pop, across the courtyard and back into the visitation quad, where all the new cons first set foot in the can. The warden was nowhere to be seen. They handed him a ream of paperwork, but nothing for him to sign. The clothes he came in with were pressed and folded in a pile laid on the counter. He reached for them and another guard said, "Hold it."

"What's the matter?"

"You've got a phone call, if you want it."

"Why wouldn't I want it?"

"Most cons who get this close to the outside on the day of their release don't turn around and go answer the phone."

Dane figured it was his Grandma Lucia, jonesing for sugar. He went back and took the call. His grandmother said, "Stop off at the bakery and get some *cannoli* and *biscotti*, will you, Johnny? And don't let the girl put you off. She's dead, that one. She doesn't know what she's talking about."

DON'T MISS

SPECTRA PULSE

A WORLD APART

**the free monthly electronic newsletter
that delivers direct to you...**

< Interviews with favorite authors
< Profiles of the hottest new writers
< Insider essays from Spectra's editorial
  team
< Chances to win free early copies of
  Spectra's new releases
< A peek at what's coming soon

...and so much more

SUBSCRIBE FREE TODAY AT

www.bantamdell.com

SF 3/05

051270

MORRIS AUTOMATED INFORMATION NETWORK

Piccirilli, Tom.
November mourns.

✓

MAY 0 9	DATE DUE	

DOVER FREE PUBLIC LIBRARY
32 EAST CLINTON ST.
DOVER, NJ 07801